Everybody Needs a Bridge

By

Colleen D. Scott

ISBN: 978-1-947832-00-8

Library of Congress Cataloging in Publication Data has been applied for.

Edited by Evelyn Fazio

Book layout and cover design by www.ebooklaunch.com

To those who give us courage….

Chapter One

What I needed was courage. Not the "jump on a grenade" kind of courage, but just enough to be scared and do what I needed to do anyway. After all, sometimes you need courage just to get through everyday things.

On my very first day in public high school, as the first period of the day began, I sat in P. E. class cross-legged on the hard-wood floor of an un-air-conditioned gym. Although it was only 7:30 in the morning, I could feel my legs sticking to the peeling varnish and beads of sweat trickling down my sides. Coach McNairy, the older coach who had extremely short grey hair, was dressed in navy polyester knee-length shorts and a sleeveless top, revealing her surprisingly muscular arms and calves. She told us that four years of physical education was a requirement in order to graduate. So there was no way out of the situation and I guess that was precisely her point.

A wall sign said that the gym had been built specifically for girls almost fifty years ago, further validated by the peeling institutional green paint and cracked stucco walls. The black metal double-doors in three corners of the gym had been propped open to let in some air, but it didn't help much since there's absolutely no breeze in southern Alabama, in the middle of August. The windows built high into the vaulted gym ceiling didn't look like they'd been opened since they were last painted, probably thirty years ago, but with the doors propped open, I could at least hope for some relief.

I probably wouldn't be sweating this much if there weren't so many girls crammed in the gym, I thought as I flipped my long, thick black hair into a pony-tail. Not quite the look I was going for on my first day of school, but my shirt was already wet and sticking to my back, so I did it anyway. I took a quick head count and figured there were almost 300 girls of every possible age, and size in that gym with me, and most of them were black. I didn't know one girl there.

"You will all dress for P. E. every day, or you will fail this class!" the same coach yelled. "Lockers are provided. Showers are available. But you will wear your P. E. uniform every day. Doctor's notes mean that you don't have to participate. But even if you are too sick to participate, you will wear your uniform," she continued, outlining our fate as she paced, military-style, in front of the other four girls' coaches standing before us.

Perfect, I inwardly groaned. *That means I have to change my clothes in front of a million strangers first thing every day*. I shrunk inside just thinking about it. It's not like I was fat or anything but I knew how mean girls could be. I didn't want to let them, or anyone else, change how I felt about myself.

I was what you would politely call inexperienced, having only started going to public school the year before and never having had to change clothes for gym. In middle school we'd spent our gym class walking around the track, still in our school clothes, since the gym had not yet been rebuilt after Hurricane Frederick had destroyed it that September. The year before that, back at my old private school, we had P. E. class but could wear our gym clothes under our uniforms and never had to undress fully for gym.

I'd known that going to public high school would be different, but I hadn't known what to expect. I'd never really been around many black people at all, and in high school there seemed to be so many. It was 1980, and the public schools had been integrated for almost a decade, through a complicated system of busing us in from the outlying areas. I wasn't a racist and had been raised to treat everyone the same. It was just that I'd never been anywhere with so few people like me. All of the girls, regardless of color, seemed so different from me in every way. They were bigger, older, louder, and most of them looked downright mean. And none of them looked the least bit scared or embarrassed about anything.

We never had any black kids at my private school. I had heard that some had applied and weren't admitted but never found out whether it was true. People sometimes say things just to prove a point. I remembered only a few black kids being at my middle school, and they had mostly kept to themselves. I guess being a new kid there, so did I. And that first morning of high school was the first time I wondered whether those kids at my middle school had ever felt like I did then - different and out of place.

Then, to my surprise, I saw an older black girl with really big boobs throw something in the direction of the coaches. Whatever it was, it went sailing over a few rows of heads and almost hit a younger, kind of pretty coach who was standing at the end of the lineup of coaches. Coach McNairy, who was apparently the head coach and in charge, jerked her head around to see where the object had come from and angrily threatened "Y'all better stop it or I'm gonna report you to the office," which made the small group of guilty girls go from giggles to angry stares, as if a switch had been thrown. When one of the girls caught me openly gawking, she made a face and flipped me off. In the weighted silence that followed, a train whistled to a stop a few miles away, echoing my feelings of loneliness.

The coach broke the silence and yelled for us to line up so "Y'all can see the locker room." So I scrambled up quickly and scanned the room again. *Maybe I can get into the locker room first*, I thought. *Maybe I can find somebody who looks less scary, and get a locker next to her.*

"Line up by alphabet! A's in the front, Z's in the back, ever body else in the middle! Lockers will be assigned in groups by alphabet, so get in line now!" yelled the young, pretty coach.

I tried to look cool, as if to say, "Who cares" although not caring was difficult for me. I asked a pretty black girl with long braids standing nearby, "What letter are you?" in as casual of a voice as I could manage.

"Just get in line, girl," she snorted back at me.

Luckily, the five coaches began to move among us, adding some semblance of order as they got us into more or less alphabetical order.

"What letter are you?" one of the coaches asked, touching me on the shoulder without a glance my way.

"P - U" I replied as helpfully as I could without looking too much like a kiss-up.

"That's right! Cuz P-U - you stink! " laughed the same black girl in a voice that was still a little too loud as she fell into line behind me. Her friends all cheered and laughed in response, rewarding her with a couple of high fives and a back slap. One girl even stomped her feet when she laughed.

Fantastic, I thought, hanging my head with the realization that this little gaggle of girls would likely have their lockers right next to mine. *Just smile and be nice. Try and stay out of the way,* I told myself, remembering years of advice from various adults.

After the coaches were satisfied with our approximate alphabetical order, we filed out of the gym and into the locker room where the suffocating heat grew even worse. The huge lights with wire cages covering the bulbs hung from the ceiling weren't turned on, probably because of the heat, and it felt like we were walking into a dark cave. The floor and every inch of the walls were covered with pale green and white ceramic tile. The ceiling was a mottled grey, and where it wasn't covered by the mildew stains, the paint peeled to reveal a different shade of grey steel. Two dangerous looking, five-foot-tall box fans stood at either side of the entrance. They were turned on full blast, but somehow didn't help much.

"Showers are to the left," one of the coaches yelled over the din of the fans as the line of girls pushed through the locker room. The new girls craned their necks in order to see, while the more experienced ones continued to chat, ignoring the coaches.

Definitely won't be using those, I shuttered as we passed. There weren't any curtains or doors separating the showers from the locker room, and no privacy of any kind.

"Here's your row," the coach waved to a bank of shelves on my right. Unlike other lockers I'd seen, these lockers were small wire baskets arranged in rows on metal shelves, each with a tag stamped with an I.D. number and a loop for a padlock.

The coach yelled, "Pick a locker, write down the number and tomorrow bring a combination lock only. Any other kind of lock will be cut off the baskets. Hurry up and go line up in the hall to get your uniforms." Then she crossed her arms with her feet apart; she obviously was ready to wait as long as it took for us to follow her instructions.

I wrote down the number of the first basket I saw, then left quickly to go line up in the hall. Once I received my gym shirt and shorts and wrote my name on each piece with a black permanent marker as instructed, I returned to sit on the gym floor and wait for the next set of instructions. The older girls quickly grabbed spots along the walls and close to the door so they could be the first to escape, so I carefully chose a spot on the floor in the middle, avoiding as many people as possible. Once safely settled, I pulled out my class schedule and the campus map, and pretended to review the rest of my day. Although I already knew my schedule by heart, it gave me the chance to sit unmolested and wait for the bell.

My next class was in the Math building, all the way on the other side of campus. Somehow, my schedule ensured that I'd cross the entire campus at every class change. The high school campus, built to resemble a large Spanish mission, was about size of a small college and looked like pictures I'd seen of the Alamo, with thick, sand-colored stucco walls and red tile roofs on all the buildings. The walls inside the buildings were thick and the stucco painted white, with floors paved in red Spanish tile. The heavy wooden classroom doors were painted with a dark lacquer and led to classrooms with rows of floor-to-ceiling transom windows.

In addition to the girls' and boys' gyms, there were buildings for arts, science, English, math, and shop, as well as a main building, a cafeteria, and an auditorium. The main building had two floors with staircases that had thick wooden bannisters and railings that reminded me of an old pirate ship. My book locker was up on the second floor of the main building, which, although near my homeroom, was as far as possible from any other class on my schedule.

Yet aside from having to scramble across campus to each un-air conditioned class, in what would certainly be a constant state of sweatiness, my schedule held reasons for hope. My placement test scores had been good enough to get me into all advanced classes, and I'd been told they were smaller than the regular ones. I even dared hope that there might be a few people I knew in one or two of them.

As I sat on the gym floor, I noticed a group of older girls had circled around another new girl and I heard them tell her with urgency, "No matter what, under no circumstances, do you ever go into the cafeteria at lunch…." I sighed audibly causing them to look over and make a face at me for eavesdropping. They didn't say why the girl should avoid the cafeteria. But since Whitney, my long-time friend, and I had already planned to meet for lunch but not in the cafeteria, I wasn't overly concerned about their warning. Our older sisters told us they always brought their lunches and ate in "the horseshoe," the driveway outside in front of the main building, so that was our plan. The horseshoe apparently was considered "the" place to meet.

I just need to figure out how I'm going to manage all of this, I thought, wiping the sweat from the back of my neck. *Rise above it. Muddle through it. Get over it.* I told myself. Even then, I knew I needed to gather my courage and do what needed to be done, despite being so scared.

• • •

Somehow I survived the events of my first day. As we began the long, hot bus ride home that afternoon and traveled the narrow streets surrounding the high school, the day's events whirled in my head. Overwhelmed with emotion, I watched as we passed the neglected wooden, shot-gun style homes and massive oak trees dripping with Spanish moss that lined the cramped streets of midtown. But by the time the streets widened and the neighborhoods, filled with sprawling ranch-style homes and well-tended lawns lined with azalea bushes, grew more familiar, I had resolved to keep my feelings about my first day of high school to myself.

So once I'd successfully made it back home, although stinking and wilted from a full day of sweating, and I called

Mom at work to tell her I was home, I curtly said, "Fine." when she asked how my day went.

I'm sure Mom genuinely wanted to hear about my day, but I wasn't ready to tell her anything, especially about how scared I'd been. I always needed time to digest everything, and to think through the potential consequences of anything I considered doing before I ever said anything to my parents.

"What time will you be home?" I asked her, intentionally changing the subject.

"I don't know, same time as usual, around 5:30, I guess. Can you start dinner?" she asked.

"Yes, ma'am," I answered quickly.

"Is Grace home?" she asked, referring to my younger sister.

"Yes, ma'am," I repeated.

"Well, can I talk to her?" she said.

"Yes, ma'am. Grace!" I yelled to my little sister, who was already in her room at the back of the house. My younger sister, with her white-blond hair and fair skin, was my complete opposite and my constant companion since I was four years old. "Pete and Repeat," my dad called us, since she'd always followed me everywhere, copying everything I did.

"Erin, do me a favor and get all your chores done before I get home tonight, please? You have dance classes starting again tomorrow, so let's start this school year off right," I heard my mom add as I returned the receiver to my ear.

"Yes, ma'am," I repeated. My mom and dad both worked hard, and naturally my sisters and I were expected to help around the house. Not that I minded having chores or helping out with dinner.

"Love you, bye," I added quickly and then handed the phone to my younger sister as soon as she walked into the kitchen.

Worried that my parents wouldn't let me stay in public school if they knew how scared I'd been that first day, hearing my mom's voice strengthened my resolve not to tell them much about P.E. or anything else that'd happened that day. My family had always called me fearless and brave due to my long history of climbing trees that were too high, jumping off of things you probably shouldn't, and getting up in front of people and doing things without being nervous. Always a confident child, I'd thought nothing of singing in front of people at church, performing during chapel at school, or dancing and playing piano in recitals for hundreds of people. None of those things were scary to me and didn't take much courage. So I knew that if I ever told them that I was even the least bit scared, they'd take me very seriously. They'd think I'd finally stumbled upon something I couldn't handle.

My parents worried, like all parents probably do, about whether they were doing the right thing by moving me to a public school. I'd heard them talking about it with some of their friends. They always told me that they wanted to do what's best for me, so I knew they'd take my concerns seriously. If they knew I was afraid, they might think it was best to pull me out and say the change was just a little too much.

It wasn't that I didn't like going to my old private school; it definitely had its advantages. It had air conditioning, for example, which was a big one. I certainly didn't have to ride a bus for an hour to get there, either. We'd always carpooled with friends. The classes had been small there, and I'd know some kids my whole life. But the biggest plus was that I'd never felt out of place or scared there, not in P.E., not when I went to the bathroom, or at any other time.

But I didn't want to go back there. It was an incredibly small school, and people always made fun of us for going there.

Even people I knew from church, who you'd think would appreciate that it was a small Christian school, made fun of us, calling us sheltered and saying we couldn't make it out in the real world. No. Going back there did not fit into my plans.

In my parents' attempt to give me everything they could, I probably had been a little too sheltered. And I needed to prove that I could make it out there in the real world because I had big plans for my future. I didn't want to stay in Alabama for the rest of my life, and I needed to go to a big high school so I could take harder courses and go away to college. I wanted to live a life like people in the books I'd read. I knew from books what was possible, and I wanted to live that kind of life, meet new people, do new things and go to many new places. I couldn't let a little fear take that away from me.

I knew it was best to keep my fears about my first day to myself. *If it ever gets too bad, then I'll tell them,* I nodded to myself as I began to unload the dishwasher.

Already I had reassured myself that what had happened in the bathroom earlier that day wasn't really that big of a deal. I'd just made the mistake of going to the bathroom during class instead of going between classes when there were a lot of girls around. But during fifth-period English class I'd asked for a bathroom pass, and swinging open the bathroom door, I'd been greeted by three much older black girls who were just hanging out, leaning on the sinks talking.

"Hey, girl - gotta casekwata?" one of the girls asked me as soon as I walked into the bathroom.

Surprised to see them and not understanding what she'd said, I just froze, and like an idiot, stared at her with my mouth open.

"Do you hear me, girl? I need a casekwata! Got one?" she asked again, wrinkling her forehead with the effort of repeating herself.

"I'm sorry - I don't…sorry," is all I could stammer in reply. I didn't know what she was asking. I'd always thought I could understand all sorts of Southern accents, but the black kids I had run into at this new school sounded completely different. And I think those girls could tell I was afraid of them.

"You don't gotta casekwata? You look like you do, lil miss white bread…" said one the girls as she half sat on the edge of the sink, smirking. After eying me up and down suspiciously for about half a minute, she bounced up off of the sink and stood up straight, looking to me like she was going to start walking towards me. Afraid she might want to do something to me, I blurted out "No - No. I don't. Sorry!" It came out a little louder than the first time, and I immediately turned and fled the bathroom. I could hear them laughing as I fled back down the hall to my class.

I wasn't sure what "Lil Miss White bread" meant, but I knew it couldn't be good. I'd been scared that they had bad intentions and their laughter seemed to confirm it. But I wished that I hadn't been so rattled.

Once I was safe at home, I realized how embarrassed I was. I never used to worry about things like changing my clothes in P.E. or going to the bathroom at school. I didn't want to be such a wimp, and I certainly didn't want anyone else to know.

It's not like I didn't have any experience dealing with people who were a little rough around the edges. When I first went to middle school, there was this guy who took a liking to me and who scared me a lot. He was 15, still in 8th grade, and he drove a motorcycle to school. I don't know his name and I didn't ever have any classes with him, but he and his friends always seemed to be in the hall staring at me.

I can't explain it, but I always had a bad feeling when he was around. He'd get this weird look whenever he saw me, and was always turning up at the strangest times, like he was following me. He was kind of cute, so I guess in some way I enjoyed the fact that he seemed to like me, but something about him and his friends set off alarms inside me. But I'd managed to get through that whole year and nothing bad had ever happened. And this was practically the same thing.

The rest of my day went pretty well, I thought as I went over my schedule in my head. I had plenty of stories I could share with my parents and sisters at supper. That's when they always asked about our day, and they were never satisfied with one-word answers. I could talk about my classes, such as Honors English, which included both literature and composition, and we were going to read quite a few books we weren't allowed to read at my private school.

Algebra and Spanish both had a few sophomore and junior boys who were super cute. Alabama history would be a piece of cake, since we'd learned most of it already back in fourth grade. Chemistry had a real lab with wet sinks, black fireproof counters, and real gas outlets, with cabinets full of lab equipment like Bunsen burners, beakers, and test tubes. We were told we would have lab at least once a week where we'd get to perform real experiments. Besides, there were a few people I knew in almost every one of my classes, mostly kids from eighth grade, but also a couple from my old private school.

They were sure to ask how lunch went, and that might end up being a little uncomfortable. I'd met Whitney out in the horseshoe as planned, along with Lizbeth, a girl I'd met through Whitney in eighth grade. There were groups of kids everywhere, walking around and talking, so just like our sisters had said, it was the perfect place to eat lunch and meet new people. But Whitney and Lizbeth didn't want to walk around and talk to anybody. It was too bad, too, to have missed the chance to make some new friends, since I saw kids from some of my classes who we could've talked to, but Whitney and Lizbeth just wanted to sit there and complain about the popular girls who used to go to middle school with us. So they just sat there on the curb and wouldn't budge.

I'd known Whitney and her older sister Alicia practically since birth. Their mom and my parents had been friends since before we were born. Whitney, Alicia, and I had played, taken dance lessons, and gone to church and school together for our whole lives. They both liked to read as much as I did, and we acted out the stories we'd read. We spent weeks and months playing out scenes from books like *Little House on the Prairie, Little Women, The Swiss Family Robinson, Pippy Long Stocking* and the Nancy Drew and Hardy Boys series. Whitney, with her fair skin, red hair, and green eyes, always insisted on playing any character with red hair. Alicia, being the oldest and tallest, would flip her long blonde hair and insist on assuming the character of her choice, threatening not to play if we didn't let her.

I'd played whatever parts were left and wrote my own stories for us to act out. We'd read stories I'd written in my spiral notebook, stories of adventures set long ago, ones that always had girl heroines and always required costumes. We'd acted out my stories enthusiastically, each of us a heroine in our own right, wearing our turbans and scarves, or coats and hats, pretending to live in tents or caves we'd made from old tarps or drop cloths spotted with paint, and pretended to make our own food from collecting acorns, grinding pine straw on rocks, and picking weeds and berries.

Much to our mothers' delight, the three of us had remained extremely close until the previous year. After Alicia went to high school, things began to change. She made other friends and understandably no longer wanted to hang out with me and her younger sister. Once we started eighth grade, Whitney changed too. She started criticizing the other girls in our classes and warned me not to be friends with any of them. Whenever I tried to be friends with anyone else, she would tell me that the other girl had been mean to her and that I wasn't her friend if I talked to that girl. I'd hoped we could stay friends and make new ones, too, but it always felt like she wanted me to choose between her and everyone else.

Stacking up my new notebooks and clearing the kitchen table so I could set the table and start supper like I was told, I decided to keep doing what they'd always told me to do: "Just smile and be nice." Maybe they were right, and if I was nice to everybody, the girls in P. E., Whitney, and any new people I met, maybe it would all work out. Anyway, it was worth a shot.

My mom and dad had always told me that I could do whatever I put my mind to, and sometimes they even called me hard-headed. I preferred the words I'd read describing the heroines in all my favorite books; words like *determined, resolute* and *persistent*, sounded better. Regardless, I knew they were right.

So the following morning, I arrived at the bus stop before daylight, determined to be successful. The air, hot and humid even that early in the morning, created a low, wispy mist that rose up from the ground in little plumes between the trees. Although Whitney and a couple of people I knew shared my bus stop, we didn't talk much. Instead, we waited, kicking pine straw and leaves around as we shuffled our feet, repeatedly searching down the street for signs of the school bus. Once on the bus, we each sat in different rows and quietly looked out the open windows, preoccupied with our own thoughts and plans, enjoying the wind on our faces.

"I don't have a combination lock yet, what am I supposed to do with my purse?" a tall blonde girl asked as I walked into the locker room.

"Put your clothes and books in the locker and bring your purse with you until you get your lock. But you'd better make sure you get one before next week," the coach told her.

Slinking quickly past the coach I put my books into the wire basket and removed my shoes, determined to change as quickly as possible without making eye contact, hoping to go unnoticed. As soon as I got my shoes and jeans off and slipped on my uniform shorts, I took a quick look around. Of the 30 or so of us in our bank of lockers, most of the girls seemed to already know each other and were laughing and talking while they changed.

Turning my back and facing the wall of baskets, I removed my top and pulled on my uniform shirt before I snuck another peek and confirmed that no one cared what I was doing. Relieved that my plan seemed to be working, I shoved everything else in the basket, pushed it into its place. Since I didn't have a lock yet either, I said a prayer that no one would take my clothes and headed for the gym to line up for roll-call.

Taking attendance in school for most people is a regular, boring activity, but for me the exercise had always been painful because of my last name.

"Pugsley, Erin," the coach shouted over the crowd. Half of the girls laughed. The other half scanned the group to see who was saddled with such an unfortunate name.

"Here!" I shouted, not bothering to look up. I picked at my shoe laces, trying to show that I just didn't care if anyone thought my name was funny.

After roll call, the coach yelled that each day we would break into groups to participate in different activities. "Wearing your uniform counts for 60 percent of your grade. Participation is 30 percent, and how you perform is 10 percent" she shouted.

All I need to do is put on the uniform and try, I thought as my resolve strengthened.

My group was assigned to the balance-beam first, so we moved to a back room that I hadn't noticed the day before. I was excited to see it contained all sorts of the gymnastic equipment. The coach told us to sit while she had an older girl demonstrate what she wanted us to do. "No flips, no spins, no Nadia Comaneci moves, no real skill required," she yelled. "Just walk to one end of the beam, turn, walk back, and repeat that a couple of times. Only one girl up there at a time. The rest of you just sit there and keep it quiet while you wait your turn."

The same blonde girl that asked about her purse sat beside me, and when I turned to her and smiled, she smiled right back. She said, "Hi, I'm Brittany."

Grinning, I answered, "Hi, I'm Erin," proudly thinking, *It worked! All I have to do is smile and be nice!*

Brittany was what my mom and her friends would've called awkward. Tall like me, at around 5'9", she stooped like she was trying not to be so tall. The bones in her thin hands and elbows stuck out when she moved, and her knees were too large for her legs. Her skin was so pale, you could see her bluish veins wherever her skin was exposed, and her white blonde hair was so thin that you could see her pink scalp. Her glasses were much too large for her face and almost hid her striking green eyes. But she had the most brilliant smile I'd ever seen. When she smiled, her whole face lit up, making her eyes sparkle.

"She's really good," Brittany leaned over and whispered to me quietly as one of the girls from our group walked easily down the beam and made the turns without a wobble.

"Yes, she is," I agreed, keeping my eyes on the gymnast.

"I can't do this - can you?" Brittany asked.

"I don't know," I told her. "I've never tried."

Out of the corner of my eye, I saw her turn and look at me a little skeptically, and my heart skipped a beat. Then she asked, "And why's that?"

"We didn't have any of this at my old school," I said with a shrug, keeping my eyes fixed on the girl on the beam as if my life depended on it.

Then she asked, "And where did you go to school, exactly?"

I answered, without mentioning the name of my old private school. Satisfied, she turned away to watch the girl return from the balance beam and sit back down among us.

"Pugsley, front and center," the coach called out, reading my name from the list on her clipboard.

No one said anything when I scrambled to my feet, but I noticed several girls silently pushing their noses up in an exaggerated gesture to mock my name, which I ignored.

Much to my surprise, I was able to walk on the balance beam without wobbling if I kept my arms out by my side. I did it well enough that the coach said, "Good job, Pugsley. Now turn."

Turning was more difficult than it appeared, but once I walked and turned a couple of times, I was almost as good as the first girl. Soon it was Brittany's turn and she walked on the beam pretty well, but had a hard time with the turns and almost fell off. "You've got to work on your turns, Rankin," the coach told her when she was done.

With her back turned to the coach, Brittany made a face at me and I grinned back at her.

"You did good," I whispered to her as she sat down.

"No, I didn't," she said with a big, carefree grin.

The coach called a girl named Roberts next. I didn't catch her first name or whether the coach had even said it. A good six inches shorter than Brittany and me, she had really dark skin. Even though she was curvier everywhere and a lot rounder in the waist, she was very muscular. When she jumped up on the beam, most of the girls cheered and said, "Let's go, Bumper!" And was she good! She pointed her toes and turned with her arms over her head like a ballerina as we watched her muscles flex. After repeating the walk and many turns with ease, she elegantly jumped off the beam and raised her hands over her head, and turned her face up to the ceiling, just like the gymnasts on TV. We all clapped and some of her friends were cheering when the coach barked, "Quit showing off, Roberts," silencing us. Bumper frowned as she walked back to her place, and her friends' looked angry, too, as they patted her shoulder or leg as she sat down. I didn't think she was showing off. She was just really good. But I kept quiet.

When everyone had taken a turn, we headed back into the locker room. As we passed the showers, one of Bumper's friends leaned close to my ear from behind and whispered, "You know Coach McNasty watches all the girls when they shower, right?" I tried to pretend I didn't hear her, but I walked a little faster anyway.

"Where do you go next?" Brittany asked as I slipped off my shirt.

When I got my school shirt back on I turned around noticing that the other girls continued talking and joking as they dressed. All round the locker room girls stood there talking in nothing but their bras, and from my vantage point, I could see several using the showers. They all looked older than me and were black, and they were laughing and joking around like it was no big deal. I admired their confidence and remember thinking, *I wish I could be like that.* I also noticed Coach McNairy standing with her arms crossed, watching the girls in the shower, just like the girl said she would.

"Hey, Erin, where do you go next?" Brittany asked me again as she pulled up her jeans. "What's your next class?"

Forcing my eyes away from the shower, I said, "Algebra, in the Math building."

"I have Pre-Algebra in the Math building, too. Want to walk together?" she asked with a smile.

"Yeah, that would be great," I said, still scrambling to dress.

"Hurry up and finish so we can go stand by the gate. That way we'll get out first and won't have to run all the way to class," Brittany said as she hurried to gather her books.

After grabbing my things, I followed Brittany and said, "I could never do that. Shower in there like that," muttering under my breath as we walked. Brittany turned and smiled, and I knew it was okay that I'd accidentally said it out loud.

"Let me see your schedule," Brittany said once we got to the closed metal gate leading out of the gym. For some reason, I didn't think to ask for hers as I handed her mine.

"Wow, all advanced classes," Brittany said as she looked up, pushing her glasses up on her nose, smiling at me again. "Looks like we have the same Spanish class. Want to meet at lunch and go to Spanish together?"

"Yeah, that would be great," I said again, grinning.

One of the coaches pushed through the crowd just as the bell rang and opened the gate to let us out. Brittany and I couldn't talk much with so many people trying to change classes, but we managed to walk together.

"Want to meet in the horseshoe at lunch?" I asked, once we began to cross the back lawn to the Math building.

"Sure," she said, smiling as we entered the building. "See you at lunch," she said as she ducked into her classroom.

Still smiling, I entered my classroom a few doors down and slid into one of the front desks as the bell rang. It was only the beginning of day two, and not only had I survived another day in gym class, I also had a new friend.

At lunch I met Whitney and Lizbeth in the horseshoe, but wouldn't sit down on the curb with them to eat. Instead, I stood and ate while I anxiously looked around, trying to spot Brittany in the crowd.

"Who're you looking for?" Whitney asked, looking up at me as I shifted from foot to foot.

"A really nice girl I met in gym class. You'll like her," I answered while continuing to search for my new friend.

"I don't know about that," Lizbeth grumbled, inspecting the contents between the pieces of bread of her sandwich.

As soon as I spotted her, I could tell Brittany had been looking for me, too. She was with another girl, and as soon as she saw me, she flashed that brilliant smile, tapped the other girl, pointed at me, and waved.

Unfortunately, Whitney and Lizbeth didn't talk to Brittany when I introduced them. Although Brittany tried to make conversation, they didn't respond with more than necessary to be polite. When they didn't bother to try keeping the conversation going, Brittany asked me if I wanted to go with her to the girl's room before the bell rang. Grateful for a reason to escape, I said goodbye to Whitney and Lizbeth and followed Brittany to the main building. In the girls' bathroom, we were nearly suffocated by the clouds of cigarette smoke. Smoke usually didn't bother me because my parents smoked, but the air was so thick in that bathroom, I couldn't breathe. Each of the stalls were filled with girls crowding around the toilets and smoking, but Brittany walked up to the first stall and said "Y'all gotta move now. I need to pee!" The girls immediately moved out of her way.

I stood outside her door and noticed Bumper and a few of her friends from standing by one of the sinks and talking. I didn't look at them but instead studied the graffiti written in lipstick and liquid paper on the black stall door.

"Hey, Pugsley-you gotta casekwata," one of the girls with Bumper said when she saw me.

You've gotta be kidding me! I thought to myself, turning around. *Not this again.*

"I'm sorry?" I said, turning and smiling at her. What I really wanted to say was "What in the heck are you saying to me?!"

"She needs a quarter," Brittany said, her voice a little muffled from inside the stall.

Oh my goodness, I thought. *Is that all? They just wanted a quarter yesterday?*

But what I said, was "Sure, I might have twenty-five cents," as I began to dig in my purse.

"I got twenty-five cents," Bumper's friend said, holding out two dimes and a nickel in her palm for me to see. "What I need's a casekwata."

"She needs a quarter. You know, a "case quarter." The vending machines only take quarters. No dimes or nickels," Brittany said and flushed the toilet.

"Oh, okay. Yeah, hang on," I said, frantically digging around in my purse until I found one and handed it to the girl.

"Thanks, Pugsley," Bumper's friend said as we exchanged coins.

"You're welcome. I'm Erin, by the way," I replied with a big smile.

She smirked as she turned away, and I saw Bumper and her other friend rolling their eyes at each other as they left the bathroom.

"Oh, my God! I couldn't figure out what the heck she wanted," I told Brittany as I followed her into the hallway.

"Where did you say you went to school, again?" Brittany asked, turning back to me with that skeptical look on her face. "How do you not know what a case-quarter is?"

"Oh, I don't know." I said and changed the subject by asking her, "What's the room number for Spanish? Is it 102?"

Once we got to Spanish class, chose seats next to each other, and class began, I was certain I wanted to be Brittany's friend. I'd only just met her, and it was only my second day, but she was genuine, full of spunk and sparkle, experienced and delightfully awkward, all rolled into one.

Chapter Two

Every night at supper, my younger sister Grace shared everything from her day, good and bad, and in excruciating detail. She talked through the important and the mundane parts of her fifth-grade life, and my parents offered suggestions to try and help fix whatever wasn't working. Meanwhile, I continued to share only what was going well, saying nothing about any of my struggles. "Life's hard enough without dwelling on all the bad stuff," my dad had always said, and I'd decided he was right.

As more time passed, it became more difficult to bring up any of my fears and struggles. Until one night, I overheard my parents talking about how well they thought I was adjusting to my new school, and how they thought I'd do well in high school. Listening to them, I knew my positive-only tactic had been the right one. They couldn't fix what was wrong unless they sent me to another school, and I was determined to stay. I just needed to keep my head down and keep working hard for what I wanted.

Mom and Dad had always told us how they'd worked hard for everything they had, and that we needed to learn to appreciate it. They'd grown up in the same small Alabama town of only a few hundred people, situated further up the river delta, about two hours north and only a few miles from the city where Harper Lee, the author of *To Kill a Mockingbird,* lived. It's the kind of town where people put value on how hard you try and how hard you work, not on how much you have.

When we went to visit my Grandmomma, I would watch out the car window as rows of hard red dirt appeared between the long rows of cotton planted in fields lined with empty, rusting rail cars sitting alongside the train tracks. Bits of cotton fluff dotted the rows of plants, stuck in the wire mesh of the rail cars and in between the gears of the rusting cotton-gin mills that sat idle under rusting tin roofs.

Both of my parents grew up during The Depression. They said that although they must have been considered really poor, they never knew it. They all grew up the same way, and although they might not have had nice things, they were never hungry, even in the hardest of times. They grew up walking to school and working in the fields before and after school, and my grandparents worked hard, too. They all went to church, raised their families, raised their own food, and worked at any job they could find. My grandparents held honest jobs, working in a textile factory, driving a school bus, managing a grocery store, being a butcher, working in the school cafeteria, operating a cotton gin and working on the railroad.

Mom and Dad said their parents didn't need money for much when they were growing up, other than to pay their taxes. They said they were lucky because a lot of people lost their land because they couldn't afford to pay their taxes during The Depression. Whenever they had any extra money left, they would buy special things like coffee, sugar, and flour and maybe some fabric for making clothes. Both of my grandmommas knew how to make dresses and shirts for their kids out of the soft cotton fabric that flour came in.

Our parents and grandparents taught us all how to work hard and to take pride in it. Before my granddaddy died, he had a small plot of land for farming and a white house with pecan and pear trees, and a chicken yard and coop with a couple dozen chickens. We went up to our grandparents' house on most weekends to help them out. We spent the morning picking lima beans, purple hulled peas, crowder peas, and green beans. And after lunch, we'd spent the afternoon shelling whatever we'd picked, sitting in rocking chairs on the front porch or in kitchen chairs out in the yard. Once we were done, my mom, grandmomma and aunts would put up whatever we'd shelled, by blanching and freezing them, or canning them. Sometimes we picked and hulled corn, dug potatoes, or picked blueberries or strawberries, which was a lot more fun since we didn't have to shell them. It was hot and dirty work, but the adults always bragged about what we'd gotten done. "Look at alla those peas she hulled," my grandmomma would say, beaming down at my bowl with her hands on her aproned hips.

Grandmomma cooked supper for all of us at night, and she made the best biscuits we ever tasted. We'd have them with fried chicken and whatever we'd picked that day, all cooked with a little bacon fat, and dessert was a cobbler made with whatever fruit she had on hand. Those dinners were better than any other meal I could remember.

After supper, we'd bathe the sweat and red dirt from our bodies and all of us kids would pile into the room that had the most windows, where we'd enjoy the cool breeze on our clean skin and damp hair, and talk in the dark about the things little kids talk about before they go to sleep. We spent most of our weekends that way, from early summer through late fall until my granddaddy passed away.

We'd lived in our town all of my life, since Mom and Dad moved there in search of better jobs after they got married. My dad went to work in a paper mill and my mom went to work in a bank and over the years, my parents worked their way up into well-deserved management positions. My dad still wore mill-worker clothes and steel-toed shoes, even though he was in management, and no longer had to work night-shifts or swing-shifts unless something broke down. My mom became the manager of an accounting office at a chemical company. Even though they made and sold chemicals, she wore pretty pants suits and high heels to work and sat behind a desk in her own office.

In time, we moved to a larger home in the same part of town, but in a better school district. As a result, Grace and I left the private school in our neighborhood and were bused into our respective public schools. My older sister Lynne had gone to public high school, but seemed to fit in better there and had been a cheerleader. Lots of boys had wanted to date her, cute ones that my parents liked and talked to when they came to the house. When she graduated, she found a job right away and went to work, which meant I'd be the first in my family to go to college.

Going to public high school was important to my future plans because, unlike my former private school, it offered a lot of advanced classes and AP courses that would make me better prepared for college. So I needed to stay and do well. My mom and dad always told us that they cared most about how hard we tried. And I was willing to stick with it and work for what I wanted.

• • •

A few months into the school year, I'd become friendly with several people in each of my classes, and spent a lot of time with Brittany. We saw each other every day in P.E., ate lunch together, sat together in Spanish class, and talked on the phone after school every afternoon and sometimes again after supper. Always talking about what we could do to make things easier in high school, we became a real team.

Even the smallest things turned out to be important in high school, and we planned everything together. We spent hours plotting how we could swap books between classes so we wouldn't have to try and get back to our far-away lockers between classes. By sharing lockers, neither of us had to carry more than two books at a time, meaning we could ditch our book bags completely. It was a little thing, but since the older kids didn't carry book bags and made fun of the younger ones who did, we didn't want to be caught dead carrying one. It was one less reason to get picked on or teased.

Because of Brittany, I enjoyed going to P.E. and didn't mind changing clothes as much, even though you'd never catch me in the showers. We tried a lot of different activities in gym, many of which I loved, but the best part was that I had forty-five minutes with my best friend each day. We met people we wouldn't otherwise meet, even if we didn't want to hang out with all of them. Some of the girls were really mean and one particular group of older white girls spent the whole gym class making fun of everybody else, picking apart what they were wearing, how they looked, what was wrong with their bodies, their hair, or any other reason they could find. We steered clear of them as best we could.

One day when P.E. was almost over, we were changing back into our school clothes and chatting when we heard raised voices. We all stopped dressing and looked at each other; it's always a bad sign to hear raised voices in the locker room. It wasn't yelling exactly, just voices talking louder than usual. Since the commotion was coming from the direction of the showers, we all peeked down the corridor to see what was going on. Just as we did, we heard Coach McNairy shout, "You need to come out of there and get dressed right now!"

She was talking to a pretty caramel-colored girl standing in the middle of the shower, covering her private parts. My mouth popped open when I saw her, not because she was naked, but because she was obviously pregnant.

"Why?" the girl asked Coach McNairy in an equally loud voice. "What did I do?"

All of the other girls scurried out of the shower and back to their own lockers, leaving only the pregnant girl standing there in the middle of the shower, alone, naked, and face-to-face with the coach.

"Don't argue with me! Just get out of there, get dressed, and come to my office. Now!" Coach McNairy said even louder, her hands on her hips.

After they glared at each other for what seemed like a long time, the girl complied. She snatched her towel, wrapped it around her, and headed back to her locker, grumbling under her breath.

"Show's over! Show's over!" the coach shouted, turning to face us, shooing us to finish dressing.

"Is she pregnant?" I asked Brittany, in what I thought was a low enough voice that only she would hear. Before she could answer, another girl said "Of course, she is!"

I'd seen a pregnant woman's belly before. It's just that I was so surprised, I felt like I had to ask out loud. She couldn't have been more than fifteen years old.

"Bet Coach McNasty didn't know 'til now," one of the black girls from my group said to no one in particular as she put on her jeans.

"They gonna kick her butt outta school now for sure," another one said as she pulled on her shirt, and in response she got several "Mmm-hmms" in agreement.

"Can they do that?" I quietly asked Brittany.

"Yes, they can do that, milk toast!" the same girl spat back at me angrily.

I didn't ask any more obvious questions until we were waiting alone by the gate to leave. I asked Brittany again, "Can they really do that? Kick you out of school for being pregnant?"

She said she didn't know, but she guessed so.

"What does milk-toast mean, anyway?" I asked, pretending to look for something in my purse.

"I dunno. Don't worry about it," Brittany said as the bell rang. All was quickly forgotten in the rush to get to the next class.

But I sure didn't forget. I looked it up in the Webster's Dictionary when I got home. It wasn't easy to find, since the word is actually spelled *milquetoast,* but I found it. When I read the definition, which means weak or timid, my face burned. It was exactly what I didn't want to be.

I wondered how some people always manage to pick on the one thing that's sure to get under your skin?

The next day, all of the girls were buzzing with the news about the pregnant girl. Although there were some things "polite young ladies" weren't supposed to talk about, a pregnant girl getting kicked out of school was big news. According to some of the girls, she'd be forced to finish school at night or to get her G. E. D. diploma to avoid being a bad influence on the rest of us. One girl said that she'd even overheard Ms. Springer, the Vice Principal, say that the girl had to leave school immediately because "pregnancy's contagious."

With the passing of time, and with Brittany at my side, I wasn't as scared going into the girl's room either. She always seemed to understand what was going on and helped me figure out the best way to handle different situations.

Typically I didn't primp in the mirror, even at home. I wasn't allowed to wear much makeup, and trying to catch a glance of your reflection wasn't worth the trouble in the overcrowded bathroom at lunch time. Girls always piled around the sinks, putting on makeup and talking. The smoke was thick and the mirrors were very old and cloudy on the edges, so it was difficult to see anything unless you were close up. But one day I happened to catch my reflection and saw that my hair was really messed up; it desperately needed combing. I didn't have a comb and Brittany didn't have one either, so I turned to see who else I knew in the bathroom I could ask. The only other person I knew was Bumper, so I asked her.

"Do you have a comb I could borrow?" I asked, but without saying her name. I avoided it since I didn't know her real name and I just didn't feel comfortable calling her Bumper. I didn't know why they called her that. And I certainly wasn't going to call her Roberts like the coaches did. She hated that.

"What?" she asked, obviously a little irritated that I'd interrupted her conversation

I repeated the question.

"Yeah, sure," she said, adding a little arch to her eyebrows as she handed me a pick from her back pocket.

I didn't know at the time why her friends were looking at me like I was weird for asking. You'd have thought that since they'd asked me to swap their change for a quarter almost every day, it would've been okay for me to borrow a comb. So I ignored them, said thanks, and quickly started combing the knots out my hair. I needed to hurry so I could get my hair back up into a pony tail before the bell rang.

"Oh, my God! What are you dooooooing?!" I heard some girl shrill.

When someone says a thing like that you have to stop, turn around, and look. And when I did, I saw four older white girls all staring at me. Everyone in the bathroom stopped what they were doing to watch.

"What are you doing, using that?!" one of the four shrieked as she flipped her long blonde hair off her shoulder.

What am I doing with what? I thought, glancing around quickly, looking for someone else to explain. Just when I caught Brittany's eye, another one of the girls explained.

"Don't use thaaaat!" the girl with the brown bangs and braces said loudly. "You'll get grease in your hair or lice, Ohmygod I can't believe you! That's disgusting!"

I looked down at the comb and didn't see anything. Once again I looked around at all of the other girls in the bathroom who were watching. Then the bell rang. Everyone began throwing their cigarettes into the toilets, putting their makeup back in their purses, and heading out of the bathroom. All except for Bumper.

"Give me that," Bumper hissed through gritted teeth.

"Sorry I…." I stammered, but she'd snatched the comb from my hand and turned to leave before I could say anything else.

"Ignore them. Come on," was all Brittany said as she grabbed my arm and pulled me out into the hall.

I followed her, still trying to pull my hair into a ponytail, my books under the arm that she kept firmly in her grasp as she led me out. Even when she let go, I felt numb, my arms and legs heavy, and my face burned with shame. Disoriented, my head swam as I walked down the crowded hall to class. I hated that I couldn't think fast enough to respond and make the ugliness stop back there in the girl's room. I should've stood up to them, even if I couldn't stop them. My head spun with things I should've said, and thought my inability to take a stand made me just as guilty.

• • •

One Friday afternoon later that fall, I rode home with Brittany on her bus and spent the night at her house for the first time. Being invited to a sleep over was an important sign of friendship and Brittany lived in an apartment, and because I'd never had a friend who lived in one, I was doubly excited.

Riding home on the bus with Brittany was much more fun than going on my own bus. She knew a lot of the kids, and many lived in her complex. It was fun talking to so many new people. Even though it also took us about an hour to get to her stop, the time seemed to fly. Her apartment complex was near the local college, and they lived there because her dad was a professor and they wanted to live close to his work. The apartments in Brittany's complex were called townhouses, with little roads and rows of apartment houses inside a tight little neighborhood. Each townhouse was connected to the next, some made of brick, some made of wood, and each a different color. Each townhouse was two stories, with two dormer windows at the top and a carport in the back.

After we dropped off our stuff at her house, grabbed a quick snack, we headed back out to the parking lot in the center of the complex to play kick-ball with some of Brittany's friends. Even though we had to play on pavement and use pieces of cardboard for bases, it was fun having so many kids to play with. We had eight people on each team, all different kinds of boys and girls, some older, some younger, black and white, and we played all afternoon until the street lights came on. That's when Brittany said we need to go "check in." As we ran across the lot, she yelled over her shoulder, promising her friends that we'd come back out after dinner and play flashlight tag.

When we went inside, I met Brittany's parents. Her dad looked exactly the way I'd expected a college professor would. He had a balding head, and his pale face was almost covered with a dark brown mustache and full beard. He sat at the dining room table, reading the newspaper and smoking a pipe. Brittany's dad barely looked up when we came in, but quietly greeted me when she introduced us before he returned to reading his paper.

Brittany's mom was in the galley kitchen, getting dinner ready. It looked like she had been in the middle of working on something and had stopped suddenly to cook dinner. There were books and papers strewn everywhere. A large back-pack with papers and books spilled out on the floor in the den next to the kitchen. When we came in, she left the kitchen and scrambled to get some of the paperwork out of the way in the den so we'd have space while she cooked.

When Brittany introduced us and her mom heard me speak, she immediately started teasing me about my Southern accent. She never said anything about my accent, but instead imitated me, repeating my words and exaggerating how I spoke. "Call me Justine," she said. But since I wasn't allowed to call adults by their first name unless they were close family friends, I just avoided calling Brittany's parents anything at all.

Brittany's mom was so different from what I expected, and very different from my mom or any of her friends. Her long curly hair was gray mixed with light brown. It wasn't styled, but instead curled long and wild about her face. She wasn't wearing any makeup, shoes, or a bra, and wore faded jeans and a tight baby blue Grateful Dead t-shirt. But what was most different about her was how she talked.

She didn't use that fake, sickeningly sweet voice to try and be nice. Instead, her deep voice was thick with sarcasm as she made wisecracks. She also didn't talk about the same things I was used to hearing either. When Brittany told her mom that I was in all advanced classes, she seemed genuinely interested and asked me which courses I was taking, then discussed each one in detail. She said she wished Brittany was in advanced classes, and told her to talk to her guidance counselor and try to get that changed. She must've told her that before, because Brittany rolled her eyes at me when she said it. When her mom asked me what else I liked to do, we talked about the books we liked to read and my dance and piano lessons. She told me Brittany used to take piano, but didn't like it so she quit. Just when I started to get uncomfortable about where the conversation was leading, Brittany changed the subject and told me her mom was in school working on her master's degree and volunteering at a woman's clinic.

Brittany's room was beautiful and almost the complete opposite of mine. She had stuff everywhere, whereas my room was stark by comparison. Beyond the normal furniture, clothes, papers, and books found in any room, she had scarves and pillows, beads and feathers, and posters and pictures everywhere. She had pink and purple wallpaper and long, flowing curtains, where my room had neutral paint and blinds. I preferred to keep my room neat and tidy, which made me feel at peace and more relaxed. But surprisingly, Brittany's room felt soft, comforting, and beautiful in its chaos.

Brittany had a window seat that looked out over the carport into the parking lot, so she could see who came and went and who was out playing. She also had a phone extension in her room, so she had privacy and could talk whenever she wanted. I had to talk on the phone in the kitchen, and only during reasonable hours of the day. Sometimes I had to sit on the floor on the other side of the island to get any kind of privacy because my sister Grace always found a way to eavesdrop. Brittany had a younger sister named Lacey who looked just like her, but she was quiet and sweet, and she left us alone, unlike Grace. They didn't seem to fight the way Grace and I did.

Brittany's family had a cat. My mom hated cats and my sister was allergic to them. We did have a dog once, but he lived outside and we gave him to our neighbor when we moved to our new house. Brittany said her mom hated dogs and thought they were stupid, dirty animals. We laughed about how different our families were, even down to our pets.

The next morning we got up early, since Brittany wanted to show me what she called "corrugation creek." It was a creek that drained from the lake in the county park a few blocks away and that ran through the woods behind her complex. We'd planned all week for our expedition, which mostly meant we were going to walk around in the woods and wear jeans and sneakers so we could get as dirty as we wanted. Brittany wanted to show me her "special spot," the place she liked to go to think. So we set out early, while it was still cool and quiet.

We talked about everything imaginable as we tromped through the mud, the sand and the rocks around the creek, and I mean everything. It was the kind of fall day that inspired conversation; cool enough to walk without sweating, but with a sky still the deep blue of summer. I'd never before had a friend who I could talk to about anything and everything with equal ease.

At some point, I asked Brittany if she was happy that they'd moved to Alabama. She said she was because it made her parents happy, and she's really proud of her mom for getting her master's degree. "It was hard at first, but I'm really happy now," she added.

"What made it hard?" I asked, since to me, nothing looked hard when Brittany did it.

"We left my grandma and my friends, and the people here are so different. When I first moved here, I didn't know anybody and couldn't understand what anyone was saying. Everyone talked funny and they made fun of my accent," she told me as we walked.

"I know what you mean! I've lived here all my life, and sometimes I can't tell what some of the people at school are saying," I told her and laughed.

"Yeah, I've noticed," she said and laughed back. I knew she was thinking about that case-quarter incident in the girl's bathroom at school.

Then I understood why Brittany didn't mind helping me learn the ropes in high school and never made fun of me for not understanding what people were saying. She'd been through it all herself.

When we took a break to eat some of the snacks we'd brought with us at her special spot on the bank of the creek, I could see why she liked it so much there. It was quiet and hidden, with a great place to sit up on a rise and watch the creek flow over the rocks for at least a hundred yards. While we were eating, she asked, "Do you know what you want to be when you grow up?"

She looked at me so seriously and intently, her half-eaten cookie still in her hand, I could tell that she genuinely wanted to hear my answer. She even stopped chewing while she waited for my answer. Brittany wasn't like most people who ask you a question just so they can tell you what they were thinking.

"I don't really know yet, but I want to go lots of places and do lots of different things." It was the most honest answer I could give her at the time.

"I know what you mean," she said, chewing again and watching the water.

I didn't ask her the same question, since I was still thinking about it.

After giving me a little more time, she pulled her knees to her chest, took a deep breath, sighed, and then asked, "If you had to use one word to describe what you want to be, just an adjective, what word would you choose?"

She sounded a little dreamy, and she didn't turn to look at me. She just stared off into the trees.

"Finish this sentence with an adjective," she said: 'I want to be…'" Then she waited for my answer.

I started to respond so she knew I'd heard her, but I spoke slowly so I could try to decide. "I…want…to be—"

Finally I gave her my adjective: "—interesting."

"I want to be interesting," I repeated, slightly faster and with a lot more certainty the second time.

"What about you? Now it's your turn." I told her.

"I want…to be…" she started thoughtfully, also taking the time between the words to think about her answer. Then she finished with, "…important."

We just sat there, letting *important* hang in the air as we soaked it all in, as if we were trying to memorize everything around us. We sat quietly, as only good friends can, each deep in our own thoughts, considering what those adjectives might mean one day.

After a while, Brittany stood up without a word and brushed off the seat of her jeans, so I got up, too, and followed her.

Chapter Three

Right before the holiday break, Brittany had a birthday party. Seven months younger than I was, she decided to celebrate with a slumber party at the townhouse clubhouse and invited a dozen girls. The club house, set in the middle of the complex, had a large party room, with dark shag carpet that could hide almost any kind of mess left after a party.

Everyone had to bring a sleeping bag so we could pile into the middle of the room, our pillows and heads together. Brittany talked about the party for weeks, and planned for all of us to spend the night listening to music, playing flashlight tag and other games, eating pizza, and having a few beers.

Brittany said she wanted to have "a little beer on hand" so the other girls didn't think that her sleepover was too childish. A grown-up neighbor friend of hers, Mr. Freeman, who lived in her complex, got the beer for her. She said he was pretty cool because he really listened to her and treated her like a grown-up, and she assured me that he wasn't creepy or anything.

I rode home with her on the bus that afternoon before the party to help get everything ready. When we went to Mr. Freeman's house, Brittany walked right in through his sliding glass door without even knocking. She yelled, "Hey! It's me!"

"In here," he called from the living room.

"This is my best friend, Erin," she said when she introduced us.

Mr. Freeman stood up, shook my hand, and said, "Nice to meet you," just as if I were an adult.

Oddly, he was shorter than we were and so thin that I doubted I could wear his pants or shoes. He was starting to go bald, but still had light brown hair circling the sides of his head, and had a thin brown mustache. He wore round wire-framed glasses that were so distracting, I couldn't tell what color his eyes were.

"I've heard a lot about you. I've really been looking forward to meeting you," he said, smiling with yellow-stained teeth. "Happy to finally get the chance."

The layout of his house was exactly like Brittany's, but he had different colored carpet, furniture, and decorations, which gave me this weird déjà vu feeling. Although the apartment was neat and clean, there was a lot of evidence that several other people lived there. Unlike Brittany's house, with all the books, papers newspapers, and magazines, Mr. Freeman's apartment instead had shoes, record albums, and empty cups strewn about. Brittany told me that he was married and had a daughter from his first marriage, and a step-son with his current wife, and that both kids still lived at home, despite being much older than we were and already out of high school. I don't know what Mr. Freeman did for a living, or why he would be home so early in the day, but Brittany certainly seemed to feel comfortable with him.

"It's in the kitchen pantry," he said, pointing and sitting down again in his chair, then picking up the TV remote. "Help yourself," he said, "but don't get caught."

We split the case of beer between us, covering our six packs with towels. As we headed out the door, Brittany told Mr. Freeman, "I'll bring back the towels tomorrow."

It wasn't anything he said or did, or the way the place looked, but the whole thing seemed weird. Maybe it was the fact that most adults weren't interested in talking to or spending time with me. Sure, they might act friendly, make polite conversation, and ask a question or two, but you could tell they're just being nice. Mr. Freeman seemed nice enough, but something didn't feel quite right and I was happy we didn't stay very long.

Once we were at the clubhouse and the room was set up, and we were ready. Brittany's mom gave her money for the pizza delivery, said "Have fun," and then left us alone. Thrilled to be on our own, and relieved that all of the girls she invited showed up, Brittany was happy. The girls she'd known since middle school were a little rougher and not very popular, whereas the ones we'd just met at our new school were prettier and more talkative, but we all got along just fine. No one got too drunk and everyone seemed to have fun together. Afterwards, although we doubted that this one slumber party had solidified any life-time friendships, we agreed that it had been a solid start and an overall success. The next morning I stayed late to help clean up, since we had to leave the clubhouse exactly as we'd found it, and we had to be very careful to dispose of the beer cans in one of the dumpsters so nobody would notice and get us into trouble.

And that's how the first semester of the school year passed, in a swirl of classes, homework, dance lessons and piano practice, punctuated by Friday night football games, a few sleepovers, and a couple of parties. Brittany and I spent as much time together as possible, and once we'd connected, we clicked together like puzzle pieces. Different in so many ways, we enjoyed our differences, appreciated them, and most of all, and recognized them for what they were. More importantly, we recognized ourselves in each other, and it was comforting never having to explain, always knowing what the other meant and how we felt.

At the holiday break, my mom had begun to notice how close Brittany and I had become, how much we talked on the phone, and how much I talked about her. One night she warned me, and said, "You really should try and have a lot of different friends, and not spend all of your time with Brittany." She went on and said, "You shouldn't put all your eggs in one basket. You're becoming way too dependent on her. She shouldn't be your only friend."

Her words, although well-intended, made me worry that showing my true feelings for my friend put the very thing I wanted at risk. As a result, I became more conscious and guarded about how much I talked about Brittany, being careful to refer to her less often and in small doses. I also made a point to sprinkle in more comments about other friends, too.

A few days later, when I told Brittany what my mom had said, she thoughtfully agreed, saying, "Hmm. She might be right. We should probably meet as many people as we can and have lots of friends." But neither of us was quite sure how to go about it.

In our high school there were a lot of cliques, and neither of us fit neatly into any of them. They had all the usual ones: football players and cheerleaders, band members, pot heads, preppies, smart kids, rich kids, trouble makers, and nerds. Most of the groups formed around activities, but sometimes smaller groups formed from a larger clique. Some people could overlap a couple of different groups, like being part of the smart crowd and a band member. But some kind of hierarchy always seemed to apply, keeping people in one group or another.

The other problem with trying to make new friends was that it wasn't as easy as people made it sound. You can meet them, talk to them, and do stuff together, but that wasn't really being friends. People can always smile and be nice without ever knowing or understanding you, or even wanting to. Brittany and I had discovered that being friends was so much more than polite conversations and shared interests or activities. We spent long afternoons talking about it on the phone over the holidays. Once again, we were tackling things together, as a team, plotting our course for two through our large, stormy high school.

"Let's start where most people think we belong," Brittany said. "You practically know all of the smart preppy kids already," she told me one night. Although Brittany wasn't in advanced classes with me yet, she said, "I'm gonna be there soon." She added, "Besides, I have a few preppy clothes, too."

Even though I knew cliques were about more than just the classes you took or the way you dressed, I agreed it was as good a place to start as any.

Excited that we finally had a plan, we looked forward to going back to school after the holiday break. Brittany even got a monogrammed sweater that was all the rage as a Christmas present. It was a beautiful green, one that I knew would make her eyes stand out even more. On our first day back to school, when she rounded the corner to our gym lockers, she had the sweater off and tied around her shoulders.

"Why aren't you wearing your present?" I asked, without even saying hello.

Although I could see the tears in her eyes behind her glasses, she didn't answer me. Instead, staring at me wordlessly, she removed it from her shoulders and held it up for me to see. Then I saw the problem: the monogram in the exact center of her beautiful new emerald green sweater, spelled out the word BRA in large, four-inch white letters.

I gasped and said, "What happened?"

Turning to shove her sweater into the basket of her gym locker and kicking the one on the shelf below hers, she shouted, "I hate them!"

"Who?" I asked.

"The stupid boys on my bus!" she said, slamming her books on top of her sweater and sitting down hard on the bench.

"I'm soooo sorry," I gushed, quickly sitting beside her and rubbing her back. Her head drifted down to my shoulder and we sat there in silence as several other girls joined us.

"What's wrong with the two of you?" one of them asked, glancing down at us as she passed by.

"Boys!" Brittany groaned as she stood, as if the effort required to get up off the bench was overwhelming.

"Tell me about it," the girl chuckled, shaking her head. We each added a sympathetic sound as we changed.

Brittany and I weren't by any means what people would call "boy crazy," but once we started making a few friends in the smart preppy crowd, the topic of boys and dating quickly began to dominate our conversations. Beyond which crowd your friends belonged, boys seemed to be all anyone cared about.

"Phoebe asked me again who I was going to the party with next weekend," Brittany said with a groan one morning as we ran the bleachers in gym class.

Not sure whether her groan was a reaction to what Phoebe had said, or the fact that we had finally reached the bottom of the wooden bleachers, I asked, "What did you say?" catching my breath.

"I said," she puffed, "I was going with you."

"Then what'd she say?" I asked, carefully watching my step on the wooden benches in front of me.

"Nothin'," she told me and puffed to a stop. "But I'm tired of givin' that answer all the time," Brittany said.

"Pugsley and Rankin, keep it moving!" the coach yelled at us from the track below, blowing her whistle for emphasis.

"We have more fun when it's just you and me," I said as we began climbing the benches again.

"I know," she puffed, striding up beside me.

We were both allowed to date, and I'd been out with a few boys already. I'd gone to Homecoming and another party with one guy, and to a ball game with another. I liked them both okay, but they were just friends. My parents were pretty good about letting me go out, probably because my older sister had dated so much when she was in high school and that had worked out well. They only had a few rules about dating. The boy had to pick me up and come to the door so they could meet him, I had to tell them exactly where we are going, and of course I had to be home by my curfew. Break one of those rules and I'd be grounded. But Brittany hadn't even been asked out yet.

"We meet more guys when we don't already have a date," I said as we reached the row below the press box at the top of the bleachers.

"Yeah, but Phoebe said the other day that Mary Ellen didn't ever date and it was because everybody thinks she's weird," she said, jogging down the bleachers. "I don't want people to start thinkin' I'm weird."

"You mean you don't want them to *find out* that you're weird!" I teased.

"That, too," she answered with a laugh.

Football season was over by then, and that had been the best chance for meeting guys. Even those of us who couldn't drive went to the games every weekend, either getting a ride or going with our parents, who would sit and talk to the other parents. At the games we would run around, talking to everyone in the student section, and then go to the pancake place or for pizza afterwards. We'd all stay out in the parking lot with the kids who were old enough to drive, leaning on the cars and talking to each other while the parents ate inside. Some of the kids would smoke and drink, and sometimes the boys would get into fights with boys from other schools. Almost every weekend, a car full of boys would ride by the parking lot, yelling things and sometimes stopping to fight.

Once football season was over, since there were only infrequent parties, we had to spend a lot of time trying to flirt with boys at school, especially during lunch. We could talk to boys between classes, but there wasn't a lot of time. You could talk to the boys in your classes, but only to the ones who ended up sitting right next to you.

But I'd already found this one guy, Emmett, who was in my Alabama History class, and who I flirted with a lot. He was super cute, crazy smart, and a lot of fun to cut up with. And he teased me a lot. We talked before, during, and after class, and since I practically knew the curriculum by heart, it wasn't like I needed to pay that much attention. Who made it to ninth grade in Alabama and didn't already know every fact about it by heart anyway?

Emmett wasn't originally from Alabama, but his parents were, and I loved that he was so different from any of the other guys I knew. He'd lived in a lot of different places, including overseas, before his dad retired from the military, so he didn't have an accent. His name, Emmett, was also unusual, but he'd explained that since his family had lived in Germany, that's where they'd heard it and liked it.

Most boys I knew didn't like that I was taller than they were or smarter, but Emmett was so much taller at 6'4" and a whole a lot smarter, those things weren't a problem. Everything about him was so big that I felt dainty around him. He was a football player and a big guy in every way, which made me feel girly just being near him. But he wasn't just smart; he also was interesting and funny. He also liked that I was smart, too, so I wanted to be even smarter and more interesting for him.

Over the weeks, without even realizing it, something clicked between me and Emmett. It was like I already knew him, or had always known him, almost like in a former life, and I wanted to be around him, talk to him, and more than anything, to make him smile. I wasn't nervous around him and could be myself, which felt good. I even liked myself better when I was with him. It felt like there was a magnet inside that drew me to him, always pulling me towards him.

I had several classes with Emmett, and although I couldn't always sit next to him, I always tried. He ate lunch with several other football players, so I'd drag Brittany to try and find them at lunch. It gave me a chance to talk with Emmett more, and it let Brittany meet all of Emmett's friends. She was pretty shy around boys, and wouldn't talk to a guy she didn't already know unless I was with her, so once again, we made a great team.

• • •

One day in late winter, I finally learned what Bumper's real name was. Our group was broken into pairs for archery. Bumper was probably paired with me because she was so good at everything and the most talented athlete I'd ever seen. She also had patience and didn't get annoyed when other kids weren't as good as she was. Bumper was helpful when people like me and Brittany stunk at whatever activity we were doing, and even if she teased us a little sometimes, she was never mean about it. Since it was just me and her that day, I decided to try to really talk to her. Over the past several months, I'd gone from being a little bit scared of her to becoming very curious.

She was helping me learn archery by repeating the instructions we were given, and by showing me how to hold the bow, place the arrow in the bow, properly aim at the target, and the release the arrow. Predictably, she hit the target every time and sometimes even got it near the center. But she told me, "Just try and hit the target. Hit it anywhere at all."

While she was helping me and adjusting my fingers on the bow, I seized my chance and blurted, "What's your real name?"

"My friends call me Bumper," she said as she moved my fingers around.

"I know that, but what's your real name?" I pressed.

"Why?" she said, fitting my arrow into the bow.

"I dunno. It just doesn't feel right not knowing, I guess," I said quietly. "I thought maybe I could call you by your proper name."

She stood still for a while, watching me shoot. She didn't say anything else until she aimed her own arrow, took her shot, and then turned to me and said, "Guess that's true. We aren't really friends, are we?" But she wasn't really asking me that question. It was more of a statement, and she studied me, waiting for my reaction.

"I think we will be. We just aren't yet, that's all," I said, trying to mimic her movements with the bow and arrow, preparing to shoot while I was talking. It turned out to be much harder than it looked. Once I shot, my arrow only made it half way to the target before it hit the ground. I turned to look at her again.

Her face had changed and was set hard. "No, we won't be friends." she spat.

"But…?" I started to protest.

"No, we're not gonna be friends, white bread." She said it quietly, through gritted teeth. "You gonna ask me to sleep over or somethin'? I don't think so." Her dark eyes bored into me, challenging me, fuming, even though her voice remained calm and quiet.

I blinked, trying to think of what to say.

"You're so stupid," she said, turning away and shaking her head. "I don't need a white friend. Leave me the hell alone!" Then she stooped to pick up another arrow.

We finished the period taking turns shooting in an awkward silence. We never looked at or spoke to each other again. Once the warning bell rang, we gathered our arrows, all of hers from the target and all of mine from the ground.

As I pulled my last one out of the sod, I heard her say quietly, "If you need to say my name, you can call me Shelby." Then she turned and stalked into the gym, quickly leaving me behind.

Later at lunch, when we were eating alone, I told Brittany about the conversation with Bumper. When I was finished, she said, "Well? Would you?"

"Would I what?" I asked, not quite following.

"Ask her to sleep over," she said, before taking another bite of her sandwich.

"I dunno," I admitted, searching my brain for a better answer.

We sat quietly eating on the curb, watching other people walk by, and I thought about her question. *Why wasn't I sure?*

What would people say? What would my parents say? Why was I so worried about what other people would think?

When we were both done eating, Brittany crumbled her bag and stood up. "I know I would."

"Come on. Let's go." She gathered her books and I followed her to the bathroom in the main building.

And that's when it started. That day was the first time I took a look around and really noticed how things were. That afternoon on the bus ride home, I noticed two black kids on my bus who lived in a neighborhood close to mine. I noticed them, not just because they were the only two black kids on my bus, but also because they were twins and in my home room. They also stood out since not only were they twins, a brother and a sister, but also because they were lighter than most of the other black kids. The other kids call them things like "mixed" and "Oreos" behind their backs. That day I watched them on the bus and continued watching as we dropped them off at their stop. Everybody talked to them when we were on the bus but never sat by them. When they got off at their stop, they quickly separated from the others who got off with them and walked home by themselves. I sat in my seat by the window, and watched them hang back until there was plenty of space separating them from the rest. They slowly made their way home but kept their distance.

After my conversation with Shelby and watching the twins walking home alone, I decided to start paying attention to where black people were in our neighborhood and our lives. I noticed that we didn't have any black families living near us. There were only a few black people at the grocery store where we shopped, not many in the library, and none at the restaurant where my family ate dinner that weekend.

We didn't have any black families who went to our church, even though our pastor always said anyone who wanted to come to services was welcome. I didn't know why they didn't. Over that weekend, I kept track of how many black people I saw, and only counted three.

That afternoon, I questioned my mom about it. "Why don't any black people come to our church?"

She said, "Oh, I don't know. I suppose there are so many churches around here, they must go to their own." She was right. We had more churches than stores, so they were plenty to choose from.

Later, as we were fixing supper, I asked, "Mom, do you have any black friends?"

She said, "Of course I do. Why are you asking all of these questions? My Goodness! You could worry the horns off a Billy goat!"

I didn't want to start a fight with Mom, but I didn't know where all of these black friends of hers were. *Maybe they were at work?* I didn't ever remember my parents, any relatives, my parents' friends, or anyone else ever having black friends visit them at their homes. I'd never even heard anyone talking about it. Not ever. I wondered what they would say if I had a black friend over to spend the night. *What would happen if I did?* But for some reason I didn't want to ask.

The only time I saw blacks and whites talking and acting like we all knew each other was at school. When we were in P.E., we'd talk and help each other. When we were at the pep rallies or football games, we were all in the student section, talking and cheering together. When we were in class together, we'd all talk and seemed to get along well. But I also noticed that although there were a few black kids in my advanced classes, there weren't very many. And even when we had classes together, not many of us would walk out of class together or talk to each other out in the halls or at lunch. It happened sometimes, but not very often.

The football players and the cheerleaders mixed it up a little more than the rest. Once in a while, the black cheerleaders or football players came to the weekend parties or to the pizza place after the games. Out of the whole group of kids, Emmett was different. He was black and he always talked to everyone, black or white, and not just in class; he was the same way in the hall and at lunch. He came to the parties and he hung out with everyone, not just whites or blacks, and not just with the football team.

As I watched, I realized that I wanted to be more like Emmett. I wanted to be friends with all types of people, not just the ones like me. I wondered how it was possible that this was the first time I'd really started taking the time to notice these things. And I wondered what people would say if I asked Shelby to spend the night or if Emmett ever asked me out.

• • •

Things with Shelby got a little better after a couple of weeks, and she began helping me again when I needed it during P.E. She even teased me again once in a while. I still didn't call her by name, not Bumper, not Roberts and not Shelby. Whenever I spoke to her, I just avoided it altogether.

Shelby, her friends, and all the kids in our group in P.E. horsed around together in the locker room. Sometimes Shelby's friends would put a song on their jam box and dance while we changed. We weren't supposed to do that kind of stuff, but as long as they kept it from getting too loud, they could get away with it. Even when a coach caught them, all they did was tell them to shut it off.

You would've thought that with all the dancing classes I'd taken, and with all of the albums my older sister and I bought for a penny from Columbia House, that I would've been a natural and fit right in. But my dance classes were ballet, tap, and modern jazz, and most of the albums we bought were Boston, Foreigner, the Eagles, and Chicago. The girls in P.E. danced to songs by The Gap Band, Cameo, Diana Ross, and practically every song on Michael Jackson's "Off The Wall" album, and the dances were different, too.

One day Shelby's friend grabbed me while I was changing and started to show me the dance moves while another girl grabbed Brittany. They thought it was the funniest thing, trying to teach us, and from then on, they'd get us to join in and taught us whatever dance they were doing. They were so confident and comfortable with themselves that it was contagious. With them, I wasn't embarrassed, wasn't afraid that they would make fun of my body, and sometimes I even danced around in my underwear.

They laughed at us even when we did the dance right, and they'd say "Y'all dance like white girls!" But they weren't being mean. You could tell they were just teasing us, making us feel more comfortable, and we would all laugh. That's how you know when teasing is okay; when everyone's laughing, then it really is a good-natured joke.

One morning we were dancing around while we got dressed for gym, wiggling around as we shimmied out of our clothes and into our uniforms, when Coach McNairy passed by and said, "Shut that off!" as she kept walking. Just as the music stopped, we heard one of the two faceless older blonde girls following Coach McNairy out of the locker room say "Look at those two dancin' around like a bunch of niggers!"

Hearing her words, Brittany and I, the only two white girls in the group, looked at each other before we turned to see if the others had heard. Although the music was turned off, they kept moving in time with the memory of the song, wiggling and shimmying to the ghost of the music. Brittany and I smiled at each other and continued to dance as well, choosing to side with the fun rather than end it with ugliness. Seeing us join in, the whole group busted out laughing, and together we continued to dance as we dressed. We even danced a little jig as our group paraded out of the locker room together.

• • •

Not long after, on Sunday, March 22, 1981, we spent a lot of time praying in church for a 19-year-old black man named Michael and his family. That was the day they'd found him, lynched. He was strung up downtown, only a couple of blocks from our high school. Our pastor said we needed to pray for him, for his family, and for all the rest of us. His sermon that day was about love, and he told us it wasn't possible for us to be Christian and to allow those kinds of things to happen. He didn't tell us anything specific we could to do to make it stop; he just kept saying, "We need to love everybody."

My parents talked about Michael's murder all through Sunday dinner. Nobody knew who'd done it yet, and my dad said, "They'll have a hard time catching whoever did it because nobody'll talk." Mom said that people were saying Michael was lynched because he was seeing a white girl.

But they did end up catching the men who'd murdered Michael. Turned out, Dad was wrong, and people did talk. And he wasn't killed for seeing a white girl; the people who had said that about Michael were also wrong. The lynch mob, bad white men, young and old, had killed Michael randomly, just because they were bad, angry people. They went looking for trouble that night, and happened upon him walking home alone from a store. But nobody knew any of that yet.

And the very next day at school, Emmett and I were separated in Alabama history class. Normally we sat in the back of the class, where we could easily talk and joke around, and since we never disrupted class and had good grades, it hadn't ever been a problem. But that Monday, immediately after roll call, Ms. Kuester, our teacher, walked down our row of desks, stood between me and Emmett, and told Emmett to "move up front so I can keep an eye on you." After pausing to make certain he was following her, she walked back up the row and asked a girl sitting in the front to switch seats with him. Since she hadn't given a reason or a warning, we were left to assume she wanted us kept apart. After class, Emmett waited for me in the hall and we tried to make light of it by nervously laughing and teasing that we needed to be less obvious in the future.

Between classes later that day, Shelby stopped me in the hall. I was walking by myself in the crowded main hall when she stepped right in front of me. Her voice low, her face close to mine, she hissed through gritted teeth. "I heard what happened in Alabama history." As she drew closer to my face, she pointed at me and snarled, "You shouldn't be playing around with him. What you're doin's dangerous." Her voice growing louder, she continued: "I don't think you even know what you're doin, but this ain't some game." The word *game* snapped at me like a whip.

Eyes wide, I stared into hers as she continued. "You need to wake up and grow up, and realize what the hell's goin' on here!" She poked me in the center of my chest with each of those words. "Leave him alone," she growled, and then continued down the hall.

Unsure of what to say, which didn't matter because she didn't stick around for a response, Shelby had explained in a few words why Emmett and I had been separated. The center of my chest throbbing with the echo of her words, I slowly continued down the hall, examining the faces of the other students who surrounded me, all unaware of what had just happened as they continued on their way to class.

Later on I met Brittany at her locker to change our books and she said, "I heard you and Emmett got in trouble in Alabama history. What happened?"

"We didn't get in trouble. She just separated us," I said as I put my books in the locker, trying to downplay the whole thing.

"How come?" she asked, leaning into the locker with a voice far more dramatic than necessary.

"We were talking a lot, so she separated us. That's all. It's no big deal. Got everything?" I asked before shutting the locker.

I never told anyone what Shelby had said to me that day, but it really stayed with me. Her warning had introduced a new fear in me and I began to worry that I might get Emmett killed, too. Although it was everywhere in the news and all over the papers, I never heard anyone at school talk about what had happened to Michael. Not the Monday after it happened, not when they caught the murderers, and not even during the trial. It was just one more thing that hung over us like a dark cloud that we pretended wasn't there. But I didn't need to hear people talk about it, and I didn't need to wonder anymore. Now I knew what everyone else would think if I ever went out with Emmett.

One week later, on Monday, March 30, 1981, I was in Alabama history when we found out that President Reagan had been shot. A teacher came to the door and motioned to Ms.

Kuester and they whispered at the door. Ms. Kuester immediately started to cry, and the other teacher hugged her before she left. Slowly she walked to the front of the class and announced that the president had been shot and that his condition was unknown.

Crying, the teacher sat on her desk, crossed her legs and pulled at her scarf. For the remainder of class, she sat talking and crying, never wiping her eyes, instead letting the tears run her heavy black eye makeup down her face. She told us she remembered when President Kennedy was shot, recalling where she was and how she'd heard about it. She kept saying, "I just can't believe it's happening again."

President Kennedy was shot before any of us were born, and our history books were so outdated that they ended with the Korean War, so we didn't learn the details about the Kennedy assassination. The only knowledge we had was from people talking about where they were when they heard the news, and how upset everyone was afterwards. Since none of us had anything to add, we sat quietly, staring back at our teacher while she cried.

Then her tears seemed to become about so much more as she looked around the classroom, asking, "Why do things like this have to happen?" and "What on God's green earth is goin' on?" Nervously we shifted in our seats, anxious to escape her questions that we couldn't answer. I watched the back of Emmett's head as he sat in the front of the class and, sensing me, he turned and looked at me a couple of times. Already able to communicate without words, we showed our concern to each other with our eyes as she continued talking until finally the bell rang.

Chapter Four

In high school, there were so many rules that people expected me to live by. Their voices began to get in my head making me question every move. These rules and expectations weren't simple ones like they'd been when I was a child, nor were they listed on a hand out, passed around in class or printed on a sign or in a book somewhere. Instead, I was left to figure it out on my own by watching, listening and reading between the lines.

When I was little, people asked me what I wanted to be when I grew up and thought it was cute when I'd say something like "an astronaut" or "a famous writer." When I started high school, grownups still asked me that question, but by then I'd changed my answer to "go to college."

"What do ya wanna study?" they'd ask. Since I wasn't sure, I tried different answers, like, "I'm thinking about studying law," or "I've thought about becoming a doctor."

At first, the typical response was a condescending pat on the shoulder and a patronizing smile. In time the responses grew more discouraging like, "Wow, that sounds really hard," or "Don't you want to have some fun while you're in college?" or included a suggestion like, "Hmm. Well, have you thought about bein' a nurse instead?"

It was difficult to figure out who I could trust. Always an avid reader, learning very early on how to escape afternoon thunderstorms by sneaking off into a good book, I frequently turned to books in search of comfort and adventure, so naturally English Literature quickly became my favorite subject. One day in class, our English teacher Ms. Woltz explained that the interpretation of poetry was unique to every individual and as a result you could essentially never be wrong. School for me had always been about learning an assignment and either correctly reciting or applying what I'd learned in exchange for a grade written in red on the top of my paper. The concept of an answer that could never be wrong was thrilling.

To illustrate her point Ms. Woltz asked us to read a poem in class telling us to "Sit quietly and consider what it means to each of you, as an individual." After some time, she asked "Can I have a few volunteers to share their thoughts and interpretations with the rest of the class?"

A boy raised his hand and shared his thoughts to which she responded "Well done Michael. Great perspective. Would anyone else like to share?" as she looked around the room.

His answer was very different than mine, so enthusiastically I raised my hand. When I finished sharing my interpretation Ms. Woltz shook her head and sourly said "No. No. No. That doesn't make any sense at all. Does anyone *else* want to volunteer?" The shame and humiliation of being tricked into believing her, only to be criticized so publically, burned my cheeks and the back of my eyes.

People were always saying one thing while really meaning another. Often as a child I was told that we're supposed to treat everybody the same, although no one obviously meant it, since there were different rules for different kinds of people. I heard evidence of it all of the time. Poor people should work harder, and those who don't work hard were called things like "no good" or "no account." Rich people weren't supposed to work at all, and those who continued to work were either greedy, or weren't really rich to begin with. Students who didn't work hard were called either "slow" or "lazy," and the ones who worked hard and got all A's were called "over-achievers." Everybody had a label of some kind, no matter what they did. And some labels were obviously better than others.

My mom had a lot of female friends and they often came over to our house. At least once a week, the group was at someone's house having lunch or coffee, or playing bridge or Bunco, and they all took turns hosting. I'd known most of the ladies for as long as I could remember, and at one time or another, we'd belonged to the same church or went to school with their kids. These ladies had been teenagers in the fifties, and consequently believed in dressing up, always wearing nice outfits with matching purses, always with their hair done and wearing lipstick.

Whenever they came to our house, we were expected to go into the living room and speak to them. And so, one night that spring, I dutifully made my appearance.

"Well, hello there," Miss Paula said from the card table that I'd helped set up in the far corner of the living room. She must've been watching the door, waiting for me to appear, since she spoke as soon as I was coming in from the foyer. "Well, now, don't you look precious?" she added, nodding in my direction to the other ladies. Always one to wear whatever was in fashion, Miss Paula was dressed in an outfit which was one size too small for her buxom frame and the colors clashed with the harsh yellow blonde of her dyed hair.

"Hi, Miss Paula," I responded politely, a little embarrassed that her greeting had caused all twenty women to simultaneously turn and look at me. They reminded me of my granddaddy's chickens eating the corn I'd sprinkled in their coop, as each lady's head bobbed up and down. Fresh from my bath, my damp hair clean and combed, and dressed in the pink flannel nightgown that my grandmomma had made at the Vanity Fair mill before it closed down, I nervously dug my toes into the carpet.

"How's school goin'?" Miss Shelby asked as the other nineteen smiled, waiting for my response. She had the same short hair style as Miss Paula, only hers was dyed an Elvis shade of black, which was much too dark for her.

"It's fine thank you." I said, looking to my mom, who smiled her reassurance.

"Your momma said you're getting' really good grades again this year," Miss Shelby continued, taking a sip from her coffee cup.

"Yes, ma'am," I said, looking down at my toes.

"Still takin' piano and dancing, too, I hear?" Miss Evelyn said and smiled. Her grey hair was like a helmet teased several inches above her scalp.

"Yes, ma'am," I said, looking up and smiling politely, just as I'd been taught.

"Gotta boyfriend yet?" Miss Paula smirked.

She knows I don't, I thought as I watched her grab a handful of chocolate covered peanuts and pop them into her mouth. Her daughter went to my high school too, and was a few years ahead of me. "No, ma'am. Not yet," I said, smiling sweetly, trying not to notice that most of the ladies were now looking over at my mom.

"Erin goes out on dates, of course. She just doesn't have a steady boyfriend yet," Mom said, smiling at them with a nod of her head, and then looking at me. "It's okay," she told me with her eyes.

Satisfied that she'd made her point, Miss Paula said, "Well, you're so pretty, it won't be long…" making her words seem ugly by talking with her mouth full, and then smiling at me with her smeared hot pink lipstick.

"Who're you goin' to Sue Ellen's party with?" Miss Evelyn asked, still shaking the dice in her hand, making her sleeves and her flabby arms flap from the effort.

"Probably with Brittany," I said smiling, but thinking, w*hy does she even care?*

"Oh?" I heard Miss Lynette say. "Brittany? I don't believe I know her," she said, lilting her voice like it was a question. She didn't bother to dye her hair, obviously preferring to "let it go salt and pepper," worn in a stiff, old-fashioned hair style.

That kind of tight-lipped smile and comment like, "Oh?" or "I don't believe I know her," always meant my answer was the wrong one. "Oh yes. She's a really sweet girl," was more of what I'd wanted to hear. The sign of ultimate success was a response like, "I think I know her momma and daddy," or "You know what? I used to go to church with her parents. They're a really good family."

Mom swiftly came to my rescue, as she often did when her friends were over, and told me with a soft smile, "Okay, honey. Time for bed. Say goodnight."

I waved over my shoulder and left with a polite "Good night," when I caught snatches of somebody saying, "Don't you think she's still a little too lanky for her age?"

Their criticisms, always thinly veiled by adding the word "little" before the other words like lanky, plain, rambunctious, and loud, were hardly ever said to anyone's face.

Later that night, when I snuck through the den into the kitchen for some juice, I'd heard snippets of their conversation over the sounds of dice landing on the card tables and ice clinking in glasses. They were discussing some poor girl who had tried out for cheerleader and didn't make it.

"Well, I guess she tried, bless her heart," I heard one of them say.

"I don't know why her momma let'er try out. We all knew she wasn't gonna make it. She isn't good enough," another added.

"Poor thing, she doesn't have many friends either," yet another agreed.

Apparently they thought you shouldn't let your kid try out for cheerleading just for fun, or on the chance that they might make it. They didn't place any value on a kid wanting something, trying, and failing.

Mom often fussed the morning after bridge or Bunko about the things some of them said, and more than once she'd made it clear that we "shouldn't pay them any mind." Miss Georgia, Mom's friend who rarely filtered her words even in front of us kids, had flat-out refused to spend time with any of the women except for Mom because of their hatefulness. I heard her tell Mom one afternoon, "I'm not listenin' to any more of their bullshit. I'm done putting' up with it. Don't even bother invitin' me anymore if any of them are gonna be around."

My parents said I shouldn't listen to what other people had to say - but how could I not? My parents told me that they loved me, that they wanted what was best for me, that I could do anything I wanted to do, and that they just wanted me to be happy. But how could I do my best, figure out what was best for me, and be happy, when people had so many rules and expectations about what I should do? Sometimes going along with what people think and following the rules made me happy, and sometimes it didn't. The threat of hearing people's opinions as a consequence of breaking one of their rules made it even harder. I wondered whether breaking certain rules would be the best thing for me, and whether ignoring their opinions would make me happy. But mostly, I was confused and unsure whose opinions I could trust.

• • •

"I don't understand, what do ya mean Shelby's not gonna be in P.E. anymore?" I asked one of the girls in the locker room later that spring as I was changing.

"She made the track team. Gonna play basketball, too," she told me as she pulled on her shorts.

"I thought you couldn't get outta P.E.?" I pressed.

"She'll go to Varsity Athletics now," she said as she left for the gym.

"What's Varsity Athletics?" I asked another girl.

"It's like P.E., but it's the last period of the day. It's only for girls on a team," she said, then she also headed for the gym.

I locked my own basket and stopped by the coach's office on my way to the gym.

"Yes?" she'd said when I knocked on her open door.

"I heard Shelby's on the track and basketball team?" I said with a question in my voice.

"Who?" she asked, not looking up as she searched for something on her paper-covered desk.

"Roberts," I said, having forgotten that none of the coaches knew us by our first names.

"Yeah, so?" she said as she continued to shuffle through papers.

What papers other than the attendance sheet for roll call do you need to run a P.E. class? I wondered. "I want to try out," I said, surprising even myself.

"For what?" she asked, finally looking up, lowering her glasses so she could look at me over the rims.

"To be on a team," I said, standing up as straight as I could manage, my fingernail nervously tracing the wood grain of the door jam.

"Ever play before?" she asked, looking me up and down.

"No, but I really want to try," I said, holding my breath.

"Well, you can't be on the volleyball or basketball team as a freshman, unless you've already played before in middle school, like Roberts. Do you play golf or tennis?" she asked cautiously, still eyeing me over her glasses.

"No. What about track?" I asked, my determination growing and fed by her obvious skepticism.

"Sure. You can try out for track. Stay after school on Friday and we'll see." She shrugged, looked back down at her papers, and with a dismissive wave of her hand, said "Go on, now. Get back to class."

"But *w-h-y?*" Brittany asked, saying the word like it had three syllables, when I finally joined the P.E. group gathered around the trampoline and told her about my conversation with the coach.

"I just wanna be on a team's all," I said and shrugged.

"But you'll have to run all the time," she said incredulously. "Why would you wanna do that?"

"I like to run" I said, setting my jaw.

Although I did like to run, my first answer had been more truthful; I really just wanted to be on a team. I had been told that playing a team sport could help my odds of getting into a good college. When I asked my mom and dad, they said it would be "just fine" and didn't seem surprised. I guess it was something they'd expected, since they'd always called me a tom-boy.

My parents never minded that I was a tom-boy who would rather rough-house than play with dolls. For Christmas, they gave me whatever toys I wanted, even if they weren't typical for girls, except the one year when I asked for a pocket knife and a BB gun. Mom bought me pants with the reinforced knees to wear, and only made me wear dresses to church. She laughed and shook her head that I was always dirty from being outside, and she never worried that I always had some kind of cut, scrape, skinned knee or skinned elbow from all of my outdoor adventures. Mom said I kept falling because I grew so tall so quickly. And that was the reason she put me in dance classes. She said, "I thought it'd help you learn how to be graceful, and maybe then you'd stay on your feet!" But I didn't mind. I loved taking dance.

As it turned out, I wasn't a very fast runner, couldn't jump very high, or throw anything very far, so I didn't make the track team. But because I could run as long as the coach wanted me to, I made the cross-country team. Unfortunately, they didn't have enough money for the girls' team to get uniforms to take home, so the school had to keep them. The morning of the meet, Coach McNairy handed each of us a uniform shirt to wear in the race, and I proudly wore mine until the meet was over and we all turned them in.

Before we knew it, our freshman year had ended and we voted for our class favorites, for kids running for student council, and for the next year's cheerleaders. Emmett was voted a class favorite, taking one of the only four spots allotted from a thousand freshmen.

• • •

Summer brought a welcome break from school and all its' pressures. I'd worked hard that year and my grades were really good, so I began to feel more confident and believed that I actually could make it in the real world.

That summer my parents rented a beach house right on the Gulf and we spent our days together out on the sand and in the water. We'd gone to the gulf, about forty five minutes away, every summer that I could remember except for 1980, the summer after the hurricane. On a Saturday, we packed the car with groceries and loaded my dad's truck with the grill, fishing rods, and nets, along with a few inner tubes, and then moved in for the week. The next morning I was up before the sun and quietly slid out through the sliding glass door onto to the large wooden deck facing the beach, just a few feet from the crashing waves. My dad was like me, already up, barefoot and dressed in shorts and a tee-shirt, sitting out on the deck.

"Mornin' baby. You're up early,"' he said softly, smiling at me above the rim of his coffee mug before he took a big swig and turned back to the crashing waves. Even on vacation, he rose with the sun. Maybe it was because he used to work before school when he was a boy, or because he had to be at work before the early shift started at the paper mill, but he'd told me more than once that it was his favorite part of the day,

Wordlessly I sank into the deck chair beside my dad and we silently stared at the waves.

"God's church," my dad said quietly. I silently nodded, and my soul agreed.

My favorite thing in the world was to get up before the sun rose and sit with my dad before taking a walk the beach alone, looking for shells. There was something so special about being the only ones up, sitting quietly together, watching the waves.

When I rose and started down the deck stairs toward the beach, my dad said, "See ya later."

Walking on the beach alone in the morning, I felt special and connected to my dad up on the deck watching me, and to God out there somewhere above the water, as He watched over me, too. I felt that same deep connection to the water, the birds, the crabs, the entire universe, and to the 'me' that lived somewhere deep inside. My thoughts felt powerful, strong, clear, and confident as they flowed through my mind.

Later that summer, I went with the youth group to church camp up at Blue Lake. We rode up together in a van, stayed in separate boys' and girls' cabins, and ate our meals together in a large screened dining hall. During the day we had Bible study, swam in the lake, hiked through the forest, and ended every night with a camp fire, singing church songs. Out in the middle of nowhere, there weren't any lights at night, so the stars shone bright and hung low. The pull of the lake and forest wasn't as strong as the beach had been, but there, too, we found God's church, and there, too, my thoughts remained strong and clear.

After camp and back home for the rest of that summer, I went running in the morning, read books during the day, and spent nights with the youth group at church or babysitting. Once or twice I hung out at Whitney's and Alicia's, who lived close enough for me to walk there. We hung out watching MTV, drinking diet soda, and eating junk food. But over the year we'd continued to grow further apart, and they'd both turned a little too boy-crazy. They were allowed to invite boys over whenever they wanted, and uncomfortable with how they acted with boys around, I stayed away.

Meanwhile, Brittany spent the summer watching Lacey, her little sister, while her mom was at school. She also hung out with her friends in her townhouse complex and told me she went over to Mr. Freeman's house a lot. She'd become good friends with his daughter Catrina, who was a lot older than we were and had a driver's license. She took Brittany around with her a lot, so she had plenty of interesting stories to tell me when we talked on the phone every day.

The only things I had to talk about were cross-country practice, the books I'd read, and the kids I'd babysat, nothing very exciting, but Brittany always listened and asked questions, especially about what I was reading. As always, she showed genuine interest. She asked about the story, the plot, the characters, what I thought it meant, and how it was different from whatever I'd read the day before.

Cross Country practice intensified as the summer ended and the season approached. We took long, several-mile runs with the track team, going from the school all the way up to the interstate overpass, which took an hour each way. Even though it was a hard run, we enjoyed it more than running laps because we could talk and fool around along the way. Somedays we jumped into the fountain out in front of the Natural Gas Company on our way back, splashing each other and clowning around in the water to cool off. Shelby, who ran sprints and hurdles, was strong and kept pace on these long runs. It was good to spend time with her again. She acted like nothing tense or unpleasant had ever happened between us, and somehow it felt like we'd grown closer. It wasn't anything that either of us did or said, but when we caught each other's eyes, I could feel the bond. Something important had passed between us, connecting us, but only the two of us knew about it.

We weren't sure how the cross-country team would do that season, but we thought the track team might be pretty good. Not only did we have Shelby and a couple of seniors, we also were getting a transfer student. We heard she was a girl who used to be a boy, and that she was super-fast. I wasn't sure they were telling the truth, since the girls on the team liked to tease a lot, and to me, someone deciding to change into a girl sounded completely made up. But everyone was excited about a fast runner joining the team.

• • •

We blinked and the summer was gone. By the first day of school, Brittany and I were beside ourselves with anticipation and hope. Fueled by the confidence I'd built over the summer, I was excited about all of the possibilities.

That first day back, we headed to the horseshoe for lunch as usual, anxiously returning to our routine of running around and talking to everyone. Luckily I had several classes with Emmett again, and we'd already planned to meet at the end of lunch that day. But after only ten minutes into the lunch period, the bell rang and all of the vice principals came outside with bullhorns. "Lunch is over. Go to your fifth period class, now!" they shouted repeatedly. Grumbling and moaning, we all moved in the direction of our next class. As we walked, we kept hearing the word *fight*.

I learned later, in the bathroom, that the fight that cancelled lunch had involved that same transfer student who was going to run track. I heard that she'd been jumped in the horseshoe by a bunch of guys. "They told her she's got no business bein' here" one of the senior girls told us. Later, in Varsity Athletics, the girls from the track team confirmed that the girl had indeed been jumped and then been sent home for the day.

The next day, the girl returned to school and made it through the entire day, but when they sent her to the boy's gym for Varsity Athletics, I guess because she used to be a boy, there was more trouble. I heard that when they took roll as they normally did, with the boys sitting in the bleachers in the gym, they chanted at her, rushed on to the court from the bleachers, and surrounded her on the basketball court. One of the coaches apparently grabbed her and pulled her out of harm's way before the boys did anything, but again she was sent home.

We never saw her after that, and I heard she'd dropped out of school. She must've been terrified. I thought she'd been so brave even to try.

• • •

Now a sophomore, I had friends in every class by then, including several with Brittany, and we continued to be inseparable. And that magnetic tug that drew me to Emmett also remained strong, and I sat by him whenever I could. He and Peter, his best friend, sat with me in Geometry, one on either side of me. They teased me that the reason they chose to sit with me was so that they could cheat off of me, but of course it wasn't true. They were both probably smarter, than I was. But I enjoyed being teased about it.

Emmett and Peter were so talented that they'd made the Varsity football team as sophomores and were both incredibly popular. The two had been friends for years and appeared to be complete opposites. Peter was shorter, lean, blonde, and fair-skinned. In further contrast, he was intense, animated and had a quick temper. Emmett obviously looked very different in size and color, and was calm, reassuring, light-hearted, and laid back.

I loved Geometry as a subject, since the theorems seemed to be the natural, orderly way of thinking about things. This was fortunate because our teacher was a complete jerk. He wasn't the sneaky type who was nice to your face but always finding ways to sabotage you. Instead, he was an overt and obvious jerk. He openly demonstrated his distaste for black people and girls on a daily basis, so he only talked to and helped the white boys in the class. If anyone else asked a question, he either ignored us or berated us, saying things like, "I don't know why you aren't smart enough to get this on our own!" Since he liked only white boys, Emmett and I gave Peter our questions and let him ask them for us.

Poor Carlee, our student body vice president, had it the worst of all, since she was both black and a girl. He constantly picked on her, looking for opportunities to criticize her incompetence. I wondered whether we accepted his bad behavior because that was "just how it is" or whether we were simply avoiding confronting him. He'd made it clear that he was prepared to retaliate in some terrible way. Whatever the reason, we silently, helplessly watched him belittle her cruelly, and watched her melt into tears on many occasions.

Our teacher's behavior and blatant disregard for decency also meant we could talk all we wanted, as long as we didn't get too loud, so I spent a lot of the class flirting and chatting with Emmett. I told him jokes when I ran out of other things to say, and they were bad, and obviously made up as an excuse to talk to him. He laughed and shook his head at whatever I said, calling me "corny with a K."

In English composition, which continued to be my favorite subject, we were assigned to read a piece of literature and then write an original piece illustrating the literary element it represented. We wrote poems and a play, and even wrote our own version of historic literature mimicking *The Canterbury Tales.* I adored writing, and wrote my historical tale based on a soldier in the Civil War. The teacher gave me an A and liked it so much that she asked me to read it out loud in class. When I finished, everyone was crying. She submitted my story in a state-wide contest and I won a second-place ribbon. The teacher was encouraging, told me I should've won first place and told me, "You know, you might want to consider being a writer one day."

Brittany asked me to read the story out loud to her since she wasn't in my class. She was lying on her bed, her chin in one hand, waving my paper at me with the other, kicking her feet with excitement and saying, "Come on! I want to hear you read it!"

Snatching my paper from her, I reluctantly agreed, and she giggled, telling me to "Read it with feeling, like you're on stage or something."

"You're killin' me," I groaned.

"Come on....It's just me," she said wriggling with excitement. "And I'm your biggest fan."

Standing at the foot of her four-poster bed, I read my tale with the proper cadence and feeling, and as I neared the end, she rose to a seated position, sitting cross-legged on her bed, with tears in her eyes. When I was done, I gave her a quick curtsey and she clapped wildly before she jumped up and hugged me.

• • •

All of the parties we went to in high school involved drinking. From the keg parties thrown out in the middle of the woods for the sole purpose of getting drunk, to the dances put on by the high school sorority, there was always going to be drinking involved and it became something of a serious sport. Like football, it was what everybody talked about all week long. And like any other sport, people made fun of you if you didn't do it well. The kids laughed if you couldn't hold your liquor, laughed if you didn't drink at all, and praised anyone who could drink a lot. So drinking became yet another barometer of whether or not you fit in.

Brittany and I had gained some experience drinking during the previous year. Both of us had been teased for being "goody goodies" for not drinking at all, and we'd seen a girl we knew get drunk, pass out, and be taken home by a guy, only to have her reputation ruined. So we decided that we needed to approach this sport cautiously. First, we agreed to always stay together, no matter what, and never leave the other one alone anytime we drank. If one of us got too drunk, even if we were out on a date, we solemnly vowed to take care of the other. Second, we decided that we should practice drinking privately, so that in public we'd be better prepared.

In order to practice, we needed a safe place to drink, and my house wasn't an option since my parents were never big drinkers. My mom told me once that one of her uncles had been an alcoholic, so that might've been the reason they didn't drink much. Brittany's house wasn't really an option either. Her parents only drank wine, which kids never drank at parties; kids drank liquor and beer, so practicing with wine wouldn't help us much.

Out of options, Brittany talked to Mr. Freeman about our plan, and although he didn't exactly condone what we were doing, he agreed we could use his apartment when he and his family weren't around. She said he always had different kinds of alcohol on hand, and told her that as long as we left him some money to pay for whatever we drank, it was okay with him to use his stock. So one weekend when I slept over at Brittany's, when Mr. Freeman was out of town, we went to his house to practice.

We ordered pizza, turned on MTV, and selected a bottle of Johnny Walker Red to mix with Coke. We used his crystal glasses and sipped the foam off the top as if our drinks were root-beer floats. Part of the experiment was to observe how much it would take to get us drunk, and so we drank, talked, ate, and danced, which is what we figured we'd be doing at a party. After two drinks, we both started to get a little tipsy, and in our silliness, we wanted to sing. MTV was fun to watch, but we needed songs we knew, and Mr. Freeman's album collection included real classics, so we turned down the TV and turned on the stereo. After one more drink, we were both drunk and no longer dancing. Instead, we sank to the floor in front of his Hi-Fi and sang at the top of our lungs. By the time we'd fixed our fourth drinks and put on the Simon & Garfunkel album, we had our arms around each other's shoulders, swaying. By the end of 'Bridge Over Troubled Waters' we were both hoarse and crying.

"I will always be your bridge," Brittany slurred as the song ended, and through her tears she grabbed one of my hands in hers. "And I will always stay with you," she promised.

"You are the most wonderful person I've ever known," I slurred back at her through my own tears, pulling my hand from hers so I could hug her.

"I love you, Erie," she said into my hair.

"I love you, too," I slurred.

And after that experiment, we established our "four-drink rule." We laughed and said, "One's fine, two's fun, three's risky, and four's the absolute max."

• • •

Fall was the best time of year, since it meant new clothes, new classes, new friends, and a new football season. For those three months, there were football games every week, pizza after the games, team parties, and school dances. Although some of our friends had gotten their driver's licenses, I wasn't allowed to go to the games with them yet. My parents didn't feel comfortable with that, since five to ten thousand fans went to the games, and the stadiums weren't in the best areas of town. I couldn't even go with my friends to our home games because the stadium seated over thirty thousand people and was located in a rough part of town a couple of blocks from campus. And what happened at our first away game that year didn't do anything to help change their minds.

As the away team, we travelled to an all-white school out in the relative sticks of the county. Although they were known to have a solid team, we were far superior in talent that year and predicted to win. The game was scheduled for a Thursday night, which made it a scramble for my parents to get us there after work, and we got a late start. We picked our way through the tall grass of the make-shift visitor's parking lot as it drizzled on us from the darkening sky. From a distance we saw our team pull up in the yellow school buses. Players usually arrived early, dressed in the locker room, and went out on the field to warm up long before the game started, so I asked Mom if we had the game time wrong. Staring at the buses, she answered slowly, "No we didn't get it wrong. They must be expectin' trouble tonight."

We managed to reach the entrance to the stadium before the boys got off the buses, and I looked into the bus windows as we passed, searching for Emmett, Peter, or anyone else that I knew so I could wave to them. But in a jumble of shoulder pads, face masks, and black and white faces, and all wearing helmets, they were unrecognizable.

"Why're they already in uniform?" I asked my dad.

"I don't know," he replied.

When we passed the open door of the lead bus, I overheard the head coach telling the boys, "Now remember, keep your helmets on and don't look up, no matter what. Jog, don't run, and go directly through the gate and out onto the sideline."

We kept walking and at the gate, the state troopers ushered us in quickly and said, "Hurry up now. Y'all need to get seated 'fore the players get off that bus."

By the time we reached the concrete steps and began to climb up into the stands, our players started to jog through the gate and out onto the field. The people from the stands, obviously fans of the home team, leaned over the railings and booed, then began throwing stuff at them. Grownups and kids alike, dressed in baseball caps, tee-shirts, wind-breakers and jeans, threw cups of soda and ice at them, along with whatever trash they had on hand, and yelled nasty words at the boys as they jogged by. As the coach had instructed, the players kept their heads down and their helmets on, and they didn't look up as the people in the crowd booed and yelled.

Just as we passed one man on the stairs, he yelled, "Go home, niggers!" and, right in front of us, threw a full cup of soda over the rail at our team.

Keeping our mouths shut and our heads down, we followed my dad as he picked his way to a spot safely near the top center of the bleachers near other families that we knew. By the time we sat down, Mom was making her "you've been bad at church" face. All moms at church have the ability to stop their kids' dead in their tracks with just one look and my mom had perfected hers. And that was the look she had on her face when we sat down that night as she muttered, "Stupid bunch of rednecks. Grown men, too." Speaking to no one in particular, she whacked her seat cushion on the bench a couple of times before she sat down in disgust.

"You're stayin' up here with me tonight," she said sharply as she pulled me down to sit on the bench beside her. I knew that I wasn't going to be able to walk around and visit classmates and friends at this game the way I usually did.

We were winning the game easily and were up by three touch-downs with only a few minutes left in the fourth quarter, so Mom and Dad said we should get a head start and scoot out early to avoid running into any more trouble. Back in the car, we began our slow creep in a long line of cars leaving early when we heard the game horn finally blow. From where we sat, we could see the state troopers standing guard at the exit gate and our players run off the field and directly onto their buses in their muddy uniforms, still wearing their helmets.

The crowd behind them roared in the stands, and people lined the chain-link fence outside of the stadium, screaming and throwing things at the buses and the players. The state troopers stood silently at the gate and by the doors of the buses, their backs straight and their hands folded behind their backs. They intimidated the opposing fans from jumping the fence, and kept them far enough away from the buses that the cups and trash they threw didn't harm the players. But the police couldn't do much to soften their vile, hateful words.

Chapter Five

Getting a driver's license was an important milestone that promised a measure of independence. As our friends turned sixteen and got their licenses, some of them also got their own cars. Going to dances and parties became easier and more fun, but having friends who could drive didn't give me the independence that I craved. I wanted to be responsible for my own schedule and to have control over what I did and when I did it. Having that freedom was important because I wanted to explore on my own terms. Going with someone else always involved a compromise and I didn't want that.

I'd started learning to drive long before I ever got my permit because my dad often took me out to practice in his pickup truck. The truck was so old that it didn't have power steering or brakes, but he said it made it better for practice-driving. He said, "You can't do anything to hurt this old truck, and once you learn to drive it, a car'll be a piece of cake."

Even though the truck wasn't much to look at, only had an AM radio, and always smelled like the paper mill, I loved that old truck. A constant in my childhood, it often carried me, my little sister, and all of my cousins to the River State Park, all of us piled in the bed of the truck. It also took us fishing in the creek near my grandfather's house underneath the railroad bridge. Whitney, Alicia and I had used that old truck as the elephant in our caravan, our ship lost at sea and our wagon that we drove across the great western frontier. The familiar smell gave me confidence and renewed my sense of adventure.

As we all became more independent, the pressures intensified. Kids at school began to ask us more frequently who we were hanging out with, who was taking us where, whether we got asked out, and by whom. Because Brittany still hadn't been out on a date, whenever she wasn't around, some of the other girls tried to come up with possible reasons. I told them, "It's not her fault! Guys just aren't looking for the right things!" But it never seemed to help. They just rolled their eyes at me and talked about what they'd do differently to increase her chances of getting asked out.

My going out every weekend annoyed my parents because they already had to drive me around, get me a ride, or set up a carpool for my lessons and practices during the week. So they really didn't like that I always wanted to run around on the weekends, too. For some reason, they preferred for me to go out on dates with boys, and this was obvious because they always said yes. But if I asked to go out with girlfriends, they'd quiz me about where we'd be going, who I'd be with, and who would be there before they gave me permission. Even when they said yes, they'd take turns reminding me to be home by eleven. Mom seemed to prefer that I went out with someone other than Brittany, and always said yes when I wanted to go out with new friends like Regina and Lorna.

Regina was a smart, preppy girl who was in a lot of my classes. She'd gone to a different private school before high school, and already had some close friends. We mostly talked about our classes or whatever was happening over the weekend, but nothing really personal or important. I wasn't sure if we were really friends, and we didn't really talk the way Brittany and I did.

Meanwhile, Brittany and I got to know two other girls, Lorna and Marsha, who were also best friends. They were in a couple of my classes and played in the band, which made it difficult to hang out with them much since they were always in the band section at games and had to practice a lot. But they were both really smart, free-spirited, and a lot of fun, so sometimes the four of us went out together to parties. But when we were with them, we always had to be doing something specific. By contrast, Brittany and I could just hang out and have fun.

Once, when I asked my mom if I could go to a party with Brittany, she said, "Why don't you go out with Regina this time?"

"I dunno. I think Regina will be there, too, but Brittany's the one who asked me to go with her," I said. It wasn't exactly the truth, because I wasn't sure if Regina was going yet. She'd only shrugged when I asked her if she was going.

"I don't like you and Brittany goin' out all the time," My mom said as she continued loading the dishwasher as if it wasn't that important.

I'd sensed her hesitation in the past, and hadn't forgotten her warning about having my eggs in one basket. But since she'd finally brought it up, I asked her point blank: "Why don't you like Brittany?

"I do like Brittany," she said, stopping and looking at me with a dinner plate in her hand. "I like Brittany just fine." She continued loading the dishes and added, "I just think you need to make a few more friends, and go out a little more with other girls like Regina, who live on this side of town."

"What does living on this side of town have to do with anything? " I asked. Brittany lived fifteen minutes away, and

Regina and Lorna lived maybe five minutes away. But why would ten minutes make such a difference to my mom?

"I just think it'd be better. Why don't you call Regina and ask if you can go with her instead?" she said with a tone of finality. Feeling that she'd closed the topic, she shut the dishwasher as if to punctuate the end of the conversation.

I didn't understand, but I'd learned that fighting with my parents never got me anywhere, and usually involved a lot more "no" answers in the future, so I let it drop by saying "Yes, ma'am," and left the kitchen.

Clearly my mom didn't understand that you couldn't just call people and invite yourself to ride along with them to a party, so I told Brittany that I couldn't go and stayed home. Brittany asked her friend Virginia, and they went to the party without me. Regina found something better to do with one of her other friends and didn't go after all.

• • •

In the spring, Regina pushed me to try out for the volleyball team. "Come on. Try out with me. Volleyball is *way* better than cross country," she said, turning around in her seat in English. Each spring, all of the teams held tryouts for the following year, and although Regina was already on the golf team, she planned to try out for volleyball, too.

"I dunno," I said. "How many girls are tryin' out?" I asked.

"Only five. You'd make six, and there are three open spots. You'd have a fifty-fifty chance of making the team," she told me.

"Let me think about it," I said.

Cross country had been fun, but the coach always asked me to run pace, which meant she wanted me to tire out the other team. Once we got about a half mile out, my faster teammates would take the advantage and sprint the last half-mile to the finish line and win. I'd rather have played basketball and had a pretty good shot, thanks to my dad, but I'd watched the team practice and knew I wasn't good enough to make it. I didn't want anyone saying, "Bless her heart, she tried," about me.

"Come on," Regina said. "Try out with me. We can go to practice and matches together. It'll be fun," Regina told me as we walked to our next class together.

"Sounds like fun," Brittany said when I asked her opinion later. "But don't listen to her, you can still run cross-country if you want."

"Wanna do it with me?" I asked.

"No way," she laughed. "But I'll come to your games."

Volleyball matches seemed like they'd be a lot more fun for her to watch than my cross country meets had been. Since most of them were on the trails by the museum at the city park near her house, she'd come to a lot of them. Other than during the final meets, we hardly ever had more than a few people watching us. You can't really watch anyone run a two- or three-mile trail unless you ran with them. But Brittany was there, along with a half dozen others, watching the start and the finish. In every race, when I crossed the finish line, always somewhere in the middle of the pack of runners, she was there, cheering as wildly as if I'd won the race.

When I asked my mom what she thought about me playing volleyball, she seemed excited and said, "Sure you can! I'll call Regina's mom. Maybe we can carpool to tryouts."

Volleyball tryouts were held in the boys' gym, which was much larger and nicer than ours, and took place over several days. Coach Carmen told us that she wasn't just watching how we did on the drills, but also how hard we tried. She spoke quietly and was reassuring, which was totally opposite from Coach McNairy's shouting, nasty approach to everything.

Coach Carmen she said she cared about how quickly we learned and got along with the rest of the team.

As always, it was sweltering in the gym and I broke into a sweat before the coach even explained the drills. But for once being hot and sweaty was helpful. After Shelby and the other older girls demonstrated the different drills, my legs, slick with sweat, slid when the coach yelled for us to "dig." Even though everyone wore knee pads, the girls who weren't sweaty stuck and squeaked across the hardwood floor, getting painful, red burns from the friction, while the sweaty ones like me slid without any problem.

Although I'd never played volleyball before, it was easy to learn and I adored being with the others girls on the team. Shelby played setter, and since she was short and had strong legs, she could get impossibly low and save the ball with a bump, which I finally found out was where she got her nickname, Bumper. As always, she helped me with tips on technique, and the other seniors cheered for us during the drills. Regina and I were taller than the others trying out so we were picked to be hitters. We both excelled at spiking the ball and defending the net. Regina's serve was better than the experienced volleyball players, making her a shoo-in to be picked for the team. And luckily, along with a freshman named Melanie, I also made the team.

• • •

The school year ended with another round of student body elections, cheerleading try-outs and voting for class favorites. Emmett and Peter were again chosen as class favorites, and Shelby was, too.

When it was time for prom, a junior who I didn't know very well, but whose younger sister was friends with Brittany, asked me to go. And because it was a big deal for a sophomore to be invited, I went. The only other sophomores who were asked were cheerleaders, so for me to be going was a big deal, even to Regina and her friends. I wore a dress that my sister had worn to her prom, and we had a good time. My date was nice and it was sweet of him to take me, but I knew we wouldn't ever go out again.

"Tell me all about it," Brittany said the next morning when she called.

"Really not much to tell," I said, rubbing my eyes and sinking to the floor of the kitchen in my usual spot behind the counter.

"Come on! I want to hear everything….!" she insisted. "You have to tell me. What was he like? Did he kiss you? Did he get you a corsage? Where did you eat?"

"It was fun. He's nice. We went in a limo. I had steak for dinner. It was okay, but not as much fun as thought it would be. I didn't really know any of his friends and wished you'd been there," I told her. I answered all her questions she peppered me with, until finally she sighed and agreed. "Yes…next year will be a lot better. We'll both go. Maybe we can double-date?"

Weeks later, I passed my driving test and my grades were so good that my parents gave me a car soon after my 16th birthday. It was a used car, nothing fancy, just a normal grey Chevy with maroon cloth seats, but it was all mine. Alicia got a Trans Am when she turned sixteen, but then, when Whitney turned sixteen, they had to share it. My sister Lynne got a cute, brand new yellow sports car, but she had to wait until her eighteen birthday, so I was incredibly grateful to have my own car at sixteen. My parents let me drive immediately, and since I was always going to dance lessons and sports practices, it felt like I was driving all of the time.

One day I invited Brittany and Regina to go to the beach. I'd spent so much time with Regina, I'd hoped that the three of us could become close friends. I drove my car and brought my jam box so we could listen to music. Regina sat in the front with me, and Brittany spread out in the backseat, playing deejay. The day had turned cloudy and cool, so we dressed in jeans and tee-shirts, but we rolled down the windows and sang as we drove. As we emerged from the tunnel and began to cross the bay on the low causeway, the strong smell of rotten eggs released by the paper mills and chemical companies that lined the northern most shores filled the car.

"Oooh! I hate that smell!" Regina said pinching her nose.

"Hey now, that's my bread and butter," I laughed, repeating what my dad had always told us kids.

"Hmpf." Regina grunted.

"So are y'all going to the fourth of July party at the VFW next weekend?" Regina asked, and Brittany turned down the sound.

"I dunno yet," I told her, looking in my rear view mirror at Brittany.

"I bet James or Robert will ask you," Regina said, putting her hand out of the window, letting the rush of air push it up and down. "It's really more of a date thing," she said. Then, turning in her seat and looking at Brittany, she added, "We've gotta get you a date, too. What about Vince? He seems to like you."

On the surface, it might've seemed like an okay thing to say. But Vince, who maybe stood at four-foot eleven, weighed ninety-five pounds on his best day, and struggled with acne, wasn't someone girls like Regina wanted to date. It felt like a backhanded compliment.

"Vince's nice, but he's just a friend," Brittany said, measuring her words. "Besides, I like to go to parties with girlfriends. It's a lot more fun," Brittany said, smiling a fake tight smile back at her.

Regina turned back around in her seat and put her hand back out the window, then said, """Well, I don't think you have to have a date, but everyone else will. You might wanna think about goin' with a guy this time."

Silently I peeked through the rear-view mirror at Brittany, who caught my eye and silently she began mouthing words and shaking her head like she was a teacher or parent fussing. We both choked back giggles, and Regina jerked around and said, "What's so funny?"

"Nothin',"' I said, quickly asking, "What about you? Who're you goin' with?" I knew she'd be distracted by the question.

"Oh, I'm going with Robert," she drawled. "I think he's so sweet. Do ya know what he said to me the other day…?"

As she continued talking, I looked back in my rear-view mirror at Brittany, who grinned at me with her eyes sparkling.

I'd always loved the beach, and although it was cloudy and colder than expected, we walked on the beach for hours and took pictures. But having the two of them together was uncomfortable. I was always either talking to one or the other, never to both. We smiled in the pictures, posing just as friends should pose with our arms locked, but it felt awkward. Exhausted from making up things for the three of us to talk about, I was happy when we finally got home.

• • •

Once again, the summer break gave me time for reflection. We'd successfully made it through yet another year, filled with both pleasant surprises and treacherous land-mines. Sharing the burden together, Brittany and I had learned how to navigate the basics, and now the routines of school were more familiar. Exploring new opportunities and enjoying more freedom, I had also unfortunately discovered even more boundaries, barriers, rules, and expectations. With so many voices crowding my thoughts, at times it was hard to know what to do, what to want, who to spend time with, and who to be. I was unsure of myself and felt pushed and pulled by other people's opinions and ideas.

Sometimes high school felt like being lost. I'd had endless advice steering my life up to that point, which I had always trusted. But the strong opinions of teachers, my mom's friends, and the kids at school swirled around me, each telling me different things that I had to consider. They told me that it mattered how much money my parents had, how pretty I was, which classes I took, and how talented I was. They told me who I dated, what they looked like, which friends I had, and how much money my friends and dates' parents had were important.

No longer sure who I could trust, these strong expectations and opinions felt as hazardous as a hurricane. And I knew firsthand the type of damage a hurricane could do. Although my family evacuated north when Hurricane Frederick hit several years before, once we returned, we felt lucky and relieved to see our house still standing. Although fallen trees littered our yard, pine straw were driven like nails into the wood siding of our house and oak leaves were pasted on everything, we had fared far better than many. The storm had destroyed schools, businesses and homes, including the home of a neighborhood friend. For weeks people worked to clear the twisted trees and power lines that lay across streets, homes and yards all across the city.

My dad told me "Work hard, do what's right, and you'll never go wrong." The pastor of our church said "Be Christ like, even when it isn't popular." My mom warned "Don't believe everything you hear. You have to learn to make up your own mind about things." Brittany told me that I was smart and a good person. She said, "You'll always know the right thing to do if you just listen to your head and your heart." Their reassuring words made me feel stronger, more capable, and less afraid. But in the face of so many other strong and damaging opinions, it was often hard to remember.

• • •

I stayed busy that summer with practice, lessons and church, and didn't really have a lot of spare time. I saw Regina every day at volleyball, and we became friends with Melanie, so the three of us hung out together during and after practice and sometimes on the weekends.

Brittany had a lot more free time, so she spent most of her time hanging out with Mr. Freeman's daughter, Catrina. Catrina worked as a waitress at night, so during the day she took Brittany with her to the beach, to play pool, to go shopping at the mall, or they just hung out with Catrina's other friends.

"We went to the beach today," Brittany told me when we talked on the phone. "Catrina drove and brought two of her friends. Cynthia had weed and we all got high. We got the munchies so bad, we ate everything we bought in like fifteen minutes. It was so funny. What did you do today?"

"Nothing really. Practice." I said, pouting. "It sounds like y'all had fun. How're her friends? Are they nice?"

"Yeah. Hanging out with Catrina's like having a big sister. Most of her friends are nice. They're just older, that's all," she told me. "I think I'm gonna get my hair cut. Catrina says I should get it cut really short. Do you think that'll make me look too much like a boy?" she asked.

"No, I don't think it'll make you look like a boy. You'll just need to be careful about what you wear's all." I answered, surprised.

"Yeah. Catrina said that, too. She says I should wear dangly earrings, so we're going shopping tomorrow to find some." We talked a bit more and then she had to go.

The next day Brittany called and said, "Okay, I did it. I only had money for two pairs of earrings, but Catrina knew how to lift some without getting caught, so she got me a couple more. Catrina thinks I need to get contacts, too. She says I gotta get rid of my glasses to go with my new look."

"Hmmm," I said and paused, not sure that I liked someone telling Brittany that she needed to change, although I agreed that her glasses were too big. "Are you gonna do it?" I asked.

"Mom and dad said contacts are too expensive, but I have babysitting money coming, so I'm gonna get 'em with my own money," she said, sounding proud of herself.

Several days later, when I went over to her house it was clear that Catrina had been right. Brittany looked fantastic with her stylishly short haircut. And freed from the large, heavy glasses, you could finally see how green her eyes were.

"I want this party to be my big reveal. Introduce the new me," Brittany said excitedly, as we walked to the convenience store to buy cigarettes early that summer evening. "This is my chance to make next year totally different when we go back to school."

"This'll be a good party to do that, for sure. Everyone'll be there," I told her. "Regina said most of the football players are coming, too. Have you decided what you're gonna wear yet?"

In preparation for what promised to be the biggest party of the summer, we spent hours and days talking about what she should wear. We agreed that she needed to dress in something totally different, something really stylish to go with her new haircut and more flattering than the kakis we typically wore. After finding that nothing she owned was right for the party, Catrina took her shopping again to find new jeans. The style they chose, which ballooned in the legs and gathered in the waist, were flattering and made her look curvier.

Brittany and I went to the party together, and all of the guys immediately responded to her new look. They flirted with her as we walked through the backyard at the party, and she got a lot of attention. No longer awkward, when she smiled and blushed, ducked her chin and looked down, attempting to tuck very short hair behind her ear, Brittany's shyness was endearing. I watched her from a distance as I drew our beer from the keg. When she talked to a guy that night and I saw the look on his face, I knew that they could finally see the real her and I knew that things had changed for her. All of the girls that night, even the rich preppy ones who could be so mean, told Brittany how great she looked, commenting on her new clothes and hair. Her big reveal was a huge hit.

Running around talking to everyone that night, Brittany finally caught the attention of Derek, the football player she'd liked for a while. When I saw Emmett and Derek leaning against one of the cars parked along the side yard, I grabbed Brittany and pulled her along to talk to them.

Once we said hello, Brittany pulled out a pack of cigarettes and lit one. Derek said, "Since when did you start smoking?"

She threw her head back, laughing as she exhaled, and said, "This summer. My friend Catrina smokes," and absently held the pack in my direction.

Thinking I could pull it off, I took one and lit it, determined to look as natural she had, but they all laughed when the smoke came out of my mouth in one large poof instead of a long steady stream like it should.

"And what're you doin' smokin'?" You're not even inhalin'!" Derek said, pointing at me and laughing as he leaned against the car, shoulder-to-shoulder with Emmett.

Brittany laughed and tried to show me the proper way to inhale.

"Now you've done it," Derek said pointedly to me and laughing. "Everybody's gonna to be talkin' about little miss goody two-shoes, drinking and smoking." Although we all laughed, I grew quiet when I realized all three of them were looking at *me*. Wasn't Brittany a goody two-shoes, too?

The four of us spent the rest of the night talking and laughing, me with Emmett and Brittany with Derek. Braver after a few beers, I stood dangerously close to Emmett a couple of times, my feet between his. The closer I stood, the stronger his magnet pulled me. I stood close to his chest, my knees brushing his legs, my face closer to his than usual.

Apparently, between Brittany's change in appearance and me trying to smoke, we caused quite the stir that night. Regina cornered me the following Monday at volleyball practice and said, "All night at the party, people were saying things like 'Can you believe how great Brittany looks?' and 'Did you know Erin Pugsley smokes?' And where did you go anyway? I didn't see you most of the night. What's goin' on with you?" she demanded.

"Sometimes I smoke. No big deal." I shrugged, secretly thrilled that I had surprised even Regina, and nervously wondered what else people had noticed, like me getting so close to Emmett.

• • •

The day before the new school year started, I went over to Brittany's for a couple of hours before volleyball practice. I parked in one of the visitor spots and knocked on the sliding glass door. Her mom saw me and waved me in. Her mom sat at the kitchen table, papers and books covering every surface as usual. And sitting across from her was a beautiful black lady. Her hair was short, almost shaved and she wore large hoop earrings. It was the first time I'd seen a black person as a guest in anyone's home.

"Hello, I'm Kayona" the beautiful woman said in a deep voice as she smiled.

"She's upstairs, Erin. Go on up," Brittany's mom said without looking up as she continued to shuffle through her papers in an obvious attempt to find something.

"Hi. I'm Erin, Brittany's friend," I said, unsure if it'd be rude to leave the room. For some reason, I wanted Kayona to think well of me.

Then Brittany yelled for me to come upstairs.

"Who's that?" I asked Brittany in a whisper when I reached the top of the stairs and entered her room.

"Who? Kayona? She's my mom's friend." She shrugged. "Look. I need your help. I'm trying to decide what to wear my first day" she said gesturing for me to look around in her room.

Brittany had pulled out every stitch of clothing she owned and everything she'd bought and spread them around the room. After a lot of intense debate, we picked out an outfit. Brittany lay across her bed, on top of clothes she'd rejected, while I sat on the floor in a spot I'd cleared by folding a few items.

"If we don't have at least three classes together this year, I'm gonna tell 'em to change my schedule!" Brittany declared, kicking her feet. "What're you takin' besides English and History? Are you taking Spanish 3?"

"Yes, I'm taking Spanish 3, and Algebra 2, Trig, and Chemistry 2," I answered.

"Well, I'm sure not taking *all that.* I'm taking Geometry and Biology 2, so we'd better get English and History together," she said kicking clothes from the bed down to me so I could continue to fold them. "Why're you takin' all that, anyway?" she asked.

"I told you. Because I want to be ready. If I take them this year, next year I can take calculus and physics," I said, dutifully folding her clothes.

"You can wait and take calculus and physics in college, you know. You don't have to take 'em all now. Have you decided where you're gonna go to college yet?" she asked, her chin resting on her crossed arms.

"Not really. I know I want to go away to school. Guess it depends on what I get on my ACT and SAT. I'm gonna try and take both."

"How come?" she asked continuing to watch me, slowly kicking her feet.

"See if maybe I can get a scholarship so I can go out of state," I said

"Why do you have to get a scholarship to go out of state?" she asked, laying her head on her arm.

"I told you already. Mom said we can't afford it otherwise. If I don't get a scholarship, I have to stay in state and go to the University." I emphasized my frustration by snapping the next unfolded shirt straight.

"My mom said I have to stay here and go to community college," Brittany said, flipping on to her back.

"What if you get a scholarship? You could you go then right?" I asked. "I really want us to go together," I told her, rising to sit beside her on the corner of the bed.

"That's not going to happen," she said softly, sitting up to face me. She saw the look on my face and added, "But hey, I can come visit you. You can take me to all of your parties, and I can stay in your dorm. Then, when you come home, you can come out with me."

"Can't you at least try?" I asked, hating the idea of us being separated. I wanted her to escape with me.

"You'll at least try, right?" I asked stretching the words out slowly. "You'll try and get a scholarship so you can go with me, right?"

"Yeah, yeah. 'Course I will," she said, dismissing me. "Let's go get something to eat." She jumped up before I could tell her I didn't believe her.

• • •

All the rising juniors met with their school counselors to confirm and plan the final courses they needed to graduate and to prepare for whatever would follow. Brittany and I ended up with three classes together, so Brittany didn't ask to change her schedule. Otherwise she didn't mention anything else about her counselor meeting. When I talked with my counselor, she said, "You'll graduate no problem, and you're taking the right classes for the college track." She told me I'd easily get in to any school in Alabama and Mississippi with my scores.

When I told her I wanted to go somewhere out of state but not anywhere in Mississippi, she told me to take a prep class for the ACT and SAT.

"What do I need to do to get a scholarship?" I asked.

She said, "That's gonna be more difficult, so you should probably start studying now."

When she asked what I wanted to major in, I told her I wasn't sure, so she asked me which classes I liked best.

"English's my favorite," I said. "I was thinking that might be a good major."

"That's fine," she said. "Most teachers start out as English majors."

"What if I want to go to law school? I've heard that a lot of lawyers major in English," I said.

"Well, that's not really realistic is it?" she said. "Don't you like kids?" Then she chuckled and said, "English's a good major if you want an MRS degree, too."

"I don't really want to teach," I explained. Then I asked, "What's an MRS degree?"

"Oh, you know," she said, waving her hand dismissively. "That's what they call it when you go to college to find a husband." She leaned back in her chair, and with another soft little chuckle, she crossed her arms across her chest to wait for my response.

I felt my face and ears go hot and knew they were turning red. The angry voice in my head shouted, *You don't know me! You don't know what I can do!* But instead of yelling at her, I stared at the books stacked in my lap. My Chemistry 2 book was on top.

Determined that I couldn't let her think I was like everyone else, that she knew what I wanted, I inhaled deeply, folded my hands neatly on top of the books in my lap, sat up as straight as I could in that hard wooden chair, and said the most opposite thing I could think of from looking for a husband.

"I was also considering engineering. Maybe chemical engineering. I like math and the physical sciences, and I've proven that I'm pretty good at them, too." I met her gaze and smiled the fakest smile I could manage.

I knew she'd gotten the message when her face instantly went hard and that simpering smile disappeared. She uncrossed her arms, sat back up in her chair, and quickly handed back my class schedule. Then she crisply said, "Well then. I would say you are - right - on - track."

In one swift move, she shut my thick folder, picked it up, and carelessly tossed it onto the top of a two-foot stack beside her. Then, through her gritted teeth, told me, "Send in the next student, please."

Without thanking her, I got up and left. In one last moment of rebellion, I didn't even tell the next student to go in. I left her sitting on the wooden bench, wondering whether it was her turn, and kept right on walking.

I didn't tell my mother about the entire conversation that night, choosing only to mention the idea of taking the review classes. She agreed, but thought one course would be enough, saying, "Pick whichever one you care about the most and take that one."

• • •

Our English requirements included a term-paper that we need to work on for the entire school year. We had to pick an author, read several of their books, research criticism of their work, and then write a paper about it, with footnotes. The paper was worth fifty percent of our grade in the course. Between the term-paper and the SAT prep, I travelled back and forth to the local college library several times a week. It made for some long days, but since Brittany lived near the campus, sometimes I'd pick her up on the way and take her with me.

I chose Dostoyevsky as my author, and Brittany chose Steinbeck. We enjoyed discussing the authors and their novels, and working on our papers together. Being at the library together, discussing academic topics, felt like everything I'd imagined college would be.

One afternoon when I didn't have classes or practice, I picked up Brittany early and we went to grab a burger before we headed over to the library. Afterwards we drove around for a bit, talking and smoking cigarettes with the radio blasting. Brittany talked about how much she liked Derek. They had been out several times since the party and she was really excited about it. She went on and on about the funny things he had said, how he'd already asked her to Homecoming dance and wondering what she'd wear, and how he always talked about all the things they would do together.

"Even though I've never really had a boyfriend before, he's exactly what I've always wanted and imagined," she said dreamily, then giggled. "Can you believe this?" she asked. "I finally have a boyfriend!"

A song that she knew came on the radio and she sang along loudly. Listening to Brittany sing the lyrics with added emphasis on the parts that had special meaning for her now that she was in a new relationship, I began to cry. I wasn't sobbing, but was moved to silent tears that I couldn't stop.

"OMIGOD! What's wrong?" she said when she saw my tears. "Pull over," she commanded.

Almost at the library, I pulled into a parking lot of one of the campus buildings and shifted the car into park.

"Are you upset about me and Derek? You know we're always going to be best friends. Nothing's ever going to change that," she gushed, grabbing my shoulders.

"No. No, it's not that." I said, pulling away from her and wiping my face.

"What is it, then? Tell me!" she said, her eyebrows knitted.

"It's hard to explain," I said, trying to pull myself together. I felt so ridiculous.

"Well, we're sitting here until you tell me why you're crying," she said and pulled out another cigarette. After she lit it. she dramatically exhaled the smoke, obviously preparing for a long wait.

"It's just that, well, I think I...*really* like somebody," I started. "I'm not sure if I do... and I'm not sure if he likes me. And even if he did..." I sputtered, stumbling to explain.

"Ooooh! Who is he?!" she squealed, leaning toward me. "Is it Robert?" she asked, sounding hopeful. "It's not James, is it?" she asked, making a face to show her dislike.

"No...No. It doesn't matter. Even if he likes me, I don't think we can ever ... go out or anything," I continued, babbling.

"Of course you can! If he doesn't ask you, you can ask him. It's almost 1983, for god sakes. Everybody does that now. Did you know that Mary Ellen asked Tim out first? It's not like it's a big deal anymore," she said.

"No, no. It's not that." More tears spilled, wetting my cheeks. "What I mean is, I don't think we ...can," I told her. Taking a deep breath, I went on: "Nobody's going to be okay with it. Not the kids at school, not my parents, not anybody. Oh, God. Just forget it. Let's just go," I said, swiping at my face and shifting the car back into drive.

"No!" Brittany said, grabbing the wheel. "We aren't going anywhere until you tell me what's going on."

"Oh, God!" I said, putting my forehead on the steering wheel "Okay." I took a deep breath and said, "It's Emmett, okay? I think I might like...might be in love...with...Emmett." Then I peeked to see her response.

"Oooooh..." she said slowly, taking another drag and then added, "Well...." and then she exhaled.

"See what I mean?" I moaned. "It's not like we can even go out, even if I do think I like him. I'm not sure how I'm even ever going to figure out whether I really love him or not. That's the point of dating, right? To figure out whether you really like somebody? But it's not like I can ever date him," I said.

Feeling safe based on Brittany's reaction, I slowed down and continued. "It's just …I can't seem to get him out of my head."

Wiping my cheeks and looking out the windshield, I quietly added, "I just feel like if I don't at least date him, I might not ever know."

Gesturing wildly, I argued with myself. "And so what if I really do like him? It's not like I can actually go out with him."

Certain that the conversation would not lead to a solution, I said, "It's just impossible. The kids at school will never be okay with it. My parents certainly will never be okay with it. All of their friends, the people at church… nobody's going to be okay with this," I told her.

And then, looking out the window into the night, I added, "I know I should totally forget about him. And I try, I really do. But I just can't…seem to do it."

I stopped talking, hit the steering wheel with both hands, and put my head down on it.

"Just forget I ever said anything, okay?" I pleaded.

Brittany, sitting back in her seat, shook her foot and, smiling at me, clucking at me. Then she said, "Well, well, well!"

"Seriously. Stop. Just forget it," I said, lifting my head, wiping my face on my sleeve, and shifting the car back into drive.

"Don't worry about it," Brittany said. "We'll figure it out." Then she asked me, "Are you sure your mom and dad really will have a hard time with this?"

"Yeah, I'm sure," I said. I was pretty sure that I knew what they would say.

That's because I remembered an incident from when I was about twelve. My family had gone out to eat, and we'd seen a white man and a black woman getting out of a car in the restaurant parking lot. The man had opened the door for the woman, and held her hand as they walked into the restaurant. I remember them looking at each other and smiling. He seemed to be reassuring her, and she looked as if she were gathering courage, as if they were determined to do this together. As I watched their faces, I heard my mom say to my dad, "I really don't understand. If they're gonna do it, okay then. But I don't understand why they've got to flaunt it. Going out in public like this, they're just askin' for trouble." My dad grunted in response and nothing else was said, until Mom told Gracie and me to "Stop staring now. Come on," as we lagged behind. So I was pretty sure what my parents' feelings would be on the subject.

As I pulled out of the parking lot and headed to the library, Brittany repeated, "Don't worry about it. We'll figure something out. It'll be okay."

Chapter Six

What began with that conversation in the parking lot consumed my thoughts as I mapped out the possible consequences. To ignore my feelings for Emmett felt weak and wrong. What if I never found out if my love for him was real? How could I ever live with myself if we moved away and I never met anyone else that made me feel this way again? He was like no one else I had ever known. He was so special, and made me feel so incredibly good when I was with him. How could I ever give that up? What kind of wimp ignores what's obviously so good, just because people might not approve?

But the thought of turning both of our lives upside down, even for what might possibly be real love, made me sick to my stomach. Genuinely afraid of what could happen if anyone else knew how I felt about Emmett, I didn't feel brave enough to face the many, possibly horrible consequences that could follow. And what if it was all for nothing? What if he ended up like all of the other guys I'd dated, and he became just another friend? What if this was just a first crush? If that's all it was, then I might be ruining both our lives without a good reason.

Even if Emmett was the one for me, what if Shelby was right, too? What if bigots lynched Emmett like they'd done to Michael? What if the guys at school beat me up like they did to that girl in the horseshoe? What if they attacked Emmett? What if my parents flipped out and never let me go anywhere ever again? What if they no longer trusted me to make good decisions and refused to let me go away to college? It all made my head spin.

But was there a possibility that people would be okay with me and Emmett dating? Brittany and her family might not have a problem with it, but would anyone else feel that way? No one I knew except Brittany's mom and Peter invited black friends over to their houses. How could the rest possibly accept me dating a black guy? Most of the kids at school used any reason, to put you down, even things that weren't true. They never let anyone forget anything, so even if Emmett and I broke up, it would follow us forever.

Thinking that the whole situation was impossible, I decided to do nothing. After all, I was relatively happy with the way things were. Why go and mess everything up now? I couldn't deny my feelings, but I could keep them a secret. At least that would give me some time to figure out whether what I felt was real. There were a lot of rules against interracial dating and I needed time to figure out if this was going to be worth breaking all of those rules.

After that night, my conversations with Brittany revolved around Emmett and Derek. We talked about every detail about when we saw them, what they said, what they did, and how they looked. She was more optimistic about my situation, and I was so relieved to have someone safe to talk to about it. She and Derek eventually became an official couple, and once in a while, if I didn't have other plans, they would take me out with them. She always drove, so I would sit in the back and watch Derek in the passenger seat as he teased her, poking her ribs and grabbing at her knee. She laughed, punched his shoulder, and ran her fingers through her hair. I laughed with them, happy that she was happy. Her awkward shyness disappeared when Brittany was with Derek.

Unfortunately, she also blabbed to Derek that I had a crush on Emmett. I reminded her how dangerous the situation was. "You can't be goin' around tellin' people!" I snapped as we walked out of the main school building. "I'm not even sure yet. And I don't know what, if anything, I'm ever gonna do about it, anyway. I've known Derek since kindergarten, for God sakes. His parents know mine. They live in the same neighborhood as some of my mom's friends. If he knows, they'll all know" I hissed.

"He promised not to say anything, and even swore on his life that he wouldn't tell anybody. He's not gonna cause y'all any problems," she said, shaking her head. "I promise I won't tell anyone else."

"Well, why did you tell him to begin with?" I said, grabbing her arm to pull her closer to me as others passed. I was shocked that she didn't understand what a mess Derek could cause if he told anyone.

"I told him because I'm trying to figure out how we can all go out together. The four of us would have so much fun," she said, hugging her books to her chest.

It was true that the four of us had fun together. We ate lunch with the boys every day. They were always with a group of other football players, and we no longer bothered going anywhere else to eat. We just made a bee-line to their spot by the back doors of the library. I sat by Emmett in class and talked to him whenever I could, just as I always had. Although I couldn't be certain, I thought he was seeking me out, too. Most classrooms for juniors had long tables and chairs in rows, but a few still had the old, one-piece desks built for smaller students. Emmett couldn't sit in those desks easily so he had to sit sideways. In those classes, he always chose a seat next to me so he could sit sideways and face me during class. As always, we could always talk about anything and everything—except how I felt about him.

I even told Emmett what the guidance counselor had said to me and how angry it had made me. I hadn't even told Brittany about that. He listened intently, and afterwards said in a serious tone, "I'm shocked that anyone would say such a thing to you. You're so smart, you could be a doctor or a lawyer, or do anything else you wanted to do."

I loved the way he said it, like it was a fact, not just his opinion. His faith in me and my abilities made me feel capable and strong.

"I told her I wanted to major in engineering," I said.

"Well, if that's what you want, you should do it. But don't ever do something just because somebody else says you can't. If you do it, only do it because you really want to," he told me almost sternly.

Emmett was so different from anyone I'd ever known. He talked to everybody and everybody liked him, not just the guys on the football team or the kids in our classes. Even the teachers loved him. Guys and girls, white and black, all wanted to hang out with him. Girls always hugged him, especially the cheerleaders. The fact that he seemed to like me, liked spending time with me, and talking to me made me feel special.

Always alert for signs of how people might react if we were together, I watched how people interacted with him. My ears perked up whenever I heard his name. Girls always said things like, "Oh, my God, He's such a nice guy!" or "He's such a great guy, I just love him!" Guys said things like, "Ya know, he's one of my best friends," or "He's so smart, and such a great football player, he'll probably go pro one day."

Sometimes, though, both guys and girls would add in a low, conspiratorial voice, "Ya know… he's not *really* black… if ya know what I mean." *Why did they think he was so different from other black people?* I wondered. *Does that mean they won't mind so much if we go out together?* But I didn't think it would make any difference.

• • •

As the holidays approached, so did the college entrance exams. Although I'd thrown out engineering in an effort to shut up the counselor, I'd decided to pursue chemical engineering. Lorna was also interested in engineering and we agreed that if we both got into the same college, we could room together, which would make the transition easier. Brittany and Marsha made it clear that they didn't intend to go away to school. I pored over the admissions documents, which emphasized that extra achievements would help our chances, so I began looking for the right kind of activities.

One day, when Brittany was out sick, I couldn't go eat with the football players by myself because it would lead to unwanted gossip. So I decided to eat with Regina and her friends. They always ate near the center of the horseshoe, so I knew where to find them.

When I walked up and said hi, the first thing out of Regina's mouth was, "No Brittany today?"

"She's out sick," I said, sitting down in the unoccupied space within her circle.

"Well, lucky us. We get the pleasure of your company today." Jessica said. Although Jessica lived in our neighborhood, had taken dance classes with me, and rode our bus, we'd never been good friends. She was quiet and kept to herself, and she seemed to only talk to Regina.

Regina snickered as she popped an orange section into her mouth.

Then Beth-Anne in her nasal voice snorted, "Won't the football players miss you?"

"Yeah," I said. "So what do y'all think of the substitute in Trig today?" I said, trying to change the subject.

No one answered my question. Instead, Beth-Anne leaned forward and hissed, "Did you hear Linda's going to Delta's party with Alan this weekend? I don't know what he sees in her. She's not even cute." With a satisfied smirk, she plucked a grape and put it into her mouth.

"I can guess," Mary Paula said through her curtain of blonde hair.

Ignoring her, Beth-Anne asked, "Did you get asked to the Delta party this weekend?" I looked up just in time to see her turn to face me. She dragged out the word you so it came out like *yee-www-uuu* and it sounded like it had three syllables.

"Yeah, James asked me to go. What about you guys?" I said, looking around at the faces in the larger circle of girls.

Beth-Anne answered for the group of girls, saying, "We have to go, since we're pledges," speaking in a sing-song voice intended to remind me that all of them had been invited to pledge the high school sorority and I had not.

After a few moments, Regina added, "You know, Erin, we were talking earlier about trying out for Camelia Belles this year. Maybe even goin' out for teen board, too. You should try out with us."

"Yeah, I bet you'd make it. You're pretty enough, and you certainly have the grades," Mary Pat added.

"Hey Beverley! Come join us!" Regina called out abruptly waving at one of the varsity cheerleaders as she walked through in the horseshoe.

I couldn't stand it any longer. Since I was almost finished with my lunch, I made up an excuse about needing to go by the office and hurried away with fifteen minutes remaining in the lunch period. Not that they cared, since by then they were busy talking to Beverley.

That night when I talked to Brittany, who had stayed home sick, I told her about the conversation at lunch. She said, "Who cares," about the sorority, and "No way," about trying out for teen board. But when I mentioned Camelia Belle tryouts, she said, "Now, *that* would be worth it!" "I've heard they're very selective and it's not just about whether you have money, or who you know. Besides," she said, sniffling through her stuffy nose, "You'd look gorgeous in the dress."

"I was thinkin' maybe it would help me get into a school like Tech. Do you maybe wanna do it with me?" I asked hopefully.

"No way!" She laughed suddenly, coughing from the effort. "I'd never make it." After clearing her throat she added, "Plus, even if I did, we couldn't afford the dress."

The following week, Brittany found an application for Camelia Belles and brought it to me during Spanish class. She shoved it at me and said, "Take this home and fill it out." Cautiously, I read through it to see if it was what we'd expected. The application described the qualifications of the program, and explained that each year the committee chose fifty rising senior girls from high schools from across the county. Selection would be based on academic and overall achievement, appearance, personality and the ability to communicate. Girls who were selected would wear antebellum dresses made within the guidelines established by the Women's League. The chosen girls would also act as hostesses at special events on behalf of the city during their senior year. "And must at all times conduct themselves in a manner that best represents the city."

When I talked to my mom about it, she said she knew about the program, had heard about it for years, and considered it a great honor to be chosen. She thought it would be great experience for me, and that we could afford the dress if I was picked, so together we filled out the application.

Since volleyball season was over, we no longer had practice, so once again I ran with the cross-country and track teams. Shelby and I paired up for the runs, and one afternoon on our way back, as we made our final turn, she asked me if I'd decided what to do about college. I told her all of my plans, talking for almost a mile.

"Why do you wanna leave so bad?" she asked.

I quickly answered, "Because I wanna go somewhere totally different where I can do totally different stuff."

"You can do things that're different anywhere. What's the *real* reason you wanna leave so bad?" she asked, without missing a stride.

After a few more paces, I told her. "I want to leave because everyone here thinks they already know who I am. They know everything I've ever done, and think they know everything I'm ever gonna do. People are always tellin me what they think I ought to do. They want me to be just like everybody else. They think I'm *already* just like everybody else, but I'm not. I want to go where nobody knows anything about me, so I can do whatever I want."

She thought for a moment and said, "Ya know, that's just geography right? People are always gonna think they know everything about you."

After falling into silence, our steps synchronized, she continued, "Everybody always thinks they already know who you are and what you can do, just by lookin at you."

I knew that she wasn't talking just about me anymore, so I kept quiet to see if she'd say more.

After several paces, she added, "You're gonna have to learn to stop listenin' to everybody's opinions on things. Ya don't do that, it ain't gonna matter where you are."

"And how, exactly, am I supposed to do that?" I asked her as we turned the last corner and headed back toward the field.

"Well, you can quit axing everybody, for one thing. You don't need to take a survey to figure out what it is you wanna do." Her voice rising like it might be a question.

"I don't ask. They're just always tellin' me what to do and askin' me all these questions. Like who you goin' out with, where you gonna go, why do you wanna do that," I said slowing to a jog.

"Well, stop listenin,' then. Most folks don't care nothin' 'bout you," she said, slowing to match my pace.

"Easy for you to say," I told her with a little pout in my voice.

"Oh, you think so, do ya?" she said.

"Well, you said it like you think it's easy," I complained, defending myself.

"Well, forgive me for not crying over alla your white-girl problems, "she said, turning to face me head on.

I knew Shelby well enough by then to know that she was done with my whining, so I said, "I know you're right. It's just hard sometimes, that's all I was sayin'." And then I turned to her and asked, "What about you? What're you gonna do? Can you ignore what everybody says?"

She replied without blinking, "Don't you worry 'bout me. I'm gonna do what I set out to do. And I already told you a couple of times, it's time for you to grow up. Life's hard. So what? We both know that already. And from where I sit, you ain't got it so bad. Why don't you just do yourself a favor and quit making up all these excuses? Go on and do whatever the hell it is you wanna do and stop your whinin'."

By then we'd reached the gate to the track and Shelby stooped down to tie her shoe. Her dark brown skin highlighted the contours of her strong muscles. She was so strong, so confident, and so beautiful. I wished I could be more like her.

Other people were on the track and close enough to us by then that they could overhear our conversation so I knew it needed to be over. She wouldn't talk like this to me when other people were around, so I ended it by saying, "Thanks Shelby. I appreciate it. And I mean that. I really do."

Looking up at me, she said, "Just remember what I said, now." And as her friends joined us, she stood and we began to jog again, ready to run our last lap and cool down.

As we took the first few strides, she hit my arm with the back of her hand. When I turned to her, she said, "And you're welcome by the way."

• • •

As Mardi Gras approached, Brittany and I talked of nothing else. Finally, we were able to drive ourselves to the parades downtown. Her parents weren't interested in it and my parents had always hated it. They never took me to the parades and wouldn't even drop me off downtown with my friends, unlike most of the other parents. To my parents, days of drinking, yelling for beads and catching candy seemed like a huge waste of time. They never went to any of the balls, and never rode on the floats like other parents either. They would never consider paying hard earned money just to be included in a mystic society. But they understood it was a big deal to the rest of us, and agreed that I could go with my friends that year. Brittany and I went to every parade and spent the entire four days of Mardi Gras weekend downtown. Roving the streets filled with revelers, we visited our friend's parents' hotel rooms, always able to fill our plastic cups with drinks wherever we went.

All of our friends were there, but they were mostly occupied with their own groups or families. Derek and Emmett were there all weekend with their football buddies, and we dropped by from time to time, but Brittany said that Derek wanted Mardi Gras to be his time with the boys. Brittany and I didn't mind it being just the two of us and preferred running around seeing everyone so we didn't get stuck with a particular group.

Joe Cain Day was the best day of the weekend, even better than Mardi Gras Day. The parades started early in the morning and continued all day, and the Wild Mauvillian's was the best crew, since anyone could join in their parade. Bands played all afternoon and into that Sunday night, and people camped out in the cemetery near the town square. I finally met Mr. Freeman's daughter Catrina and his son Tucker that Sunday, among a large group of twenty-somethings, all camped on old beach blankets, mismatched camp chairs, and Igloo coolers arranged between the mausoleums. Grouped together in chairs, their feet propped up on their coolers full of iced beer and tote bags of food, they appeared as at home as they were in their living room. Brittany knew almost everyone there, so we hung out for hours, talking, eating, and drinking. The girls chatted freely with her and the guys flirted shamelessly. Brittany and I wore stacks of beads we'd caught in parades and they hung thickly around our necks. One of the guys flirting with Brittany kept fooling with her beads, stroking her neck and touching the exposed skin on her chest, intentionally brushing her boobs. Not only were these guys significantly older than we were, they also were pretty wasted, so the guys flirting with Brittany made me nervous.

I knew enough about how older guys acted after they'd been drinking to know when to worry. Some guys pretended to be interested in you and thought it was funny if their attention made you nervous, but other guys intentionally tried to take advantage of the situation and I knew these guys didn't have good intentions. Luckily, when I suggested we leave, Brittany didn't object and we left them safely behind.

"You know all those guys?" I asked as we headed away to listen to a band playing in the distance.

"Yeah, sure. They're friends of Catrina and Tucker," she said as she pulled a cigarette from her pack with her lips.

"They really seemed into you. How old are they, anyway?" I asked, watching her carefully.

"I dunno. Somewhere in their twenties, I guess," she said.

"Do you like any of them?" After all, I'd watched her flirting right back.

"Yeah. They're alright. Just fun to hang out with," she said, exhaling.

I was glad to be safely away from the group, but the worry I felt for Brittany gnawed at me. She'd spent a lot of time with the Freeman's when I wasn't around and I didn't know what went on when she was there.

• • •

Meanwhile, the football team practiced in the spring and summer, preparing for the next fall season. We were predicted to win the state championship in the coming year, and a lot of talented players on the team were already being recruited by colleges from all around the country. Emmett, one of the most talented defensive lineman, larger than most and with an extremely high grade-point average, became one of the most highly sought-after recruits in the state. Given the success of the team and the attention from recruiters, he also got a lot of attention at school, in the city, and county-wide. It wasn't uncommon for him, Peter, and their other friends from the team to be interviewed on the local TV stations and get their pictures in the sports section of our local paper.

One day that spring during practice, someone accidentally hit Emmett's knee the wrong way and blew out his ACL. "He had to have surgery," Peter told me the following day in class. "Since he'll be out of school for a couple a weeks, a bunch of us are gonna go see him and cheer him up this weekend when he gets outta the hospital."

"Is he okay? Did they fix it so he can play again?" I asked, concerned.

"I think so. Should be able to play. But he's kinda down in the dumps about it, so it'll be good for us to go cheer him up."

Afterwards, Peter gave me Emmett's address, told me how to get there, and said, "We can meet up over there. A group's going over Friday night."

Emmett's family lived in a brick ranch house similar to mine, and only about a mile away, but I was uncomfortable showing up at Emmett's house by myself. So I asked Brittany and Derek to go with me, and pick me up on their way. That night, there must've been thirty people at Emmett's, and cars lined the street and the driveway. And inside the house, football players, preppies, cheerleaders, pot heads, kids from every group, were all crammed into Emmett's bedroom, talking and laughing.

Emmett's spirits were lifted, but he was in the largest foot-to-hip cast I'd ever seen. His legs were muscular and as big as tree trunks, and that heavy cast on his left leg it must've weighed seventy-five pounds. People came and went the whole time we were there, walking through the house, going back and forth down the hall to his bedroom. Emmett's parents were incredibly lovely and hospitable, and I found out that his dad was a retired Air Force master sergeant who now worked as a real estate agent, and his mom was a middle-school teacher. They opened their home to all of us and seemed thrilled to have us there. Their home was filled with sounds of laughter, the aroma of food cooking in the kitchen, and so many books in the floor-to-ceiling shelves in the den. Beautiful, exotic -looking items were everywhere, from places like Turkey, Germany, and many other places where they'd traveled and lived.

The school administration let Emmett make up all of his schoolwork while he was out and I volunteered to take him his class assignments for Trig, swinging by his house most afternoons. His parents made me feel welcome, which quickly helped me overcome my shyness over being there. I missed seeing Emmett every day at school, especially during lunch, so I looked forward to my visits. Even when a phone call would've worked, I instead went to visit and enjoyed our afternoons, especially because now we had the chance to talk without being watched by everyone at school.

Becoming closer with Emmett and more comfortable with this new level of intimacy, during one visit I finally confessed how I felt about him. I was elated to find out he felt the same way. We talked over the potential reactions to making our feelings public, and were relieved that we shared equal concerns. Although he didn't think his parents would mind us dating, he was concerned about the coaches, teachers, and our classmates and friends at school.

Uncomfortable in the spotlight, he also worried about the public at large. "I'm not sure I'm ready for all of that," he said, wringing his hands. So we agreed that, at least at first, we'd keep our feelings to ourselves and keep things within our tight circle of trusted friends. He also told me that it was okay if I still wanted to date other guys.

Thrilled to be able to spend time with him without ruining everything, since we didn't know whether it would last, I continued to see Emmett as often as I could. When he was up on crutches and back at school, he still couldn't drive or go out on the weekends, so groups of us continued to go to his house. Sometimes it was only a few of us, and other times it was as big as a party. If kids were drinking, they handed their beers in through his bedroom window and walked through his house politely speaking to his parents. But sometimes they didn't bother coming in through the front door and instead crawled through his bedroom window, right behind the beer.

Brittany, desperate to set up a double-date for us so we could all hang out together, invited us to Mr. Freeman's when his family was out of town. We ordered pizza, had a few drinks, and tried to watch a movie on the VCR, but instead spent most of the time laughing and talking. Eventually Brittany and Derek disappeared upstairs, leaving me and Emmett alone downstairs, sitting on the couch, with Emmett's huge cast propped up on a nearby chair. Once in a while they reappeared, barreling down the stairs laughing, Derek chasing Brittany, catching her, and tickling her, and all of us laughing. Being with Emmett felt incredibly right, completely comfortable, and totally normal.

A few weeks later, James showed up at my house unannounced. We'd gone out off and on over the last couple of years, sometimes going to parties and football games, and once to a dance, but we'd never dated seriously. Although he was nice enough and we had fun together, I'd told him repeatedly I didn't want to be his girlfriend and had kissed him only once or twice. He'd been to my house only to pick me up, so it was strange for him to show up unexpectedly.

When I answered the door, I said, "Well hey, this's a surprise. What's goin' on?"

"We need to talk. I gotta ask you something," he said, shuffling his feet, both hands deep in his jeans pockets.

"Okay," I said. "Do you wanna come in?" I wasn't sure if I should invite him inside.

"No, I just want to ask you if it's true," he said, shifting from foot to foot on the doorstep.

"Is *what* true James?" I asked, leaning on the open door.

"Is it true you're goin' out with Emmett?" he finally said, looking at me and making my heart skip a beat.

"What're you talking about?" I stammered.

"I heard that you're goin' out with him now, and I wanna know if it's true."

"James what're you doing?" I said, shaking my head sadly.

"What's wrong with me?" he continued "I've taken you out lots of times. We had a good time. I know you said you didn't wanna be my girlfriend. But why not? How could you do this to me? I wanna know!" he said, his voice rising.

"Why would you choose somebody like him over me?" he continued, raising his voice another octave until it cracked.

"I'm not listenin' to this. Not wanting to be your girlfriend has nothing to do with anybody else," I said, feeling my face and ears getting hot. "Look, I like you, James. You're a good guy. A good friend. Like you said, we've had fun, but I told you. I'm not lookin' to be your or anyone else's girlfriend."

"So you're saying it's not true," he spat, and I could see that his hands were now in fists, even though they were still deep in his pockets.

"I'm saying you've got no right to come over here and ask me this. You need to go!" I scolded, moving half of my body behind our front door and glancing behind me. I didn't want my parents or sister Grace to hear any of this.

"So it is true?" his said, his voice cracking again at the end on the word *true*.

"Just go, James," I said as I shut the door and locked the bolt.

Looking through the peephole, I could see that he paused on the top step, staring at the closed door for a minute or two, and then turned and walked down the front walk to his car.

My mind spun and careened with worry. *Who knew? Who was out there talking?* I thought as I continued to watch through the window next to our front door. I saw him look back at the house once more, before he finally got in his car and sped off down the street. It wasn't until he'd driven off that I realized I'd been holding my breath the whole time. Forcing myself to exhale, I tried to remain calm, telling myself it was okay. *They might think they know, but unless we go public, they won't ever really know.*

Chapter Seven

As we neared the end of our junior year, I felt on top of the world as my plans all came together. Brittany and I weren't considered popular, but we had plenty of friends. Emmett and I continued growing closer, but since neither of us wanted to turn the world upside down, I could still date others guys. I'd made the volleyball team again, joined the newspaper, and become co-editor. My grades were so good that I was inducted into the National Honor Society, my scores on the ACT and SAT tests were solid, and I was selected to be a Camelia Belle, one of eight girls from my high school who were chosen.

My mom's friends were all a flutter over it the next time they came over to play bridge, since none of their daughters had ever been selected to be a Belle. When I said hello that night, they stopped their card games to ask me questions about my dress, whether I was excited to have been chosen, and whether I intended to try out for the Junior Miss pageant, too. Smiling politely, I answered all of their questions, accepting their praise modestly. As I said good night, I heard Miss Lynette say, "I don't know why Jessica made it. She's not very pretty." I paused just beyond the doorway and continued to watch and listen.

Miss Paula said, "I don't know why they picked Clarice, either. Don't you think it's weird to have a black girl wearing an antebellum dress? Why would they do that?"

"These days I guess they have to pick at least one or two. And she's a lot prettier than most," I heard someone else say. She looked up and saw me watching. Our eyes locked as she reached forward to play her card, loudly snapping it down on the table.

Pulling away from her stare, I looked to my mom across the room, who was quietly watching me as I listened. She just shrugged. Answering her with a roll of my eyes and a shake of my head, I wordlessly turned and retreated to the safety of my room.

• • •

Several weeks later, I was asked to the prom by a senior who had asked Beth-Anne first. Since she already had a date, she'd told him no and he asked me instead. Although I resented being second choice, I accepted his invitation, along with her gloating, without complaint. Since Emmett and I couldn't go to the prom together and no one else had asked me, saying no would've meant missing prom, which somehow seemed worse.

As the end of the school year approached, senior cheerleaders were chosen, student council elections were held, and once again Emmett, Peter, and Shelby were voted class favorites. Emmett's cast was off by then and his knee healed, so he began working out again and the doctor cleared him to play football during senior year.

Continuing to ride high tide, in June I received a scholarship for a high school summer program at a college in Montgomery. A six-week program, it was designed to allow rising high school seniors to take college courses over the summer and live on campus in the dorms. Since the college was well-known through our church, and with the expectation that the experience would better prepare me for the following year, my parents agreed that I could go without much persuasion.

With less than a thousand students enrolled, the entire college was smaller than our freshman class. Although it was in a sketchy area close to downtown, the campus insulated itself with tall, beautiful stone walls and a large, guarded iron gate. Inside the walls, the grounds were landscaped like a secret garden, and brick roads wove between the brick and stone buildings that were arranged on small streets circling a large grass field in the center of the campus. Most of the buildings and dorms were closed for the summer, since barely two hundred students attended summer school, so the older continuing students were easily separated from the inexperienced high school students. Resident assistants stood guard at the desk located at the entrance to our wing, where only the participating high school students were allowed. The dozen of us, hailing from high schools all over Alabama and Georgia, were nice, polite, very smart, and all white. We ate all of our meals together at long tables in the cafeteria, slept in our dorm rooms, used a shared bathroom located on our respective same-sex wings, and watched TV together in the rec room every night after class.

My roommate, Sue Ellen, took the same pre-calculus class I did, which we agreed wasn't any harder than our classes back in high school. Over the first couple of weeks, she and I settled into a routine, and in the process we met several upper classmen. One sophomore in particular named Lawrence paid her a lot of attention, and often after class, she dragged me along to help her find him. As an upper classman, Lawrence was allowed to have a car, and one day he invited Sue Ellen out for a burger and a movie. "You have to go with me," she begged, squeezing my arm, and I agreed. Later that week, Lawrence, his friend Zack, Sue Ellen, another guy named Ted, and I crammed into

Lawrence's beat-up Celica. After the movie, Zack, passed around a bottle of cheap wine in the car. Although I had only a few sips, by the time we returned to campus, I felt woozy and sick to my stomach, and so did Sue Ellen and Ted.

Once we parked, and before I saw where the others went, Zack helped me out of the impossibly small back seat and led me out to the quad near the amphitheater, saying, "You need some fresh air." With his hands on my shoulders, he pushed me across the grass. Finally we sat on a bench under a large tree and he said, as he put his arm around me, "Now ain't this a lot better?"

Nodding slowly, my stomach protesting, he leaned in and kissed me. The closeness made me nauseous, and I pulled away quickly, jumping up from the bench. Stumbling away from Zack, I grabbed the trunk of the tree and threw up. "Aww," he said as he joined me, rubbing my back as my stomach emptied the cheeseburger, fries, soda, and popcorn. Once I finished, I continued spitting, attempting to rid my mouth of the foul taste of wine. Without a word, he joined me, and at first his hands offered comfort, rubbing my back, but then they turned threatening as they moved everywhere else, up my shirt, under my bra, and even down the front of my pants. Pushing at him, I said, "Stop it!" and tried to move away, but the large roots and acorns of the Live oak tripped me and I fell, sliding on the small leaves.

With a laugh Zack acted like we were having fun and fell quickly to the ground beside me. Unfazed, his hands continued to roam under my clothes, and he moved on top of me, his legs pinning mine. Pushing at his shoulders and turning my body from side to side, I struggled to free myself from his groping hands and heavy body. Then, from somewhere in the dark, I heard a man's stern voice say loudly, "Hey! What's goin' on over there?"

Embarrassed and thankfully unable to see the face that belonged to the voice, I seized the opportunity to scramble up and away from Zack as he turned to say, "Oh, hey, Cameron. Uhh," and with a chuckle continued. "She got a little sick, so I'm tryin' to help her up. Get 'er back to the dorm."

"You're not helping her up," the deep voice in the dark said. "Get out of here, Zack, before I call campus security."

"Oh, come on now. I'm not doin' anything," he said, rising from the ground with a laugh as he brushed his hands off on his knees. Having made it several feet away, once again stumbling on the roots of the tree, I attempted to pull down my shirt and straighten my clothes.

"I mean it, Zack. Get outta here," The man said, moving forward quickly, nudging me gently to get behind him, and placing his hands on his hips. He stood solidly between Zack and me, and warned him once again, "Go on now, Zack or I'm calling campus security." Pointing away from me, he repeated, "Go on now. I mean it!"

"Alright, alright," Zack slowly said, chuckling under his breath, still brushing himself off, and began to walk in the direction of the dorm. After several steps, he put his hands in the air and made a motion like he was throwing something away, and said, "Whatever, man."

Once Zack was far enough away, the man Zack had called Cameron turned to me and asked softly, "Are you okay?"

"Yeah, I'm okay," I said as I brushed myself off, trying to rid myself of leaves, dirt, and the creepy feel of his hands, but also reassuring myself that I wasn't hurt. "I'm really feeling sick though," I told him.

"Let's get you back to the dorm," he said, gently reaching out as if he wanted to take my arm, but then he hesitated and pushed both hands deep into his pockets.

Slowly we headed to the dorm without speaking, until we reached the entrance, when he asked again, "You sure you're okay?" When I nodded, he asked, "Do ya think you can hold it together long enough to get past the R, A.?"

"Yeah, I think so," I said, once again pulling down on my shirt while he picked a leaf from my hair.

In the light of the lobby, I kept my head bowed, but managed to catch a glimpse of his face as I quickly glanced back at him at the door, then hurriedly walked past the R. A. at the desk. With a nod of his head, I turned and walked quickly down the long hall to my room. The locked door told me Sue Ellen was still out somewhere, and I fumbled to let myself in with my key. Without turning on a light or removing my clothes, and after carefully locking the door behind me, I collapsed onto my bed, kicking off my shoes and pulling around me the quilt my grandmomma had made. I was relieved to be safe, finally.

The next morning, I slept past breakfast and woke with a terrible headache. Sue Ellen had returned and snored softly in her bed, so I shuffled down the hall to join the small, quiet group assembled in the rec room, watching TV. Less than thirty minutes later, the R. A. walked halfway down the hall and called out, "Erin, you have a visitor."

Unmoving and unblinking, the other kids remained where they sat, sprawled over the green vinyl furniture. Their jaws slack and their eyes glazed, they stared in the direction of the TV as I rose to leave the room. After rounding the corner, I was finally able to see the lobby and my heart flipped in my chest at the sight of Zack standing there, waiting just beyond the R. A.'s desk. He smiled and waved, which instantly made me sick to my stomach again as my mind raced. I never wanted to see him again, but he was there, and the R. A. was there, so I doubted whether I could avoid him without making a scene or having to answer a lot of questions.

Willing myself to hurry up and think of the best thing to do, I slowed my pace and stared at the carpet under my bare feet. My mind raced. *What should I say? How can I make him go away and leave me alone?*

A flash of summer sunlight caught my attention as the double doors to the dorm opened, and I saw a dark silhouette walk into the lobby. As I watched, Zack turned to face the open doors and walk towards the silhouette. As the doors closed, the shadow became the man from last night, the one who Zack had called Cameron. I watched as they spoke. Zack shook his head no and looked back down the hall at me. Cameron stood with his feet wide apart, his arms crossed as he slowly shook his head no at Zack. Cameron said something and he put his hand on Zack's back and gave him a push. Involuntarily, Zack took a few steps towards the double doors. Twisting away from Cameron, with a swipe of his hand, Zack removed Cameron' hand from his back. But he continued walking towards the doors, and when he reached them, Zack briefly turned to look down the hall at me again before he pushed the door open, blinding me with the flash of the bright summer light. His dark silhouette went out and I heard the heavy door close behind him with a loud thunk.

Cameron walked across the lobby to lean on the ledge of the reception desk. I watched as he smiled and said something to the R. A. Obediently she looked up from her book with a smile, and with a laugh, she flipped her long blonde hair off her shoulder. Now within earshot, I heard the R. A. say with a giggle, "Yeah, I guess so. Must've changed his mind." Cameron turned to shoot me a smile, even as he whispered something else to the R. A., making her giggle in a higher pitch. Ignoring her, I entered the lobby, looked at him and said, "Cameron?"

"Nice to meet you," he said, smiling as he held out his hand to take mine.

"Hi. I'm Erin," I said, as I accepted his hand, and with a sheepish smile, added "Thank you for last night."

Holding my hand in his, he took my elbow and turned. As if we were dancing in a ballroom, he spun me smoothly, guiding me towards the double doors of the lobby. "Would you like to take a walk?" he asked, smiling down at me before shooting a parting smile over his shoulder at the R. A., who sat chin in hand, smiling at him from behind the desk.

"Yeah, that would be great," was all I could say as we walked out into the bright sun.

As we walked down the steps, I spoke hurriedly, saying, "I'm so sorry about last night. Thank you so much again. I don't know what happened."

As we walked across the brick driveway and out onto the quad where he and I first met, I gushed with the story of my roommate Sue Ellen and Lawrence inviting us to grab a burger and a movie, the wine Zack brought, and how I didn't drink much but that it'd made me sick, adding weakly, "That never happens."

"Unfortunately, you're not Zack's first victim," Cameron said and nodded solemnly. "I'm sorry that happened to you. He put something in that wine. I'm sure of it. I wish we could catch him one day so he'd get kicked out of school. But unfortunately it's always just rumors and things that almost happen but don't, so we haven't been able to do anything about it yet."

"Who's we?" I asked.

"My fraternity. Unfortunately Zack's one of my fraternity brothers." He answered, scratching the back of his neck.

As we continued to walk slowly around the campus grounds together, the conversation soon moved away from Zack. I told him about myself in response to his polite questions, speaking brightly of my current activities and future plans. In the course of the afternoon, I learned that Cameron was a senior taking one last class that he needed to graduate. As he pointed out the president's home, the prayer gardens, and the dorm he'd lived in previously, he shared his plans to get his masters in theology and become a Methodist minister.

Over the next several weeks, we continued to spend our afternoons together, and I learned he'd majored in history, loved books on the Civil War, and was so fascinated by fire-fighters that he even had a real fireman's suit, complete with boots and a helmet. Like me, he loved the beach, but he also loved the mountains, and felt as I did that he could always feel God there. He asked me questions, listened to my answers attentively, and always remembered what I told him. With his dark brown hair, olive complexion, and dark brown eyes, we looked like we could've been brother and sister. He was smart and funny, silly and sweet, handsome and tall, and he dressed like a Southern frat boy. He spoke often of his close-knit family. They had moved to my home town from upstate New York, when he was in high school. He'd graduated from an expensive private all-boys' school, and had a younger brother two years older than me. I could tell that he really liked me, and I liked him, too. He was different and special, and he made me feel special, too. And he was everything that people would approve of in a boyfriend.

After summer school, Cameron planned to return home to work at an auto-parts store while he studied for his entrance exams and applied to seminary schools. Before we left, he warned, "Your parents might be worried about us seeing each other, since I'm twenty-two and you're still in high school. So as soon as we get back, I need to come over and meet them." And just as he expected, when I told my parents about him, my dad said, "Well I don't know about this. We're gonna have to meet him."

But Cameron was unlike any of the other guys I'd gone out with before. He didn't just come over to pick me up, say a sentence or two to my parents, and then hurriedly take me out. Instead, he came over and stayed around. We ate supper and watched TV together, and he seemed genuinely interested in getting to know my parents my sisters. He was so nice and polite, so well-mannered and well-intentioned, that my parents grew comfortable with our relationship after just one visit.

• • •

I hadn't been able to call Brittany for weeks, since making long distance calls wasn't allowed, so when I got back, we had a lot of catching up to do. Bursting with news, I wanted to tell her about my class, the dorm, Sue Ellen, the other high school program kids, Zack, and, of course, Cameron. I knew she and Derek had gone out a lot over the summer, and that she probably had been hanging out with Catrina and Tucker and their friends, too, so we made plans to spend the following weekend together and get caught up on each other's lives.

We spent the night at Brittany's house, staying up late and talking about every detail, rather than going out anywhere. Her mom called us "little magpies," and told us to stay in Brittany's room so she could hear herself think. Each story I told Brittany reminded her of one she had for me, and by the next morning, it was as if we'd never been apart. The following day we spent walking in the woods, and we went back to our spot by the creek.

"This is gonna be our best year ever," she said as we sat looking at the creek flowing beneath us.

"I can't wait," I replied.

"You know, by this time next year, everything will be different, right?" she said, turning to look at me.

"It doesn't have to be. You could come with me, you know," I scolded.

"Won't matter," she said, smiling. "Things will be different. But we'll always be together, no matter what we do and no matter where we are."

"I know, but I really gotta get outta here," I said. "I feel like I'll explode if I stay," I told her, missing her point entirely.

"That's not what I meant," she said. "And why do you always do that anyway?" she asked.

"Do what?" I said looking at her, confused.

"That thing with your feet." She said pointing down at my feet, where the toes of one foot rested on top of the other.

"I dunno. Stop changing the subject!" I said and laughed.

"Let's get out of here," she said, laughing as she rose from her rock. "Let's go see what Tucker's up to. I want you to meet him again."

Over the summer, Tucker had gotten his own place in the same complex with a few of his friends. I'd only met him that one time during Mardi Gras, and as we walked back, she talked about how she wanted me to meet him again so I could see how cool he and his friends were. When we got to his back door, she knocked loudly on the glass, but didn't wait. Walking in, she hollered a loud "Hello," and we could see three guys in the living room, sitting on mismatched lawn chairs. Until she reintroduced us, I didn't remember which one of them was Tucker.

"Y'all sit down. Wanna beer?" Tucker asked, without getting up. He was wearing shorts, a tee-shirt with a wrinkled button-down shirt over it. Barefoot and with one foot propped up on his other knee, I could see the tops of his feet were hairy and the bottoms dirty. His dark hair was all messed up, and the cowlicks told me he'd just woken up. The dark stubble on his unshaven face told me he needed to shave often.

Brittany said, "Yes, please. I'll get it," and immediately left me in the living room as she flew to the kitchen.

Unsure whether I should follow, I sat gingerly on the edge of the worn-out sofa, which had obviously been handed down to help furnish the place. I watched Brittany take two bottles from the refrigerator and it dawned on me that she'd done this before. She knew exactly which drawer held the bottle opener, and that the small white plastic trash can was in the cabinet under the sink. She handed me a bottle, then plopped on the couch.

"So, Brittany says you went to college this summer," one of the other guys said.

"Yep" I answered, taking a nervous swig, and refusing to make eye contact.

"Where'd ya go?" he asked, lighting a cigarette. He appeared to have just woken up, too, and like Tucker, was also in need of a shower and shave.

"Up in Montgomery," I told him, then examined the label of the beer bottle to avoid looking at him.

"She said you're a Camelia Belle, too," the other guy said.

"Yeah, I am. My dress's yellow," I told him, not sure why I felt the need to say that. I looked at Brittany and silently pleaded for help, and from the corner of my eye, noticed

Tucker studying me as he shook his foot. I grew increasingly uncomfortable under his gaze and desperately wanted to leave.

"What're you guys doing t'night?" Brittany asked, smiling at me before looking at Tucker.

"You're lookin at it," Tucker said, stretching his arms wide before pulling one last swig from his beer. With the sucking sound of his lips leaving the bottle, he asked Brittany to "Get me another one, will ya?" as he pointed the butt of his now empty bottle at her.

"Sure," she said, hopping eagerly off the coach to grab his empty bottle and return to the kitchen to get another beer for him.

After about an hour, during which I was glad we'd stopped talking about me, Brittany finally said, "Welp. We gotta go."

"Come back over tomorrow after Erin leaves," Tucker shouted as the two of us walked towards the sliding glass door. "We're thinkin' about havin' a couple of friends over."

"Okay, see you tomorrow," Brittany said as she pulled open the heavy slider, once again looking down and tucking hair that she no longer had behind her ear.

"What in the world is goin' on?" I asked her, as soon as the door closed and we were outside on the patio. "Are you seein' him now? Or what?"

"Kinda," she said shrugging. "It's no big deal, really. I'm still seeing Derek and all, but we've been fighting a lot lately. Derek's always telling me what to do. Besides, Tucker and his friends are fun to hang out with."

"How old are they?" I asked, horrified, and with extra emphasis on the word *old*.

"No older than your college boy," she shot back in the bitter tone she usually reserved for her mom.

Ah, so this is when you're supposed to use the word touché, I thought to myself. But to Brittany I said, "Yeah, but something's not right with him. I don't know what it is but you gotta be careful."

"Stop bein' such a baby," she snapped.

Unwilling to fight with my best friend over a guy, I never said anything else to her about Tucker. Instead, I reassured myself that giving her a hard time about him was as bad as what I worried people would do if they knew I went out with Emmett.

• • •

My Camelia Belle dress was ready before the summer was over. The seamstress had taken all of my ideas sketched in crude pencil drawings and translated them perfectly into a gorgeous dress. My dress, my hat, my parasol, my long gloves, and even my pantaloons were exactly what I'd wanted and everything I'd imagined. There was plenty of lace, but it wasn't overdone. There were bows in the folds of the skirt, just as I had specified, but not too many or too large. My waist looked incredibly small in the off-the-shoulders dress with the corset drawn tight, and the bodice fit perfectly in gauzy poofs that added volume to my otherwise flat chest. The three different layers of skirts began at my waist and fell in fluffy poofs, soft pleats, and ruffles of gauze, silk, and taffeta. The skirt was held wide in six-foot panels backed by a sturdy white cotton hoop skirt. The buttery yellow color of the dress, hat, parasol, and gloves highlighted my coloring and whatever beauty I had to offer. In that dress, I looked every bit the part of a beautiful young southern belle.

Our senior year began much as the three previous ones had, in a flurry of classes, lunches, practices, parties, football games, and dates. I took a full load of courses, even though I only needed another year of P. E. to graduate. Half of my classes were AP courses, which I hoped would help me earn college credits if I scored high enough on the tests. Although I no longer had dance classes or piano competitions, I stayed busy with the scheduled appearances all around town for the Belles, and I had responsibilities with the school paper, including articles to write, editions to plan, articles to review, and ads to sell.

Brittany was in a few of my classes, but since I was seeing both Cameron and Emmett, and she was dating Derek and Tucker and hanging out with Catrina and her friends, we didn't do as much together on the weekends anymore. We were still inseparable in every other way, before and after school, and during lunch. We made up for lost time by writing each other cryptic notes during school and talking on the phone late into the night. My mom clucked her tongue in disapproval many nights as I sat talking to Brittany on the phone from the floor of our kitchen saying, "You two are as thick as thieves!"

Emmett again shared several of my classes, and sat with me in both English and Physics. He was back playing football, and as busy working out and at practice as ever. We tried to see each other whenever we could outside of school, but it never was as often as either of us would've liked. My feelings for Emmett grew deeper with every passing day, but so did my conviction that we couldn't go out together. We simply could not risk it. We both had too much at stake, and dating Cameron was far easier.

Cameron, unlike any other guy I'd dated, took me out to dinner and the movies, opened doors for me, remembered things I told him, didn't mind hanging out at my house with my parents, and never got annoyed with my younger sister. My parents liked him, and everyone else did, too. Although Camelia

Belles kept me busy with appearances, Cameron followed me, always proudly waving to me. A history buff, he loved revisiting the local historical sites that we were assigned, snapping pictures of me posing in my dress in the expansive gardens and on the steps of the carefully restored antebellum homes along the oak tree lined streets of downtown.

Cameron introduced me to his family, even his grandmother, and I enjoyed the normalcy of being with him. I could talk about him freely, and we dated often. He told me he wanted to see me as often as possible, but like Emmett, he also said I shouldn't stop dating other guys. "It's important," he said repeatedly, "for you to go to dances with other guys, guys from your school. Go to parties with your girlfriends. Go to every football game and school event. You need to enjoy your senior year. I've already had mine so I know what it's like and I understand. Don't worry about me. I don't want you to miss a single thing. It's a very special time in your life," he said.

In the blink of an eye, we had been dating for six months and it was the holidays. Cameron wanted us to open our presents at my house in front of the Christmas tree in the living room. He opened my gift to him first, and like a little kid he put on the wool sweater I'd given him as soon as he opened it. He gave me a CD and a card, and then handed me a small box. He obviously had not wrapped the small gift himself, and I ripped off the gilded paper and bow. Inside a black velvet box was a beautiful pearl ring.

Seeing the one big question in my eyes, his face glowed with the lights of the Christmas tree when he said, "I don't expect you to make or keep any promises in accepting this ring I just got it for you because I know how much you like pearls."

When I showed my mom the ring later that night after he left, she told me, "I don't care what he says. I think he's serious about you. If you're not just as serious about him, you'd better be careful. Don't you lead him on, Erin. That wouldn't be right."

• • •

Our first day back to school after the holidays, in January of 1984, our English teacher assigned the book ***1984***, and for weeks we tore it apart, listing all of the things it had predicted that had not happened yet. By then, most of us knew where we were going to college. We'd won the state football championship, and because of the team's success, a record twelve players were offered football scholarships that year. Emmett, Peter, and three others signed with the University. I didn't get any academic scholarships, so I knew I was going too.

Cameron was accepted to seminary and was moving to Atlanta in the fall, Lorna was accepted to a Tech University out of state, and Brittany refused to commit to going anywhere. Sometimes she talked about coming with me to the University, and sometimes she talked about staying at home and going to community college. She said she had to wait and see how much financial aid she could get before she made her decision, so I waited, hoping and praying she would join me.

Late in January, the Camelia Belles traveled to Florida, where we participated in a half-time show, visited a theme park and marched in a parade. Traveling in a huge Greyhound bus, each of us had our huge antebellum dresses, tote bags full of makeup and hair curlers, and enough matching outfits for a week. Staying four girls to a room in various hotels, each room with two double beds, not enough towels or electrical outlets, we somehow survived.

The day after we returned, Brittany called. "I have so much to tell you," I started to say as soon as I knew it was her on the phone. "So much has happened."

"I need to see you right away," she said in a tone much too serious for stories about my trip.

"Oh. Okay," I said. I'll be right over," I stammered, already thinking of the excuses I'd need to get out of the house again so soon.

"We can't talk here," she said in a hushed tone. "Just hurry up and get over here to pick me up."

Once I pulled into her complex, Brittany crossed the parking lot before I was out of the car. She was lighting a cigarette, which wasn't a good sign. Her parents didn't know that she smoked, so it was obvious that she didn't care if they saw her. She jerked opened the passenger door, hopped in, and said, "Let's get out of here!" as she slammed the door shut.

"Where do you wanna go?" I asked, putting the car in reverse.

"I don't care, just drive," she said, rolling down her window.

I pulled out of the parking lot and reached down for one of her cigarettes, lighting it as we rode in silence to the college. I parked in the same lot where I'd told her how I felt about Emmett, and where one Sunday afternoon, she'd taught me to drive her parents' stick-shift car. Once I parked the car and shut off the engine, I demanded that she tell me what was going on.

Brittany sat there in the passenger seat, her hand out the window holding her cigarette. She blew three perfect smoke rings, then turned to me and said, "I'm pregnant."

Chapter Eight

"Oh my God" I sighed. "Are you sure? What're you gonna do?" I asked and threw my cigarette out the window. Suddenly the smell of it made me sick to my stomach. Waiting for her answer, I stared at my hands still gripping the steering wheel.

After a long exhale, Brittany said, "Yeah I'm sure."

"Well, have you told Derek yet?" I asked, letting go of the steering wheel.

She made an annoyed face at me, one I'd seen her make at her mom, before she turned to stare into the trees lining the parking lot and quietly said, "It's not Derek's."

"Well? Whose is it, then?" My voice sounded shrill in my ears. Why was she so calm?

"It's Tucker's, Erin!" she said with an angry look. Then she snapped, "What's wrong with you?"

"Okay," I said, taking a deep breath. "So? Does Tucker know? What did he say?" I tried to sound calmer and apologetic.

"Yeah, he knows. He went with me to the clinic," she said as she looked out into the night. The only sound I heard was the pounding of my own heart in my ears.

"Have you even had time to really think about it yet? About what you're gonna do, I mean?" I asked, trying to remain as calm as she looked.

"I'm going to have a beautiful baby, that's what I'm going to do," she said, inhaling deeply. "I'm going to finish school. Get a job. Save my money. And then, sometime this summer, before the baby comes, we'll get married." She turned and faced me, and I watched as tears pooled in the corners of her shining eyes. "Tucker says if we start now, we can get our own place by the time the baby comes."

"How far along are you?" I asked.

"Ten weeks. That gives us 'til sometime in September," she said and nodded.

"You still have time, you know. Any time before twelve weeks you can still—" I started to say, my voice betraying me and rising again before she interrupted.

"I'm not going to abort this baby," she snapped, putting her other hand protectively on her abdomen. "God, Erin. I'm Catholic! Besides, at ten weeks, the baby is already a child, already has fingernails. Did you know that? I don't care what anybody says, I'm not killing my baby."

"You're not Catholic," I snorted, incredulous. "Since when do you even go to church?"

"Stop it! I was raised Catholic. And I don't have to go to church every Sunday to be Catholic!" she shouted, clearly ready for a fight, even with me.

"But what about school? What about everything we said we wanted? Everything you said *you* wanted to do? You were going to be a counselor and help people! We were going to travel together! What about everything we've always talked about?" Feeling helpless, I knew I wasn't helping. But I couldn't stop.

"This isn't the end of the world, ya know. I can still do whatever I wanna do!" she said. "Besides, most of that was what *you* wanted. Not me." She was angry now.

"Alright, alright," I said, putting my hands up in surrender. "Wow," I said with a deep exhale.

"Yeah? Well, tell me about it," she said, as she flicked her cigarette butt out the window.

"What did your parents say?" I asked, almost afraid to hear the answer.

"About what you'd expect," she said. "They're pretty mad. But I think they'll come around. Eventually, anyway. Mr. Freeman's really being great about it. I think it'll be okay. They just found out, and it's a shock, ya know?"

We remained quiet for a while, my own mind spinning in the silence.

Then Brittany said, "I wanted you to know before anybody else, but you were gone. I didn't know how to get hold of you, so I had to go ahead and tell them."

I didn't know what to say. *Should I say I'm sorry?* I was sorry. Really sorry.

Brittany seemed more resigned and angry than sad and upset, and I wanted to ask her how she felt. But all I said was, "Are you okay?"

"Yeah, I'm okay," she said, sighing.

"It'll be okay," I said, testing how the words sounded, turning them over, and trying to decide if it was true. *Will it really be okay?* I asked myself. Feeling a little more certain, I told her, "It'll be okay, Brittany."

After a few moments, I turned in my seat and said, "You know, you could still go off to school with me. We could get an apartment together. We could work and go to school, and both of us could take care of the baby. You don't have to—" I was thinking out loud and wondering, *Why do all of our plans have to change?*

Brittany laughed and shook her head. "I don't know about all that. Look, don't tell anybody about this yet. I'll tell people when it's time."

"I won't say anything," I vowed, shaking my head, too.

"I should go home now. We're supposed to have another big discussion with the parents tonight. So take me home, okay?" she asked.

When we parked at her house, I grabbed her arm before she could open the door, and, pulling her to me, I hugged her tightly. We sat holding each other for a long time, and I talked to her quietly as I rubbed her back, saying soothing things as I held her. I didn't want to let her go. She kissed my cheek before finally she pulled away and got out of the car.

I cried the whole way home, wondering how this had happened. Did she really not want all of the things we'd talked about doing? Were those dreams really only mine? How had I missed that? All of those nights when we'd talked and talked, was it really only about what I wanted? But she'd wanted it, too. She said so. I knew she'd meant it. Why was she now saying that she didn't?

I cried bitterly for her, for what she was going through, for what she was giving up, and for everything she would have to endure. But some of my tears were for me. It felt like I was losing my best friend.

Before she got out of the car, she'd said, "It's time ok? You've gotta sail on. I know you can do this," and I'd understood instantly what she'd meant. She expected me to keep going, and this time to do it all on my own. It felt like a goodbye.

Later that night, I fainted. One minute I was in the bathroom brushing my teeth, and the next, I awoke lying sprawled on the bathroom mat with my mom wiping my face with a wet cloth. She and my dad helped me up and got me into my bed, where immediately I fell into a long, deep sleep.

These fainting episodes began during my junior year in high school, and at first we thought they were caused by allergies. As a little kid, I'd been sick a lot from allergies, and even took daily shots for a while. But these weren't typical sinus headaches; they were crushing and exhausting, and unlike sinus headaches, didn't start with pressure behind my eyes. Instead, these headaches started as a sharp point of pain that widened as it crawled across my scalp until it crushed my skull in a helmet-like vice. Once the pain had a firm grip, relief only came with sleep. Mom said I was probably going out and doing too much, and that I should rest more and drink more water. But no amount of sleep or water prevented these attacks. After several months, things got even worse, and as the first spears of pain began, my hands, arms, and face would tingle, my speech would slur, and I would get light-headed.

The first time I'd fainted, it frightened my parents so much that that took me to a doctor who admitted me into the hospital. For three days, I had CAT scans, EKGs, ECGs and MRIs. Sticky electrodes were attached to my head and connected to nearby machines that beeped, flashed lights, and printed lines noisily on paper. Once the results were in, the doctor told my relieved parents that I didn't have a brain tumor or heart problems. He explained that these episodes were migraine headaches caused by restricted blood flow in the blood vessels to my brain. The doctor said, "Migraines are a condition that can be worsen by changes in hormones or stress and in Erin's case, it's most likely both." He prescribed a medicine to help cut down on the frequency of the migraines and told my parents to try and help me avoid stress. My parents nodded and I wondered: *How am I supposed to do that?*

The morning after Brittany had told me the news, I woke up and groggily walked into the kitchen, my insides hollow and sore. Judging by the smells wafting through the house, I could tell that Mom was somewhere nearby, already busy with her Saturday cleaning chores. Even with the windows open, the familiar smells of Comet, Pine Sol, bleach, and a faint hint of ammonia hung in the cool, almost-spring air.

"How're you feelin'?" Mom asked, popping her head around the corner as soon as I entered.

"I'm better," I said, opening the refrigerator with a glass in my hand.

"Have you been takin' your medicine?" Mom asked, holding a sponge as she watched me carefully.

"Yes, ma'am," I answered from behind the refrigerator door. Feeling it necessary to hide my feelings, I hid inside the open refrigerator, pretending to need time to decide on what to drink.

"You need to stay home this weekend and get some rest. You've been doin' too much lately," she said, pulling a damp rag from the pocket of her apron.

"Yes, ma'am, I will," I said, burying my face further behind the refrigerator door.

"I mean it, now," she said. "And don't stand there with the door open. Pick something and shut it."

"Yes, ma'am," I said once more, pouring juice into my glass and kicking the door closed so I could quickly turn my back to her. I drank my juice standing at the sink.

"Somethin' botherin' you?" Mom asked. "You know what the doctor said. Stress causes these episodes."

But before she could continue her line of questioning, I interrupted and said, "No ma'am. Nothing's bothering me." Draining the juice from the glass and carefully setting it in the sink, I added, "My period's due next week. That's probably it." I knew it was stress. But I just couldn't tell her about Brittany. I wasn't ready and I needed time to think everything through first. My parents were worried about me but I wasn't ready to face their concerns yet.

I stayed home all weekend, just as I'd promised, spending most of the time alone in my room. I didn't have a lot of homework anymore, since the school year was almost over. But when I spread my books and notebooks out across my bed, my parents gave me more privacy, so that's what I did. The first time I called Brittany's house that weekend, Ms. Justine said, "Brittany can't come to the phone right now." The second time I called, she said, "She's not home." The third time, she told me, "Brittany's going to have to call you back later." The fourth time was late Sunday afternoon, and when Ms. Justine answered the phone and heard my voice, she covered the receiver and yelled Brittany's name.

"Hey," Brittany said when she picked up the phone.

"Hey. How are you?" I asked.

"I'm okay," she said. "I can't really talk right now. They took the phone outta my room." and then she suddenly started to yell at the top of her lungs, "And now my mom…follows me around the house all day…and listens to every word that I say!" It was as if she wasn't talking to me at all, and was instead yelling at her mom. Considering how loud she was, her mom could've heard her from anywhere in their house.

"Why don't I pick you up in the morning and we'll ride to school together," I said.

"Sounds good, I'll see you then." As she hung up, I could hear her yelling again.

"I don't know what else you think is going to happen—" but then the line went dead.

The following morning when I pulled up to her house, Brittany was waiting for me, a book and notebook under one arm, her large red leather purse thrown over her shoulder, and she was holding a lit cigarette. She opened the door and jumped into the car before I'd even come to a full stop.

"How was it?" I asked, accelerating to get her out of there as quickly as possible.

All the way to school she ranted about her parents. "Mr. Freeman's the only sane adult around here," she said. "I told my parents that I just might move in with him before Tucker and I get our own place if they don't stop making every moment of my life a living hell."

"Now I have to tell Derek," she said, sighing. "And then, once he knows, I'll withdraw from school, probably next Monday. After that, you can tell everybody else."

"I'm not going to tell anybody. It's none of their business," I told her.

"I know, I know," Brittany said. "What I meant was, well everyone's gonna find out anyway. But by Monday, it'll be okay for you to talk about it. If somebody asks you about it, I mean." She sounded nervous.

"Why can't you go ahead and finish school? You're about to graduate anyway," I said, trying not to whine.

"I'm already showing," she said, rubbing her abdomen. "It's like overnight, you can already tell. You know they won't let me stay in high school pregnant. I'll finish at night school. Besides, I need to hurry up and find a job so we can move out."

Brittany was right. As soon as you knew to look, you could clearly see the baby bump below her waist band. She'd always been so skinny that whenever she ate, her belly would swell. And although she wasn't even three months along, she wasn't going to be able to hide it for much longer. And once the administration found out, they'd make her leave.

"Do you need me to go with you when you tell Derek?" I offered, desperate to find a way to help.

"No, thanks," she said. "Just be ready afterwards." She sighed.

Later that day, I sat in Spanish class, nervously watching the door, waiting for Brittany. She was almost late and walked in just as the bell rang. I gasped when I saw her. Just as I feared, Brittany's face, eyes, and even her ears were bright red. It was obvious that she'd talked to Derek.

"Tomar su asiento Britinia," Ms. Wagner, our Spanish teacher, said. Then she closed the class room door.

Brittany ducked her head and slunk into her seat beside me, as murmurs emanated from the rows of kids. "What's wrong with *her*?" a girl's voice said, sounding snide.

"Are you okay?" I mouthed. She just shrugged her shoulders and put her head down, resting her forehead on her crossed arms on top of her books.

Twenty minutes into class, during which Brittany never lifted her head, Ms. Wagner walked over, put her hand on Brittany's back, and whispered, "Te sientes bien?" which translated into "Are you okay?"

Brittany sat up and silently shook her head no. It was obvious she'd been crying.

Ms. Wagner looked to me and said, "Llevarla a la officina, por favor," which meant she wanted me to take Brittany to the office.

Anxious to follow her instructions, I frantically collected my things and signaled to Brittany with a jerk of my head towards the door, softly saying "Let's go." Obediently she rose and followed me out of the classroom to the murmuring of the other students. She rested her chin on the top of the books she carried, keeping her eyes focused on the floor.

As I closed the door behind us, I heard Ms. Wagner say to the class, "Calmarse, calmarse, esta enferma," Which meant to calm down and that Brittany wasn't feeling well.

"We goin' to the office?" she sniffed, rubbing her nose as she followed me down the empty hall.

"No," I said. "I'm takin' you home."

"You'll get in trouble," she said weakly and without conviction. But she marked her protest by stopping in the middle of the hall.

"No, I won't. I still have my off-campus pass from selling ads," I told her, retracing a few steps and putting my arm around her shoulders. "Come on. Let's get you out of here."

On the way home, she told me through hiccups and tears what I already knew. Derek had taken the news badly.

"Maybe you should've told him over the phone, or somewhere other than school," I told her.

"No, he deserved to hear it face to face," she said. "And I didn't trust myself to see him anywhere else."

He'd made a scene by punching his locker, yelling at her, grabbing her arm, and then pushing her away. Although she didn't tell me everything, it was obvious that he'd said a lot of hurtful things.

As soon as we went inside her house, her mom pounced. Ignoring the fact that we were home from school so early, she asked me, "Well, what'd ya think of our little girl now, little Miss Camelia Belle?"

Before I could answer, Brittany snapped back at her mom, saying, "Leave her alone!"

"I just wanna know what she thinks of our little girl, who's now going to be a high school dropout and married with a kid, all before she turns eighteen," Ms. Justine said and took a puff from a cigarette. I'd never seen her smoke before.

"I'm going to be a grandmother before I even turn fifty! Did ya know that?" she said, exhaling, this time addressing me, although her eyes followed Brittany as she walked past her into the kitchen.

"Please, Mom. I've had a really bad day. I just want to grab us something to eat," Brittany said as she opened the refrigerator.

"One of many bad days to come, I'd expect," her mom said, looking back at me and swirling her cigarette dramatically in the air with a weird smile.

"Cheese weenie?" Brittany asked as she held up a package of hot dogs with cheese filling.

"Sure," I said.

"Oh, that's really good for the baby," her mom snorted.

Then to me, as she pointed at me with the hand that held her lit cigarette, she said, "Erin, you need to stay away from all this. Do yourself a favor and go to college." Then with a large sweep of her hand she said "And get as far away from all this as you possibly can."

Frozen in the middle of the living room, I silently nodded my head.

After the beep of the microwave, Brittany said, "Let's go," as she grabbed the paper-towel wrapped links and several pieces of white bread. "We'll be back," she told her mom over her shoulder as she pulled me toward the sliding door.

"Can't wait!" her mom yelled behind us as we hurried outside into the parking lot.

"Where to?" I asked as we headed to the car, expecting to drive us somewhere.

"Our spot," she said, striding towards the woods.

Once we sat on our favorite rocks, she wrapped one of the hot dogs in a piece of bread and handed it to me. "Sorry about my mom," she said glumly.

"It's okay. She's just upset," I said taking a bite of hot dog and chewing slowly.

"She doesn't have to be this—" she hesitated, searching for the right word, then said, "—evil."

"She's not evil. She's just hurt and upset. You know that," I told her. When she didn't respond, I added "My mom would probably say a hell of a lot worse!" I shuddered at the thought.

"I can still go to college, you know. I'll get my diploma at night school or my G.E.D. Once we're married and the baby comes, I can take a few classes." Although she tried hard to sound confident, it sounded more like a question.

"Of course you can," I said, trying to reassure her.

"It's not like my life is over," she said, again sounding unsure.

"Of course not," I told her.

We sat in silence, listening to the wind in the trees and the sound of the creek. It was a beautiful day. The kind of day we loved, with its deep blue skies, a slight chill in the air, and a bright warm sun.

"I just.... I just really wanted ...." she said and stopped.

"I know," I said, nodding in true understanding. "It'll be okay."

"Yeah," she said, getting up and looking across the drainage gulch that we'd pretended was a creek and at the scrub of trees that we'd pretended was a forest.

"Yeah" she said. "It'll be okay." She turned and started for home and I quietly got up and followed her.

When Brittany didn't show up at school the next day, I went to the newspaper office instead of going to lunch. I called her house that night but no one answered. The following day, she came to school in the morning, but by lunch, I couldn't find her. Her friend Virginia, who was in a morning class with her, told me Brittany had already gone home for the day. Still hanging onto my off campus pass, I left school and went to her house. But nobody answered. If anyone was home, they refused to answer the door. Unsure what to do, I stood in the parking lot, looking around. I didn't want to go to Tucker's or Mr. Freeman's. Just the thought of seeing either of them left a bad taste in my mouth. Not wanting to go home that early, I decided to drive back to school.

When I returned, I crunched through the shell parking lot behind the boy's gym, making my way to the main building, when a male teacher assigned to patrol startled me. "Just where do you think you're goin' young lady?" he boomed, making me jump in surprise.

"I'm—" I said, putting my hand to my heart, "I'm going back to class!" I must have looked guilty because he said, "Let me see your pass!"

After digging through my purse, I nervously handed him my off campus pass. With only a quick glance, he snorted, "This pass has expired, young lady. Let's go."

Taking my elbow firmly, as if I would try to make a break for it, he pulled me along. Once we arrived in the lobby of the main office, he pointed to a bench and said, "Have a seat," then ducked into Mr. Stevens' office, to my relief. He was the young black Vice Principal with a reputation of being fair compared to Ms. Springer, the older, angry white lady who had a reputation for ruining people.

"Care to explain why you were skippin' school, Ms. Pugsley?" Mr. Stevens asked as I entered his office.

"I had a pass to be off campus," I responded politely.

"Not a valid pass. Where did you go?" he asked, drumming his fingers on the desk.

"I don't understand. Why isn't it valid?" I asked as innocently as I could, praying that my face wouldn't betray me.

"The school newspaper doesn't sell ads in the spring, as you very well know. Where did you go, Ms. Pugsley? If you tell the truth, maybe you won't get suspended," he said.

"I had an emergency. But I'm back now and would like to go to class, please," I said, still trying to sound innocent.

"What kind of emergency?" he asked.

"A friend of mine's in trouble, so I just had to leave for a little bit," I said, instantly sensing my mistake.

"And which friend would that be?" he asked, leaning forward in genuine interest.

"My friend Brittany," I said, hanging my head.

"And what kind of emergency would require a student to leave during school to go help a former student, Ms. Pugsley?" he asked with an evil smile.

"Former student? What so you mean? Did she withdraw?" I asked incredulously. She'd said she was going to do it, but not until Monday.

"Yes, she did. Just this morning." He told me, grinning. *Why is he so happy about this?* I wondered, staring down at my lap, avoiding the self-satisfied look on his face and praying for mercy.

"You should be more careful about who you call a friend, Ms. Pugsley. Friends like her will get you into trouble," he said, clasping his hands in front of him on the desk. "You have a bright future. You should be more careful."

I looked up and said, "Yes, sir."

"Let this be a lesson to you. Friends like that are bad news," he continued.

"Yes, sir," I said, once again hanging my head.

"One day in-school suspension, Ms. Pugsley. Have all of your teachers sign this form," he said, holding it out. "Report to the cafeteria first thing tomorrow morning."

"What? Why?" I asked, involuntarily looking up and into his sneering face.

"To teach you a lesson, Ms. Pugsley. Get new friends before you really screw up," he said, shaking the form at me.

As I took the Disciplinary Form from him, I saw that he'd written "in-school suspension." It had lines for each of my teachers to sign it, and at the bottom, a space labeled "parent signature."

Stumbling out of his office and into the hallway, I heard a rushing sound in my ears. *My parents are gonna kill me*, I thought as I moved into the crowd, not knowing where I was going until I stumbled straight into Regina.

"Hey. Where're you goin'? English's this way," she said, pointing in the opposite direction.

Without a word, I turned and followed her to our next class, not daring to walk beside her, but choosing instead to follow a few paces behind.

"I don't understand why you'd do such a thing," Mom yelled as she moved pots, pans, lids, and dishes from counter to stove, stove to sink, and sink, to dishwasher. "Why? Why would you risk your entire future? Why would you skip school so late in the year?"

"I just needed to leave, is all," I grumbled from my chair at the kitchen table, picking at imaginary crumbs on my placemat.

"Why? *Why* did you need to leave? You'd better tell me or I'm takin' your car away, young lady." She continued slamming, clinking, and clanking, making far more noise than necessary.

"I told you, I'm sorry. It's just that Brittany was really upset. I needed to leave to find her. I was worried!" I said, trying to tell some of the truth, to make it sound reasonable, and also show that I was sorry.

"Why's she so upset?" Mom said, running out of dishes to bang. "And what does that have to do with you?"

"She broke up with Derek," I said, reassuring myself that this was at least partially true. *They did break up*, I thought.

"Well, that's not your problem, is it?" Mom said. "Why would you need to leave school? You could've called her when you got home. Why would you do this when you've worked so hard? Tell me!" she fumed, scrubbing the counters furiously.

"I dunno, Mom. I said I was sorry. I won't do it again. I promise. It's just a one-day in-school suspension. It won't mess up anything," I told her, my hands clasped on the table as I shamelessly begged. I couldn't tell her that Brittany was pregnant. I just wasn't ready for that conversation. But I knew, even as I apologized, that I'd also missed my chance to tell her about Brittany.

"I just don't even know what else to say to you, young lady," she said, flinging the dishrag in the direction of the sink.

"I'm sorry, Momma. Really. I won't do it again. I promise!" I vowed. Experience had taught me that by the time she said," I don't know what else to say," it meant that the conversation was over.

"You'd better not," she said as I got up from the table and slowly made my way to the den, afraid that any sudden movement would set her off again.

"Yes, ma'am. I'm sorry," I murmured guiltily as I reached the doorway to the den and quickly fled in the direction of my bedroom.

When I tried to call Brittany that night, Ms. Justine answered and said, "She's not home."

• • •

In-school suspension meant the students who were being punished had to sit in the cafeteria for the entire school day at the reserved tables along the far wall. The aroma of breakfast still hung in the air when I arrived, and the greasy smell of eggs and sausage made me feel queasy. As the day progressed, the mostly black cafeteria workers in their white uniforms and hair nets began to cook lunch. Like breakfast, lunch smelled thick with grease. I didn't know anyone else in suspension so I sat alone, although most of the kids there seemed to know each other. I passed the time by doing schoolwork, reading my assignments, and catching up on Spanish translations. When I'd done all of that, I organized my papers and folders. The others either didn't have school work or they didn't want to do it; instead, they doodled, played games, slept, or just stared out of the cafeteria windows.

News traveled fast, and most people had heard the news of my in-school suspension by the following day, and I did my best to behave as if nothing was wrong. When people asked, "Is it true that you got suspended?" I just laughed, shrugged, and said, "Yeah. It's no big deal." Sometimes I added, "Whenever I do anything wrong, I always get caught."

Derek refused to look at me, and only a few people were brave enough to ask me to my face about Brittany. The few that asked said, "Is it true Brittany dropped out of school because she's pregnant?" I found I could quickly close the topic by answering curtly, "Yes. She's gonna get married and she's happy about it."

Emmett didn't ask me any questions during class. We kept our conversations brief and shallow, but several times I saw him eyeing me suspiciously. After school that day, he ran to catch me in the parking lot and asked, "Hey. How're you doing?"

I started to laugh and shrugged. I began with my canned response, but Emmett interrupted me, took my arm gently, then said, "No, really. How're you doin'?"

"I'm hangin' in there, I guess," I told him and looked around at the other kids passing by on their way to their cars. "Can I maybe come by this afternoon?" I asked softly.

"Yeah, of course," he said, then glanced around the parking lot.

Alone together at his house, Emmett did most of the talking while I cried. He already knew everything and repeated over and over how sorry he was about what had happened to Brittany. "I know how it feels," he said. "It's like you're losin' her," he said.

I was so relieved hearing his words. He knew me so well. And even in this crazy, mixed-up mess, he already understood how I felt, without me having to explain anything.

"I know it probably feels like you'd be doing something wrong if you kept going, if you keep doing what you've always done, but you're really not," he said.

"But how am I supposed to just go on? What about Brittany? How do I just keep going and act like nothing's happened?" I protested.

"You just do it," he told me firmly. "You have to."

Then he added, "You know, Brittany doesn't expect you to stop your life, either. She knows you'll always be there for her."

Later, pulling out of his driveway, I was exhausted. But knowing that someone understood me made me feel a stronger. And that helped me to at least keep going through the motions.

By the end of the week, the whole school knew about Brittany and everyone stopped talking to me about it. Slogging through my days, I knew they were talking behind my back by the obvious way they shushed and nudged each other when I walked by. But I was relieved, too. I spent the rest of the week focused in class, eating my lunch alone in the newspaper room, and carefully avoiding everyone who was talking behind their hands. But most of all, I missed my best friend.

I made it through the week, and that Friday afternoon in Varsity Athletics, we began the period as we normally did, stretching out in the grass. The large group dwindled as one by one, each girl peeled away to run laps, until only Shelby and I were left.

"You okay?" Shelby asked as she stretched.

"Yeah, I'm okay," I grunted, as I lay back on the grass.

"Are you sure about that?" she asked, looking up and resting her chin on her knee.

"No," I said, choking on the lump in my throat.

We didn't talk that afternoon, but Shelby stayed with me, stretched with me, ran laps with me, cooled off with me, and walked with me back to the locker room. Once we collected our stuff and the final bell rang, we wordlessly began the walk across the shell parking lot. When I stopped beside my car and fished for my keys, Shelby stopped beside me and stared beyond us at the track.

"I'm really sorry ya know," she said. Not waiting for my response, she slowly walked away.

"I know. Thanks, Shelby," I said, even though I doubted she could hear me.

• • •

That night, home early from work, my mom started yelling as soon as she hit the door, announcing her arrival by screaming, "Why in the world, young lady did I have to hear at Bunco last night, that Brittany got pregnant and dropped out of school? Why didn't you tell me?"

Lying on the couch, staring at the TV without really watching it, my first thought was, *Oh Shit!* But instinctively I asked, "What do ya mean?" I tried to sound innocent.

"Why! Did I have to hear! That my daughter's best friend! Is pregnant? And dropped out of school? And why! Didn't my daughter! Tell me herself?" Mom continued yelling, punctuating each phrase with a pause and the sounds of her slamming the door, tossing her briefcase on the chair, and throwing her purse on the table as she stomped her way towards me.

"I dunno," I mumbled.

"That's NOT an answer!" she shouted, even though I was only three feet away. "You're done, young lady. This is it! You're NOT hanging out with her ANYMORE!" she yelled.

See. I knew it, I thought, but then I sat up and screamed back, "I'm NOT going to stop being her best friend just because she's pregnant! That's not what friends do!"

Exhausted from the effort, I dropped back on the coach and burst into tears.

"I didn't say you couldn't be her friend," Mom shouted back, but not without a note of sympathy.

Not bothering to respond, I covered my face with my arms, trying to shut her out.

Mom took a deep breath and added, "I only said that you can't hang out with her anymore." Then she went on, saying "You can still be her friend. But she's gonna have a baby now. She needs to get her life together. She doesn't need to be goin' out anymore."

Still crying, I finally managed to say, "Yes, ma'am," silently begging her to stop.

"You just have too much to lose," Mom pleaded. "You need to concentrate on finishin' school and goin' away to college. And Brittany needs to concentrate on getting' married and whatever else she's gonna do. I just don't know why you didn't tell me about all of this. What is goin' on with you?"

When I still didn't respond, Mom sat on the end of the couch and rubbed my leg, and added in a softer voice, "Look, you just need to stay focused for just a few more months. And then you'll be off to school, anyway."

I said, "Yes ma'am," still hiding my pain and praying that God would make all of it stop.

She sat on the couch, quietly watching me, and then she eventually left the room.

When Cameron came by later that night to pick me up and take me to the movies, I couldn't wait to get out of the house. I hadn't told him anything about Brittany on the phone since I had no privacy. But as soon as he saw my face and my mom's tight lipped smile, he knew something was wrong. His face wrinkled in concern, he quickly ushered me out the front door, saying brightly to Mom, "Sorry we've gotta go! We don't want to be late for the movie!"

After opening his passenger door for me, he jogged around to the driver's side, got in, and asked, "What in the world is going on? I can tell you're both upset about something."

"Please, Cameron, just drive!" I told him, resting my forehead in my hand.

Then I told him everything, that Brittany was pregnant, and that it was Tucker's baby, and everything else, including my suspension and that Brittany had dropped out of school. Somehow I didn't cry, and Cameron just listened quietly as he drove.

We didn't go to the movies. Instead, Cameron drove to a liquor store, and got a six-pack of my favorite dark beer, and then said, "Let's go to my house so we can talk."

At his house, we spoke briefly to his parents, then headed into the kitchen. He opened a beer, handed me the bottle, then called and ordered my favorite pizza. Then he took my hand and led me outside onto the patio. He settled me into a cushioned wicker chair and set an ashtray on the table in front of me. He brought over another chair and sat down, saying softly, "What you need tonight is a safe place to talk it all out."

While we drank and ate, we talked and I smoked. "Your mom's right," he repeated. When the night grew cool, he brought me one of his sweatshirts and said, "Brittany needs to focus on her baby right now, and to try and work it out with her soon-to-be husband." He stroked my cheek and said, "You should focus on your future, too."

Cameron sat, then took my hand and said, "It was just a matter of time, Erin. When you graduate from high school, this is just what happens. Everything changes. Everybody goes off in different directions. They go to different schools, get married, and go to work. You get new lives and you make new friends. It's all just part of growing up."

After we ate, Cameron cleaned up and, I sat alone, looking out past his parents' manicured lawn, wondering if what everyone was telling me was true.

"You can always stay friends with Brittany," Cameron told me later when he kissed me goodnight at my door. With his arms around me, he added softly, "It's just going to be different now. That's all."

Chapter Nine

I slept in that Saturday and stayed home all day, just lying on my bed, reading. I called Brittany's house every hour on the hour until I finally reached her. I could hear my mom in the laundry room while I was on the phone. She stayed in there, I assumed so that she could listen to my conversation, but I didn't care.

"How're you doin?" I asked Brittany.

Sighing deeply, she said, "Better. My mom's a lot calmer now. How're you?"

"Fine. I'm fine." I told her.

"Heard you got suspended last week for skippin' school. Is that true?" she asked with an edge to her voice.

"Yeah. It's no big deal," I told her, thinking, *I'm getting pretty good at sounding like I don't care.*

"The hell it isn't! Where-in-the-hell were you goin'?" she demanded. She sounded really angry.

"I was looking for you!" I hissed. "I was worried."

"God, Erin. Please, please don't make this worse!" Her anger turned into a moan.

"How am I gonna make this worse?" I hissed back.

"If you screw up now, everybody's gonna blame me, that's how," she said, "Please don't do this!"

"I'm not gonna screw anything up. Come on, Brittany," I groaned, but then I sighed, knowing she was right. If I messed up, everyone would blame her. She didn't need that. She didn't deserve to be blamed for anything else.

"I was just worried," I explained. "I keep calling but you're never home."

"Don't worry about me. I'm fine. And yeah, I'm not home much. I've been out looking for a job, and trying to get into night school. I kinda have a lot going on, ya know?" She sounded frustrated that I didn't get it.

Sighing, Brittany said, "Look, why don't you come over next week and we'll talk, okay?"

"Yeah. Sounds good. Next week would be good. I miss you," I told her.

I knew she wasn't fine. She was my best friend and I knew her. But I also knew we couldn't talk over the phone about anything important, not with both of our mothers eavesdropping. So I agreed to see her the following week.

"Miss you, too," she said, hanging up.

• • •

We were on separate paths, and that made it harder to see each other. As weeks passed, I went to school while Brittany went to night classes. And when I was free on weekends, she spent her time with Tucker or was at work. Catrina helped her get a waitressing job at the place where she worked, and Brittany picked up every shift she could to save money for the baby.

Over the phone, Brittany seemed cheerful and always full of stories. She said she loved her night classes and would graduate in the summer, and as usual, had made a lot of new friends. "They all have such interesting stories," she said. "Everybody's so different." One by one she described the other students, sharing their stories. The juvenile delinquent that had been expelled, the middle-aged, divorced white lady who needed her diploma to go back to work, the much older black man who said, "It's just time," and another pregnant teenager who was barely sixteen.

Brittany's parents moved past their anger and began to accept things, and then became excited about becoming grandparents. "They're already buyin' things for the baby, and we don't even know what it is yet!" Brittany giggled. "My dad wants to go with me to pick out a car-seat this weekend."

Forging a new path, Brittany volunteered at the woman's clinic and was excited when she was assigned to work on the teen suicide hotline. Growing stronger in her opposition to abortion, she put a bumper sticker on her mom's car and carried a grotesque key chain with a fetus on it. She didn't talk about Tucker often, but seemed eager to be a part of his family and often talked about Mr. Freeman and Catrina.

She remained interested in my life and always asked about school, my teachers, assignments, and classes. She often asked about Emmett, and about Cameron and some of my other friends. I knew she still talked to a few of her friends from middle school, and sometimes she quizzed me about them, wanting to compare notes.

Melanie and Lorna knew I was lost without Brittany, and like friends do, they rallied around me. Although Melanie was a year younger and had a boyfriend, she made time for me on the weekends. Lorna and I had a lot of classes together, so she hung out with me at school and we ate lunch together. We talked about leaving town, how different college would be, and how we couldn't wait to start our new lives. Lorna and Melanie both liked Cameron, and they often went to Emmett's house with me.

• • •

In the spring of our senior year, the class broke into different cliques based on what lay ahead after graduation. Some of us were going to the University, some were going to State, some were staying home and going to community college and others were getting jobs locally. A few had found a way to go to a college out of state.

After weeks apart, one Sunday when Brittany didn't have to work, I made an excuse to my mom about needing to go to the library and spent the afternoon with her. When I knocked on her door, her mom saw me through the sliding glass door, and to my surprise, she jumped up, opened the door, and hugged me hard. Seeing her papers and books scattered everywhere as usual, along with a new car-seat on the floor by the couch, made me happy.

"It's so good to see you. How've you been?" she asked, holding my shoulders and smiling.

"Great, thanks. How're you?" I said, relieved to see her being her old self again.

"I'm going to be okay," she said with a smile, then told me, "Our girl is upstairs." With a gentle push, she added, "Go on up. She'll be really happy to see you."

Brittany's wonderfully messy bedroom, always soft and colorful, no longer felt exotic. Instead, it felt familiar and comforting. We chatted for hours. Her belly had grown large and she kept rubbing it. We laughed and teased about it, admiring how fat she'd become.

"So what're you gonna do about prom," she asked.

"I asked Cameron to take me," I told her, blushing slightly. Even though I'd been excluded from so much in her new life, I wasn't comfortable talking about things she no longer was a part of, like prom.

"Hmpf!" She grunted. "Why aren't you goin' with Emmett?" She wrinkled her brow when she said this.

"Well, we talked about it," I sighed. "I mean, we both wanted to go, you know, together. But he said we'd be a spectacle if we did. Ya know, no one's ever done it before, I mean, black and white dates to prom. And he said he didn't want us to get all dressed up just to have everyone stare at us all night."

"You think it'd be that bad?" she asked, rubbing her belly thoughtfully.

"Yeah. I know it would. The teachers and the principal would probably freak out. And my parents would probably freak, too. And even if they didn't, everybody'd talk about it. So I don't think we really could stand it," I told her, my voice flat.

"But Emmett said he didn't want me to miss out, and he knows senior prom's a big deal and all. So I asked Cameron to take me." I told her, attempting to sound casual.

"Are you sure Emmett's okay with that?" she asked.

"I dunno. He said he was. I told him I was gonna break up with Cameron before school's out. So I guess he doesn't mind too much. He really didn't say a lot about it," I told her picking at the carpet.

"I thought you really liked Cameron," Brittany said.

"I do. I like him a lot. But I'm leaving and he's leaving. I don't really ever see us together, ya know? Not forever or anything," I said, lying on the floor and staring at her ceiling.

"Ha. Yeah well. I can't really see you bein' a preacher's wife!" she said and laughed.

"I know, right?" I chuckled.

"But you can see you and Emmett together, right?" she asked more seriously.

"I dunno. I think so. I'd like to be, anyway. It's weird because, I mean, Cameron is everything I *should* want. My family loves him. He's a really great guy. He'd always let me do anything I want and everything's so much easier with him. I dunno. It just feels like I'd be settling." I sighed, "He's such a great guy. He really deserves someone who's really into him. So I think it's better if I go ahead and break it off."

"I guess I know what you mean. It'd definitely be easier with him. But I agree. You shouldn't just stay with him just because it's easy," she nodded.

"But why pick someone who's basically impossible? I mean, I love Emmett, but I still don't know how we'd ever work it out. We'd have to move somewhere far away where it wouldn't be such a big deal. Who knows, maybe it'll be different up at college," I said, looking to her for reassurance.

"I dunno. Maybe," she said and nodded thoughtfully.

• • •

At the end of our senior year, Emmett, Peter, and Shelby were once again voted class favorites. Our freshman class had welcomed over one thousand students, but four years later our graduating class had just over four hundred students. *What happened to the other six hundred people?* We all wondered.

The graduation ceremony was held at the stadium, where all of our home football games had been played, and we received our diplomas in alphabetical order. My row included Shelby and the other girls from our freshman P.E. locker room. My grade point average ranked in the top twenty of the class, high enough to qualify me as a top-tier student, but not high enough for a scholarship or other distinction. During the ceremony, I wasn't allowed to wear the National Honor Society tassels because of my suspension, although they still had to list me as a member in the program. They'd changed the rules just because of my minor infraction, and although they couldn't kick me out, they punished me in the only way they could, by withholding my tassels at graduation.

One of the cheerleaders was pregnant, and although we all found out in the weeks leading up to graduation, she'd managed to keep it a secret from the administration so she didn't have to quit school. She and her boyfriend planned to get married over the summer, but since no one knew about the pregnancy, they were both able to participate in the ceremony. Brittany should've been there with us that day, and she should have been seated with me in my row. It just wasn't fair.

The ceremony took a long time, and afterwards most of the graduates threw their graduation caps into the air. I didn't. Instead, I grabbed Shelby's arm before she could leave the field, twirled her around, and surprised her by hugging her tightly. Her head only came up to my chest and I had to yell over all of the cheering when I said, "Thank you, Shelby, for everything!"

She'd won a track scholarship to a small school somewhere in Louisiana, and thinking I'd never see her again, I hoped that my hug would express how much she'd meant to me. She laughed when I finally let her go, pumped her fist high in the air, and yelled, "Let's go get 'em!" before she quickly disappeared into the crowd.

My mom's friends threw me a graduation pool party at Miss Paula's house, but Brittany couldn't come since she was working. The celebration was fun but felt incomplete without her.

I went on our senior trip to Fort Walton Beach, but again, Brittany couldn't go with us. Months ago, four of us, Lorna, Tia, Brittany, and I, had booked a room, in a hotel right on the beach. Many of our other friends, including Emmett and

Derek, were also staying there. But by the time we'd graduated, so much had already changed, only Lorna and I ended up going.

Lorna and I drove the two hours to the beach with the windows down, and talked nonstop about how our lives were going to be so different now that we were out of high school. Then we spent the week in our bikinis on the beach. Some nights we went out eating raw oysters, drinking beer, and dancing, but mostly Lorna spent her time running around the hotel, meeting different guys from different schools, while I spent time with Emmett on his balcony, watching the crowds of drunken kids on the sand below.

Then we all went our separate ways. Emmett, Peter, and the other football players who'd committed to the University went up for the summer to start football practice and classes during summer school. I spent the summer working at my mom's company. In preparation for my new life, I proudly opened a bank account and deposited every penny I earned. I spent hours planning and making lists of what I needed to buy and pack. Ready to move on, I preferred to stay home, dreaming and reading, rather than going out.

I was anxious to see Brittany before I left town, but it wasn't easy with her always at work or with the Freemans. Running out of time, at last, I hunted her down at her waitressing job. When the hostess touched her arm, informing her that she had a visitor, I saw her look of surprise turn to genuine pleasure when she saw me. Smiling at each other across the crowded restaurant, I realized how much I'd missed my best friend. Just the way she smiled at me with her whole face and her sparkling eyes made me feel warm inside.

After telling her manager that she needed a break, the two of us hurried outside to the front porch to talk. Although she was nearing her due date, she hadn't gained weight anywhere other than her belly. Everything else looked exactly the same. The red sweater she wore stretched disproportionately over her huge belly. She once again rubbed the baby bump the entire time we talked, putting my hand on it a couple of times and saying, "Can you feel that? Can you feel it kick?"

After some idle chit-chat, Brittany exhaled and said, "So! You're going off to school!"

"Yeah," I said and sighed as I watched a group of people stumble up the stairs and into the restaurant.

"I'm so excited for you!" she beamed.

Helplessly, I started to tear up as I searched her face. Holding up her hand, she said "Nope. Don't do it! If you cry, I'll cry, and I can't be crying at work!"

"I wish you were coming with me!" I gulped, trying to control how much I already missed her.

"I'll always be with you," she grinned, pushing my shoulder. "You're my best friend! And just think, when you come home for Christmas, you can come over to my new place and see the baby!"

"Yeah," I said and grinned sheepishly, ashamed of my sadness.

"I can't wait for her to meet you!" she added, beaming at her belly.

"Her? It's a girl?" I gulped again.

"Yeah, it's a girl! Can you believe it?" she said, glowing with pride.

• • •

I packed and repacked, anxiously consulting my lists as I tried to balance between being able to fit everything into a dorm room and not leaving anything behind that I needed. Ready to start a new life, I carefully packed the items that reflected who I wanted to become, not who I used to be. I was determined to be a serious college student on the brink of forging my new life, doing what I wanted and with anyone I chose.

Finally, I thought, *I can see Emmett whenever I want, do whatever I want, and be whatever I want!* I imagined my new life would be free of watchful eyes and other people's expectations.

My parents glowed with excitement whenever we talked about college. I was the first in our family to go to college, and they repeatedly told me how proud they were. They also reminded me about what a great opportunity it was, and I solemnly agreed.

On my final day at home, I hugged Grace, good-bye, wishing her luck as a freshman in high school, said good-bye to Lynne, wishing her luck, too. Now married, she'd just begun her own new life as a wife. And then, my parents drove me to school in their Buick sedan. I didn't look back.

Freshman girls at the University lived in a thirteen-story dorm named after the first woman college president in the state. Known as an advocate of both education and prison reform, it seemed appropriate that the dorm was named after her, since it included both features. The dorm had extensive security to protect innocent freshmen girls, and in my role as a serious college student enrolled in the chemical engineering program, I chose a room on the top floor, which was designated a quiet floor. Surrounded by similarly serious female students, I expected to avoid the less serious ones living on the other twelve floors below us.

Once we arrived, my parents helped me move in, unpack, and settle into the room. The size of a large walk-in closet at just twenty feet by ten, the floors were covered in grey tile, with concrete block walls painted the same institutional green as the girl's locker room in high school. My new home had two built-in closets, two built-in chests of drawers, two desks, two chairs, and two beds. The bathroom shared by the entire wing was located directly across the hall from my room. To my delight, it was not only clean, but also had doors and curtains shielding the toilets and showers, unlike our old locker room. After briefly meeting my roommate Joanna and her parents, who had already arrived and picked the bed by the window, my parents kissed me good-bye and left. Thrilled that I'd finally made it, I cheerfully waved good-bye as they drove away. At last I was on my own.

Joanna, my new roommate, was from Kentucky, and her accent, although distinctively southern, had an unfamiliar twang. She was petite, with light brown hair and fair skin. After chatting briefly, we set out to meet our new neighbors. Tricia, an aeronautical engineering student from Virginia, and Gayle, an electrical engineering student from Homewood, Alabama, lived in the room on our left. Across the hall was Savanna, a mechanical engineering student, was from Illinois, and her roommate, Amy, a pre-med student, wasn't very friendly. She sniffed and said, "Thanks, but I don't really care to meet anyone. I won't have time for friends." A set of identical twins from Birmingham lived in the room on our right. Their dark skin and short, curly hair immediately reminded me of Shelby. They were friendly and talkative, but they looked, talked, and dressed so much alike that there was no way to tell them apart.

After our brief tour, once back in our room, Joanna sighed, saying, "Well, I guess we're lucky they're twins," as she sat on her flowered Laura Ashley bedspread.

"What do ya mean?" I asked, sitting on my own bed topped by my grandmother's quilt.

"Because otherwise I mighta ended up with one of them as my roommate," she said, pointing at the wall that separated us from the twins. "Ya know, my mom thought you might be black," she added with a laugh.

"Why?" I asked, confused.

"Your last name. There's lotsa black folks with your last name, ya know. But thank goodness you're not. Otherwise I woulda had to try and move! Let's go get somethin' to eat," she said, hopping up.

I was dumbstruck. My mind raced for the words to voice my objection. But finding none, I guiltily followed her out of our room and down to the cafeteria on the second floor. I hated that, after all this time, I was still shocked into silence when things like that happened.

Not knowing anyone else, Joanna, Savanna, Tricia, Gayle, and I ate our first dinner together, chatting excitedly about the dorm and our plans while we ate from plastic trays. As we walked back to the elevators, we heard a commotion outside in front of the dorm. There, marching up the driveway, were hundreds of black guys dressed in black pants, white shirts, with top hats and canes! As the guys chanted, clapped, stomped, and popped the canes in stunningly perfect synchronization, I was reminded of the marching bands in the Mardi Gras parades. Hundreds of squealing girls lined the sidewalks along the u-shaped driveway and hung out of the lobby windows to watch and cheer.

In the elevator, as we chattered about how amazing the spectacle had been, Joanna filled us in. "Yeah, that's a black fraternity. They do that sorta thing during rush. It's called steppin'." Happy to be the expert, her status was affirmed when we only murmured in response. She continued, saying, "I'm gonna rush, too, but since I'm a legacy for Zeta, I'm really just doin' it for show."

"I'm a Zeta legacy, too!" Savanna responded and they both squealed.

According to Joanna, there were white sororities, whose antebellum houses lined the street closest to our dorm. "Each one has a reputation," she explained. "There's one for smart pretty girls, one for smart not so pretty girls, one for slutty girls, one for dumb girls, one for pretty and rich girls, and so on."

"What's Zeta, then?" I asked.

"Rich, good girls," she answered smugly.

She went on, explaining that the white fraternities had even larger colonial style homes lining the streets facing the center of campus, while the black fraternities had small houses several streets off campus and the black sororities didn't have houses at all. Joanna told us that rush was always held in the first weeks of the fall semester, and that freshman could apply, or "rush" to join. During those weeks, all of the different Greek organizations hosted parties and open houses so they could meet the applicants.

That night as I fell asleep, I stewed about yet another elaborate system of applications and interviews set up to segregate us beyond just race and sex. My hopes of no longer being ranked and labeled by things I couldn't change seemed dashed. I knew that fitting in with a sorority would mean putting up with a house full of girls who always talked about rules, always telling me what to wear, where to go, and who I should date. *That's not why I came here*, I fumed, tossing and turning in my bed.

Determined to forge ahead, instead of rushing, I registered for a full load of credits. Heady with the seriousness of my academic courses, I sat alone in the cafeteria at breakfast that the first morning of classes, nodding with satisfaction at my schedule. Just like in high school, all of my classes were in different parts of the campus. But this time it would be exciting. Calculus 2, Chemistry, Computer Programming, Econ, and Intro to Engineering were all in different buildings, so with my textbooks and a T-square loaded into a large backpack, I proudly headed off to each of my classes.

I was the only girl in two of my courses, and just one of two in my Calculus class. But Econ and Chemistry held the most promise, each having hundreds of students. In the large, stadium-style classrooms, I saw representatives of everyone enrolled, frat boys wearing button downs, shorts and baseball hats, sorority girls wearing skinny jeans and t-shirts, athletes wearing sweats and larger t-shirts and everybody else mixed all in between.

Intro to Engineering was the most difficult class, but not because of the course material. It was also the furthest away, in the Engineering building high up on a hill, a thirty-minute walk from my dorm, and I the only girl in the class made up almost entirely of Iranians. Each man a varying shade of dark skin and black hair, and they were all older and spoke English only to the instructor. Although dressed like most college guys in jeans and button down shirts, they also wore heavy cologne. They sat scowling in class, and excluded me even more by talking among themselves in a language I didn't understand. Even their words sounded angry.

That first night, Emmett called and asked me to meet him out on the quad. Happily I agreed, and as I pulled my shoes on, Joanna looked up and asked, "Where're you goin?"

"Oh, just to meet this guy I know from high school," I blurted, anxious to see and talk to him. We had so much to discuss.

"Oh? Is he your boyfriend?" she asked, smiling.

"Um, well, we've been out before. Not sure he's really my boyfriend yet. I guess so…maybe," I stammered uncertainly.

"So, what's his name?" she asked, seeming to lose interest as she turned back to her books.

I hesitated briefly, remembering what she said about our twin neighbors. And just the way any lie begins, without a thought to the consequences, I said, "Peter," as I dashed from the room.

• • •

After only a week at college, it was apparent that I'd escaped nothing. The expectations, segregation, and overwhelming need to sort everyone into categories seemed far worse than ever. Reluctant to cut myself off before I knew what was at stake, I fell back into my old habits of trying to fit in and get along.

Joanna told me that she struggled in school and needed to study a lot, and although she spread her books and paper across her bed every night, she spent most of her time talking long distance to her boyfriend back in Kentucky, or else she was over at the sorority house. Gayle studied at the library during the week, and went home every weekend to see her boyfriend. Tricia rushed a different sorority than Joanna and spent most of her time with her new friends at the house. Savanna's grumpy roommate Amy quickly moved into a single room, and although Savanna also rushed a sorority, we began spending a lot of time together in her room. Almost every night, we studied together. And on weekends, we ordered pizza and stayed up late, talking far into the night.

Emmett lived in the football dorm, and roomed with Peter. In addition to their classes, they had football practice, workouts, and position meetings every day. They also had to eat their meals in their own cafeteria with the team. We couldn't go out together to the nearby bars on the Strip, since they carded and neither of us was nineteen. We also didn't want to hang out in the common areas of our dorms together, so we often met on the quad at night. Holding hands, we'd walk across campus or sit on a bench under a tree in the dark, talking. Once in a while, Emmett borrowed a teammate's car and we drove around, or else we went parking, but not very often, since driving around off campus made us nervous. Back home, we'd known where it was safe for us to go, but in the small town known as the birthplace of the Klan, we were afraid to venture off together to unfamiliar places.

With so many girls trying to get into sororities and guys into fraternities, conversations all over campus began to sound sadly familiar. At first, all the talk centered on who was asked to pledge and where, but then people shifted to who had been asked out by whom. The Greek letters soon became shorthand for how smart, rich, or attractive they were.

But it wasn't just harmless fun. Shortly after rush, a large cross was burned on sorority row. The dorms buzzed with the rumor that it was intended to prevent a black sorority from moving into a house on white sorority row. No one was ever charged with the crime. The horrifying incident served as just another reminder that this wasn't a game. And once again my hopes were replaced with fear.

Football games on the weekends were also a familiar focus and quickly became the reason for everyone on campus to party. The stadium, which seated over sixty thousand people, held three times the student body and attracted fans from across the state. Arriving days in advance, the spectators' RVs and their occupants parked in the stadium lot and behind our classroom buildings. Savanna and I walked through the lots before games and the atmosphere reminded me of Mardi Gras weekend back home.

But even the football games were influenced by the Greek system. Although every student received season tickets, and the student section was technically open seating, early Saturday morning, the white fraternities sent their pledges over to reserve seats for their upper classmen and their dates. So unless you went to the game with a guy from a fraternity, you didn't get very good seats. Once again, there was a pecking order to everything, no matter how much I detested it.

• • •

Several months into the fall semester, Emmett reinjured his knee during practice and had surgery on his ACL once again. Peter called me when it happened, and because I was worried about him, I begged a ride to the hospital from Gayle on the day of his surgery. I ran into his dad outside his hospital room. Remembering me, he hugged me and thanked me for coming, but warned me that Emmett probably wouldn't remember I'd been there. "I'll make sure and let him know you've been here," he said. Unsure of what to do, I nervously waited with his dad out in the hallway. We talked about school and other polite topics and before I left, he let me stick my head into Emmett's room. But Emmett only screamed in pain so I got out of there in a hurry, hoping his dad would tell him that I'd been there.

Once Emmett was released from the hospital and back in the football dorm, the coaches assigned him a tutor so he could keep up with his courses. They moved him to a first-floor room, and since they allowed visitors, I went to see him one day after class. A coach greeted me at the reception desk, and although he looked surprised to see me, he led me down the hallway to Emmett's room.

The young coach stood at the doorway, shuffling his feet with his hands stuffed in his pockets. "I really shouldn't leave you two alone," he mumbled. Surprised, we both turned to look at him. But when neither of us responded, he said, "Well, make it quick and keep the door open. Ya hear?" Then he hurried back down the hall. He clearly wasn't comfortable leaving a white girl alone with a black guy.

• • •

A few weeks later, we all returned home for Christmas break. Everyone tried to catch up with one another in the time we had before we had to leave again. Cameron and I spent a good deal of time over the holiday together, even though we had officially broken up. He loved the seminary and excitedly told me about his studies. When I was with him, I focused on all of the positives about college, and he loved hearing about my classes, the dorm, and the football games.

I got to see Lorna, who looked great in her new short haircut and stylish punk clothing, and she told me she enjoyed being at Tech, although her classes were difficult. She already had a boyfriend who was in the ROTC. The Greek system wasn't strong there, and she told stories of bon fires, football games, and line dancing at the local bars.

As soon as I got home, I arranged to see Brittany's new apartment and meet her new baby, who they'd named Amy. She and Tucker had rented a duplex in midtown, several blocks from our high school. It had a big front porch that the apartments shared, and matching front doors. Inside Brittany's small living room sat the weathered old couch, chair, and table from Tucker's old place, with a blood-red carpet covering the middle of the wood floor. There was a black and white tiled kitchen, with a matching bathroom. Amy's crib was in the smaller of the two bedrooms, with a changing table on a braided rug.

Brittany looked amazing, and the baby was gorgeous. She'd already grown a lot and I couldn't believe what a natural mother she was. She was playful and cheerful, yet very efficient and everything a great mom should be.

She said she wanted to stay in because "Tucker's working tonight, and I hate to ask my parents to babysit since they help out while I'm working. You don't mind, do you?" But I never cared what we did. I just wanted to spend time with my best friend.

After we played with Amy, gave her a bottle, and put her to bed, Brittany made us fried hamburgers and macaroni and cheese from a box. She also made us drinks she called "Fuzzy Navels," which she'd learned to make from the bartender at work.

"Tell me all about it," she said, sitting at her tiny kitchen table and lighting a cigarette. "I want to hear absolutely everything!"

We talked for hours. Being able to talk to Brittany again, I was surprised by how relieved I felt. How good it felt to be able to be myself again! Every story seemed funnier, my hardships trivial, and my goals and dreams far more achievable when I was with Brittany. She told me she loved being a mom, loved her volunteer work, and said that she made good money waitressing. It was like old times, the two of us tackling life together.

"I'm thinking about enrolling in classes in the spring," she said.

"You should!" I told her. "You'd make a great counselor. You should major in social work."

"Maybe I will," she said. Then she laughed, jumped up from her chair, and said, "Help me clean up."

We washed the dishes, singing along to her new favorite song, an old one by the Mamas and the Poppas called "California Dreaming."

We talked and giggled late into the night. When I left, she hugged me and said, "See, I told you. When you're best friends like we are, it doesn't matter if we don't see each other every day." And she was right. It was like we'd never been apart.

• • •

Back at school for the spring semester, I was determined to ignore everyone's expectations and do what I wanted. My plan was to meet new and interesting people, and I explored different parts of campus life. I joined a co-ed intramural volleyball league at the sports complex, and although the kids were polite, I wasn't allowed to play much because they took the game way too seriously. I also joined Encore, a student union group that arranged for campus speakers and events, and even met the members of the band The Go Gos before their concert, along with Jimmy Carter and Charlton Heston before they each made speeches.

But no matter how many people I met or how interesting they were, I didn't really click anywhere. Maybe it was because we were still divided by our majors, Greek affiliations, race, and nationalities. Everyone seemed to be searching for people that were just like them, rather than enjoying our differences. The people I met never became part of a lasting group of friends; instead, I cycled in and out of their circles with courses and activities, and was easily replaced.

In the spring, Emmett's cast at last was removed and he began the excruciating program of rehab exercises. Watching his dream of a football career slip away, he grew frustrated and discouraged. Having turned nineteen in November, he'd started going out to bars with other football players and friends, and as a result, he developed a far more interesting social life than mine. Walking together in the dark, and occasionally driving around with me in someone else's car, trying not to get pulled over by the police paled in comparison to everything else that was now available to him. Although we wanted to continue seeing each other, we officially agreed to start seeing other people.

"I'm tired of feeling like I have to sneak around all of the time," Emmett said in frustration one night on the quad.

Sad, and yet also relieved, I consoled myself that it was probably better for both of us. I desperately wanted us to be together, and be able to be a normal couple who did normal things. And although I hated the thought of him with anyone else, I was also sure we'd never survive what we'd have to face as a couple at that point. It was hard enough to fit in at college; if we were together as an interracial couple, it would only make things worse. My only hope was that, one day, we could be together somewhere else.

I fell asleep every night listening to the cassette mix-tape that Emmett had made for me. Night after night, I searched for his feelings in the lyrics of the songs by The Temptations, The Spinners, and Rod Stewart. And night after night, I stared at the ceiling and wondered if we'd ever have the courage to fight for what we wanted, and whether our feelings for each other would survive the wait.

• • •

I spent spring break at Savannah's, and as the spring semester ended, Savanna and I made plans to room together the following year in a dorm that was closer to the center of campus. Our friends were moving out; Joanna and Gayle were going back home to be with their boyfriends, and Tricia was moving into her sorority house, so there wasn't anyone left.

Savanna and I each went home to work for the summer; she was working for her dad, while I worked at my mom's company again. Meanwhile, Emmett stayed at school to take classes and continue his rehab. He moved out of the football dorm, got a new roommate, and took several trips to Florida and the Bahamas with a group of his new friends, including girls from the gymnastics team.

During my summer at home, I saw Brittany several times, but not often enough. The two-month break passed too quickly, and on that last night before I went back to school, we sat in her kitchen after putting Amy to bed. She made us Long Island Iced teas and we ordered pizza.

When I asked about Tucker, she shrugged and said "He's okay. We're just having a hard time, that's all." Instead of talking about him or their relationship, we focused on being together and discussed the other details in our lives.

When she asked about Emmett, I told her, "He's fine. We broke up." Responding with a sigh, she didn't ask why or press the point. Instead, she only said, "I'm sorry," with a sad look.

"I'm taking two classes this fall," she told me brightly. But then she sounded sad when she told me she had to stop volunteering. "I had to pick up more hours at work," she said.

"But I thought you loved it there! Couldn't they hire you at the place where you volunteered? Maybe you could work there part-time?" I said.

"You have to have a degree to get hired, and they already have all those people from the community college who want the few paid positions they have. And I gotta work, so if I want to go to school, I can't volunteer anymore," she said with a hint of bitterness. "It's expensive living on your own, and my parents can't always help us out every time we need something."

Frustrated by our own struggles and the barriers thrown in our way, we talked a lot about the past that night. We reminded each other of our favorite memories, each trying to outdo the other by remembering the most obscure details.

"Oh, I got you something!" she said, jumping up from the kitchen table. "Be right back!"

Then she handed me a brown paper bag, saying, "It's not wrapped or anything, but I saw it and thought of you."

We both laughed as I pulled a green and grey coffee mug out of the bag. It had feet, and one of the feet had its toes crossed.

"You know how you always do that with your feet?" she beamed, laughing. "I saw it and just had to get it for you. Ya know, I have a picture from the beach with you doin' that. Come look."

Following her to her bedroom, I watched as she walked to the dresser and took down a picture that had been stuck into the mirror's frame. She handed it to me, saying, "See!" It was a picture of us at the beach, sitting up on the lifeguard's stand. Regina must've taken the picture. It seemed like so long ago. Brittany was still wearing her big old eyeglasses and her hair was still long. The sky was dark and the wind blew our hair over our smiling faces.

"Look!" she said pointing at the picture. "Look at your feet!" And sure enough, my toes were crossed.

That night we talked again about how we'd always be best friends. We said this not in promise but in sacred declaration. And we spoke the words out loud to reaffirm our commitment, the same way a congregation repeats the benediction at the end of a church service. That night, we began a new dream and a new future, with us always together as friends. Cheerfully we laughed and said that one day our kids would be best friends, that we'd both have fabulous jobs and make a lot of money, and that we'd travel the world together.

• • •

When I returned to school in the fall for sophomore year, I continued my search for belonging, but took yet another path. Savanna and I were roommates, and through her I met friends of the guys she dated and went out with several of them. We double-dated, going to frat parties and football games, and since we were both nineteen, we went to bars with the intention of meeting other guys. Although we preferred the bars on the strip since we could walk there, and they were filled with frat boys, now that she had her car, we began to expand our search by frequenting other bars off campus. Once in a while, we went as far as Larry's, the small dirty bar where the football players hung out, drinking and playing pool.

One night after a visit to Larry's, I confessed my feelings for Emmett to Savanna. "I think I'm still in love with him," I slurred, "But we broke up. I'm not sure it'd ever work out, anyway."

Solemnly, she nodded drunkenly and said, "I understand, but that wouldn't really be ideal. Keep looking. I'm sure you'll find somebody else."

One night out at Larry's, Emmett and I introduced Savannah to Peter, and the four of us ended the night together at the on-campus apartment where the guys lived. Somehow, even a little tipsy, she saw a similar challenge in her attraction to Peter, proclaiming, as we left that night, "I don't care what my parents would say, I could live the rest of my life in a shack with Peter."

Through Savanna I also met Jeanette, a member of the Zeta sorority, who was going through her own rebellion. Friendly and willing to go out every night, she considered herself a groupie and tried to meet every guy who played in a band. I liked people who considered themselves artists, believing they were less judgmental, and so began to hang out with Jeanette when Savanna was busy.

Although my grades were average, the courses were difficult, and since I'd quickly lost interest in my science and math courses, I decided to take a few humanities courses that semester. English Lit was taught by a skinny graduate assistant with long hair who often kicked off his shoes and sat cross-legged on top of his desk to discuss the pieces we read in class. Unlike my high school teacher, he genuinely entertained even the wackiest of interpretations, and graded based on the substance of our analysis, rather than judging the conclusion.

I enrolled in an Intro to Religion class, thinking that my extensive Christian education would lead to an easy A. But I was happy to find it was far better than what I'd expected. Instead of being a deep dive into Christianity, the course covered all religions. As we studied each religion, I became convinced that they all were basically the same, with mostly superficial differences. And my Intro to Philosophy course challenged me with both a new way of thinking and a new way of thinking about it. But one of the best surprises was meeting new types of students in these classes: a girl with a pierced nose, a guy with tattoos who only wore black, and a guy who was thrown out of his previous school for performing his theater project naked on stage. In religion I met a girl named Elise who invited me to her apartment one day after class to study. She'd spent the summer in France, wore a beret and talked of nothing else but living abroad. We drank expresso and smoked cigarettes while she showed me photos until I was so jittery my eyes couldn't focus on the words in our text.

Encouraged and excited about my new courses, I met with my advisor to discuss changing majors. "You shouldn't change majors to anything in the liberal arts," she said, shaking her head adamantly. "You'll lose too many credits and end up having to stay in school longer. And if you don't want to be a teacher, there's really nothing else you can really do with a liberal arts degree. Why don't you consider something in the business school or nursing?" she suggested. I was disappointed, but adamant about not extending my time in school, so I reluctantly agreed to take an accounting course in the spring semester.

When I saw Brittany over the Christmas holidays, I told her, "I like the artist types in these new classes. They're kinda different. But most people still care too much about who you know, who you date, and if your parents have money. Most everyone's in sororities and fraternities, and they don't like anyone else. The football players and other athletes keep mostly to themselves, too."

She shook her head and said, "I'm sorry, but it sounds just like high school. I thought it'd be different. Do you think it's different anywhere else?" she asked.

"God, I sure hope so," I said.

When I asked about Tucker, she told me, "He moved out," adding, "We're not really getting along."

"What're you going to do?" I asked. I didn't want to say, I'm sorry, since I wasn't sure I was. I never thought Tucker was good for her.

"My mom and dad are going to help me until I can find a better job," she said, lighting a cigarette as we sat at her kitchen table. "I can't keep relyin' on tips. Sometimes I don't make that much, so it's hard to budget," she said, running her fingers through her short hair.

"Stay in school as long as you can," she told me, swinging her foot. "I know it's hard, but let me tell you, it sucks even worse out here in the real world."

• • •

In the spring semester, I quickly discovered that the principals of accounting came easily to me, so I changed my major to Business and Savanna did, too. Adjusting to our easier course-loads, we spent the semester doing everything together, going to bars several nights a week, dating frat guys on the weekends, and occasionally meeting up with Emmett and Peter. On Sundays, we'd put the top down on her red convertible and drive out to the cliffs, where we'd spend the day studying, reading, and sun-bathing on the rocks above the river.

At the end of the semester, my parents gave me a new compact car for my twentieth birthday, as another year and summer sped by. Like the previous year, Savanna was back at home, working for her dad, Emmett was at school and traveling with his friends, and I spent my summer working at my mom's company.

Although we talked often, Brittany kept apologizing that she couldn't get together whenever I called. "Sorry, I'm just so busy working, taking care of Amy, and trying to get back in school that I just don't have time right now."

Then, one night on the phone, she told me, "Well, it's final. Tucker and I are divorced."

"How're you doin'?" I asked, worrying about her.

"I'm fine," she said. "I'm ready to start dating again."

"Really?" I asked, not sure what I should say.

"Oh, yeah." she said, exhaling her cigarette smoke. "It's definitely time to move on."

One night early in the summer, I ran into Derek. And in the following weeks, we started dating. We had a lot in common and enjoyed hanging out, so I ignored any feelings of guilt. I convinced myself it was okay. Emmett and I had been seeing other people for a while. Brittany had a kid, was divorced, and was dating again. Her time with Derek was long over.

As another fall approached, Savanna moved into her sorority house and I arranged to sublet a one-bedroom apartment. Juniors who still lived in a dorm were looked down on, and since I didn't belong to a sorority and had nobody to room with, my parents agreed to pay my rent, as long as I worked and covered my other expenses. I left town early to get settled into my new place, with my new car, so I could find a job before school started. I didn't get to see Brittany before I left.

When I called to say goodbye, she said, "I'm sorry I've been so busy, Erin. But we don't have to see each other to stay close, right? We'll be best friends no matter what. Besides, we'll see each other over Christmas. It'll be here before you know it." I was sorry not to see her, but knew I knew she was right, and I'd be back soon.

Once I was back at school, I quickly found a part-time job at the mall. Proud of the progress I'd made, I began to look forward to the new school year and beyond. Living alone, working part-time, and mastering my courses, I finally felt independent and confident. I could picture the day when I'd be a businesswoman with an office in a high-rise, living in a big city, maybe even in New York City.

One night early that fall, the phone rang as I sat studying. It was already after 10:30, so I thought it must be a friend wanting to go out. I answered the phone, pretending to have been asleep. I was surprised that it was my mom, since we'd already talked earlier that evening. "You asleep?" she asked. She sounded out of breath.

"No," I said, clearing my throat. "No, I'm studying. What's wrong?" I was instantly alarmed.

"Are you alone?" she gulped.

"'Course I am," I told her. *Why would she think I wasn't by myself?* I wondered.

"Do you have a friend you can call?" she asked. She sounded tense.

I said, "Yeah, Mom. What's wrong?!" I started to panic.

I can't recall the rest of the conversation, but she started by saying, "Well I was watchin' the news and—" And then she told me the worst thing possible.

I remember my knees buckling. I was sitting on the floor when I promised Mom that I'd call a friend to come over as soon as I hung up.

I called Emmett as I sat there crying with my back pressed to the wall.

Brittany had been murdered.

She was only nineteen years old.

Chapter Ten

I don't remember whether I went to class that week, or if I went to work, or if I spoke to anyone, or if anyone went home with me on the three-hour drive home.

What I do remember was talking with Emmett that awful night.

Within minutes of my call, he was at my apartment. He sat with me on the floor among my books and papers as I cried. Leaning on the coffee table that separated us, I told him what Mom had said about Brittany's death.

Her body was found on the floor in the den of her apartment. Every time I thought about it, I tried to shake the image of her body, lying on that blood red carpet in her den, out of my head.

The news report had said that when her parents couldn't reach her, they became worried. They'd made plans to get together, and when she didn't show up, her dad went by the apartment to check on her. Although the lights were on, she didn't come to the door. Unable to see through the fogged-up windows, since the air conditioner had been left on full blast, he realized something was horribly wrong. Frantic, he called the landlord and the police.

They found her with her throat slashed. It had been an obvious and protracted struggle and her other injuries included multiple bruises and lacerations. The apartment was in disarray.

She had a phone cord wrapped around her neck. Thankfully, her daughter was found crying in her crib, unharmed.

The news report had said, "Based on evidence found at the scene, the victim's ex-husband was taken into custody and subsequently charged with murder."

Days later I picked up Derek at his parents' house. We drove to Brittany's parents' complex and I held Derek's hand tightly as we walked across the parking lot to her sliding glass doors. Brittany had been cremated and her ashes spread in a small family-only ceremony. Her parents had invited close family and friends to a visitation at their home.

We walked into the den crowded with people, but I don't remember who was there. I don't recall seeing Brittany's baby, her dad, or any other friends, but they must've been there. I only recall talking to her mom, who thanked us for coming. She said our being there helped her remember all of the happier times. I hugged her tightly and cried so hard that I couldn't speak.

To my surprise, she comforted me, rubbing my back as we hugged, and holding me close for a long time. She said, "You were such a good friend to Brittany," which made me cry even harder. *Was I a good friend?* I wondered.

What stands out most about that day was her little sister. It'd been several years since I'd seen Lacey, and when she walked into the den, it took my breath away. She looked so much like Brittany, their features and frames nearly identical. She'd grown into a lovely teenager in my absence. The most striking resemblance was in their mannerisms. The way she crossed her long skinny legs, the way she pushed some of her hair behind an ear, and the way the bones of her hand and wrist moved and protruded. I recognized all the gestures. When she responded to something someone said with a nervous giggle, tucked her hair behind her ear, ducked her chin, and looked up again with a bashful smile, I lost whatever control I still had.

In that moment, watching that familiar gesture and endearing smile, everything inside me gave way and a large emptiness yawned. The room swirled as I fell, silently imploding and collapsing into my own dark sorrow and grief. And I was terrified.

Chapter Eleven

Exactly one week after my mom called to tell me the horrible news about Brittany, I was on my way back to school, shoving the dark emptiness down. The lump in my throat, large and sharp, tore at my throat with every swallow, and when it eventually sank, it sat, sharp-edged and deep in my gut.

I changed jobs, leaving my minimum-wage job at the trendy shop in the mall for a waitressing job. I could earn more money in tips as long as I smiled and pretended to care about my customers. Busy with my full-time load of classes, I sat in my large business courses, pretending to be just another student. I went out as often as possible, pretending to party and trying to appear interested in the people I was with. The dark emptiness, although hidden from public view, waited patiently until I was alone. Yawning wide and deep, it grew stronger when no one was around. Pretending to be ok when I was alone quickly became impossible.

I was traumatized by Brittany's murder to the point that I was scared of everything. Afraid to take a shower, certain a stranger would sneak up on me when I was most vulnerable, I left the curtain open and watched the door. Afraid to light my gas stove, sure that pent-up gases would make it explode, I opened all of the kitchen windows before I lit a burner. Certain that the flame on my cigarette lighter would make the gas heater explode, I kept the apartment cold and only lit my cigarettes outside on the landing. I couldn't even eat comfortably in my apartment. My throat closed and I choked, so whenever I could, I ate at the restaurant where I worked or else at the student union. On the few occasions when I cooked or ate at my apartment, I ate only food that was soft, and was careful to take small bites and chewing laboriously so I could get it down.

At night, the dark emptiness inside me extended outward, until it became one with the shadows around me, where it threatened to swallow me whole. Frightened by what lay in waiting, I left the lights and TV on all night. Afraid to let myself fall asleep, I studied, read, and cleaned, fighting my desperate need to rest. Eventually I ran out of distractions, I inevitably nodded off, only to jerk awake soon after. Once I was startled awake, my hands and legs shook and my heart raced uncontrollably.

After many nights of this terror, I discovered that I could regain control over my body by doing jumping jacks. Once exhausted from the exertion, my heart slowed to a steady pace and my trembling stopped. The constant cycle frayed at my nerves, making me dread sundown and be grateful for morning.

Exhausted and frantic, and desperate to avoid being alone at night, I came up with a reckless strategy. I went to class, studied for a few hours, went to work, and then went out partying, ending the night by either crashing at someone else's place or else staying out all night. Jeanette and her roommates quickly became an important element in my self-destructive behavior.

Jeanette had continued with her own form of rebellion and had abandoned school altogether to be a waitressing full time and moved into a dodgy rental house behind the stadium. Her new roommates, two sorority sisters named Carol Anne and

Laura May, were fifth-year seniors who weren't allowed to live in their sorority houses as their final semesters loomed. Their priorities were to graduate, to party endlessly, and to find future husbands, the order of importance varying by the day.

The reputations of these three girls were widely known, and people showed up at their house looking to party every hour of the night and day, so it was easy for me to show up and pretend. We went out almost every night, watching various bands perform, and partied with them into the early morning. I discovered that when people were partying, they didn't question people's motivations. Drinking and getting high allowed me to fall asleep, and all the partying kept me from feeling so alone. I could control my fears when other people were around, letting me keep my secret safe. Being in a crowd helped chase the darkness away.

Savanna would've listened, would've tried to help, if I'd given her the chance. But the normalness of her life made me feel even more like a crazy person. Jeanette would've listened too. She loved sharing in the dark dramas of her friends. But the thought of her using my pain as a source of entertainment kept me from sharing my feelings with her.

Emmett listened whenever I opened up to him, and he was the only person at school who knew my secret. During those first weeks, I'd relied on him to watch me eat and sleep, but the uncontrollable fear embarrassed me, even with him. He and his roommates hung out with cute, perky, fun-loving gymnasts who bounced when they walked and giggled when they talked. I couldn't let myself become "that girl who has issues" to him. Growing up, people used to say, "You gotta try and not let your crazy hang out," so that's what I did. I tried to hide my crazy.

By the Christmas break, I was numb and exhausted. I recalled very little from the months that had passed, and my self-destructive lifestyle had taken a huge toll. Once back home, I slept through the first three days and my parents were worried.

Dad said, "I think you're tryin' to do way too much. You're wearin' yourself out!" And I solemnly agreed.

Cameron didn't come home for the holidays, but Derek did, and we went out a couple of times. Overwhelmed with the guilt of dating Brittany's ex-boyfriend, I couldn't talk to him about her, and couldn't tell him how afraid I'd become. So I avoided him and pretended to be busy.

When I finally tracked Lorna down, I found her overwhelmed by her own problems. She'd broken up with her boyfriend, withdrawn from school, packed up and moved home, mourning the loss of her fiancé, and her dream of graduating from Tech. I tried to be a good friend, and listen to her, and console her, but I didn't have a lot left to give. I certainly couldn't burden her with my own pain and fears.

My grades, when they came, were terrible. How could they not be? Seeing them plummet nearly made my parents lose their minds. Concerned, disappointed, and furious, they were the endless topic of our conversations during the break.

After relentless questioning, I finally broke down and told them selective parts of the truth.

"Ever since Brittany died, I've had trouble sleeping," I told them and I started to cry. "I'm afraid I'll die all the time. My heart races and I can't concentrate. It's hard to study." I described what I'd been through, sparing them the gory details of my fears and my attempts to avoid them, and hoped that what I'd shared was enough.

They said they understood, and tried to reassure me by saying things like, "I know it's hard, but it's time to put all of that behind you." But they were also telling me to try and move on.

My dad said, "Loss is an unfortunate but unavoidable part of life. Everyone goes through hard times like these. You're just gonna have to learn how to work through it."

As if a laundry list of the grief of others would somehow ease my pain, they provided multiple examples of loss from our family history. The point of the stories being that everyone went through hard times, lost people they loved, and yet found a way to move on.

They told me that they wanted the best things in life for me, which I believed. "You have so many opportunities," they told me, which I also believed. But when they said, "You can do this," I didn't believe them.

How could I just move on? She was my best friend. I wanted to talk about Brittany. I wanted to miss her, wallow in my loss, cry about it, and have somebody willing to listen to my every thought and feeling. My fears were crazy, but they were real. How could I go on smiling and acting as if nothing was wrong?

"Do you want to move home?" my mom asked. "You could finish up here."

"No way. Absolutely not," I said, shaking my head. I couldn't throw away all of the independence and freedom I'd gained. As hard as it was, I had a shot at finding the courage to be myself away at school. Moving back would mean suffocating under the oppressive expectations of everyone who had known me since childhood.

"Well, we have to do somethin', Mom said. "You can't keep goin' like this. You're makin' yourself sick. Why don't we find you somebody to go talk to while you're home?" she suggested.

Paying someone to listen to me sounded like a great idea, so I agreed to see a counselor.

"Go and talk to somebody, and if you feel better about things and your grades are good next semester, then you can stay. Otherwise, you don't have a choice. You'll have to move home," Mom said.

"We just can't afford to pay and have you go throwin' it all away," Dad said, and I had to agree.

My mom made the appointment, gave me the name and address, and before I left the house on the day of the appointment, she offered to go with me but I just shrugged a wordless no. She nodded slowly, handed me a signed blank check, and said, "Ok then. Just let me know how much it is."

I met the counselor in her office and sat in a chair before the counselor's desk. Her office seemed more like a law office than one for a mental health professional. The deep green plush carpet, heavy wooden engraved furniture, gilded framed diplomas and books lining shelves on every wall screamed complicated legal issues not emotional ones. A greying blonde, she was thin and bird-like with big glasses like Brittany's.

She began by clearing her throat and saying, "So. Tell me why you you're here."

I told her about Brittany, her murder, not being able to sleep and my all-consuming fears, all the while crying so hard that she repeatedly handed me tissues. I told her about the darkness, how my heart raced at night, and the way my throat closed, choking me when I ate. I told her how I spent my days and nights imagining the various ways that I could die while showering, eating, driving, and walking down stairs. I told her how everyone around me had moved on, and that I didn't know how. She remained silent, nodding her head from time to time, and kept handing me tissues until I was spent and fell silent.

"What do you do when your heart races?" she asked as I sat there, sniffling.

Surprised by her question, I answered slowly. "Well…I do jumping jacks. If I do 'em long enough, my arms and legs stop shaking and my heart slows down," I told her.

"Have you ever tried deep breathing exercises?" she asked.

When I said no, she explained them to me, demonstrated them for me, did them with me, and watched me practice them on my own. After I had proven that I could inhale to the count of five and exhale to the count to five, she said, "Good. Now, you should breathe like this whenever you have a panic attack."

"Is that what this is?" I asked.

Ignoring my question, she went on. "After you give this a try for a little while, if you're still unable to control your panic episodes, come back and see me. But I think you should give it at least a month," she said.

I watched in disbelief as she rose from her chair, clearly signaling that our session was over.

Confused, I rose and stumbled behind her, leaving her office, and heading into her waiting room thinking, *How could that be it?*

Incredulous, I shook her hand robotically. She said, "It was nice to meet you. And if I don't see you in a month, good-bye and good luck."

I even said, "Thank you. It was nice to meet you too," in response, even though I was dumbfounded.

"Remember, give it at least a month," she said over her shoulder as she walked back down the hall to her office.

Anxious to leave, I filled out my mom's check in the amount the woman at the front desk indicated, and then left.

Driving home, I was so angry I could barely see straight.

That counselor hadn't even said she was sorry about what happened to Brittany. She didn't even seem to care. She didn't tell me whether or not what was happening to me was normal. What had she called it? A panic attack? She didn't tell me if I was crazy. She didn't give me medicine, didn't tell me how to make it stop, nothing. Instead, all she'd told me to do was to count to five when I breathe in and out. How could that be it?!

I hated her. She was horrible. Who spends all that time getting all of those degrees and then thinks it is okay to tell someone who's freaking the hell out just to count when they breathe? Try it for a month and see if that works? Talk about a waste of my parents' money.

"How was it?" mom asked as soon as I hit the door. I knew she'd been watching for me.

"Fine," I answered in a hoarse voice, my eyes and face visibly red and swollen.

Grabbing the bathroom door before I could close it behind me, she asked, "Think it helped?"

"Yeah. I do. I think it helped," I said, in between splashes of water hitting my face. I carefully avoided looking at my lying face in the mirror.

"Hope so. How much was it?" she asked, obviously worried. I could tell she wanted to hear more. She wanted to be sure she'd done the right thing sending me, and wanted to hear me say that I thought I was going to be okay. But I couldn't give her what she wanted.

"It was a hundred fifty," I answered with my face buried in a towel.

"You know," she said, "I was thinkin'... you probably shouldn't mention this to anybody." She smoothed my hair. "You don't want this gettin out." She was smiling at me.

"Who would I tell?" I asked, staring back at her image in the mirror.

"Exactly. Just gives people somethin' to talk about, anyhow. Ya know how people are," she said, taking the towel from me. "Once this's all behind you, you don't want all of them knowin'. They hold things like this against you later." She folded the towel and hung it on the rack.

Wordlessly, I turned and left the bathroom and headed down the hall for my room, when I heard her say as cheerfully as she could, "Why don't you go lie down for a little bit?"

• • •

Several days later, I decided to write down everything I could remember about Brittany. My head swam with memories, and since there was no one to listen, writing helped. Everything we did together, every place we went, anything I could think of began to fill an empty spiral notebook that I'd found in my room. Written in the form of a letter to her mom, in which I shared everything about her daughter that I could remember, I figured she, of all people, would want to know how I felt.

I wrote down silly things, like when we talked on the phone for hours while we both ate ice cream. How sometimes at school, we ate our lunches before ten in the morning and took turns buying chocolate candy bars from a band member just for the coupon for burgers, which we'd buy and share after school. How she called me Erie when she was happy, and how I called her Bridge whenever I needed her. Innocent memories, like the night we danced like the Solid Gold dancers until our sides hurt from laughing, and the not so innocent, like when we bought a quarter and pack of Jokers, and then rolled and smoked our first joints together. I wrote about everything we'd done, everything we'd said we wanted, everything we'd dreamed about doing, and everything we'd planned to do together someday.

All week long, I wrote in the spiral notebook. At night when I couldn't sleep, I searched my brain for more details, often waking in the morning with my first thoughts of Brittany and something else to add. When I wasn't writing, I slipped the notebook under my bed so it stayed out of sight but never far from reach.

But I should've known better. Everybody knows that you never put stuff like that down in writing. Teachers and parents always find it. I was asking for trouble.

And sure enough, one afternoon when I walked into my room, my mom whirled around and said, "What're you thinkin'?" and waved my spiral notebook.

"I dunno," was the only response I could give her.

"I can't believe you! You smoked pot? What in the world? Who were you writin' this to anyway?" she screamed.

"It's for her mom," I answered flatly.

"Why would her mother ever want to hear any of this?" she continued, waving my words at me.

"I dunno," I repeated, staring down at my toes as they dug into the carpet.

"If I had known all this was goin' on, I would've never let you hang out with her to begin with!" Then she whirled out of my room.

Waving my notebook in the air over her head for me to see as she walked down the hall, she added, "And I'm throwin' this away before your father sees it."

My notebook gone, my mom angry, and my parents worried and watching my every move, I stayed in my room and stewed. Absolutely no one understood what I was going through.

Why didn't anyone want to talk about it? Why wouldn't anybody let me talk about it?

I was angry at my mom, angry at everyone. I hated everyone, including myself.

Why was I so weak and so scared?

Lying on my bed, I pulled the quilt around me in a hug. My grandmamma had made it for me when I was eight. I'd taken it everywhere with me. Tattered with use, that quilt was always perfect, no matter the weather. It was cool like a sheet and warm like a blanket, and it was the one thing I had to have wrapped around me whenever I felt sick.

"How could she do this to me?" I said out loud, when a force like a lightning bolt hit me. Was I talking about my mom or Brittany? Was I was mad at Brittany?

But it wasn't her fault, I thought, as I felt my mind spinning. I knew it wasn't her fault. Tucker had killed her. I was shocked at myself. Aghast.

How could I be mad at her? The police said she'd fought back, and hard, too.

No-it couldn't be her fault. I couldn't be mad at her. She'd done nothing wrong.

Drained, I lay back on my bed and stared up at the ceiling and groaned out loud, "Why did she go out with him?"

I'd known he was trouble the first time I saw him. Why hadn't she listened to me?

I'd told her he was trouble, hadn't I? Why did she have to get pregnant? I thought, flipping over onto my stomach. And even then, why did she have to have the baby?

She'd had choices. If she was set on having the baby, and so against abortion, why did she have to keep her? Even then, if she'd wanted to keep her so much, why did she have to go and marry Tucker? Her parents would have helped her. I wanted to help her.

How in the hell had she let this happen? And why in the hell did she go off and leave me alone?

She'd promised me she'd never do that!

Anger slowly replaced the emptiness, where it had hidden unseen. And like the emptiness, the heat of my anger grew in size and strength. Unlike the original lightning-bolt of realization, this anger grew gradually, like a dial slowly being turned. Over the remaining days of the holiday break, hidden and protected, that flame burned brighter and hotter inside me.

Tired of being scared, and exhausted from pretending to be something I wasn't, I was angry about everything, most importantly at my own lack of courage. And so I decided to stop cowering. I just didn't have it in me to care anymore.

If courage is being afraid and doing it anyway, I would go and do everything I'd ever wanted to do, no matter how scared I was.

I wasn't just going to leave what had happened to Brittany behind me. If I had to leave her behind, I was going to leave everything else behind, too. All of the past, all of the rules and expectations, all of the pretending and trying to fit in, I was leaving it all behind.

Stewing in determination I called Derek and broke up with him over the phone.

"Can I come over so we can talk about it?" he asked.

And I said, "No. There's no point."

"This is because of Brittany, isn't it?" he asked, sighing sadly.

"Some of it. But no. Mostly it's because of Emmett," I said firmly.

"Well, we're all friends. I can talk to him." He sounded hopeful and said, "I'll explain it all to him. It'll be okay."

"No, you don't understand. I want to be with Emmett," I answered in a measured tone.

"But he's seeing other people. You told me so yourself," he said, his voice rising and almost cracking.

"I don't care," I told him, and it was the truth.

Feeling strong, I called Emmett. "I need to talk to you. Can I come over?" I asked.

Face to face with him, I announced "I've broken up with Derek. And I don't want to see anyone else from now on. Only you."

Unimpressed, he shook his head and said, "I'm just not sure that makes any difference. Maybe I want to keep seeing other people." With his elbows resting on his knees and hanging his head, he said, "I just don't know anymore."

"That's fine," I said, and smiled because it was true. "You can see anybody you want. That's completely up to you. I just wanted to let you know that I'm not going to see anybody else. I've made my decision and I just wanted you to know. That's all."

• • •

In preparation of my return to school, I spent time convincing my parents that I was okay and would continue to be okay. More determined as my anger grew, I committed to once again focus on my studies and graduate as soon as possible.

I didn't care about accounting, but it was easy, I was good at it, and once I graduated, I could get a good job anywhere with that accounting degree. I didn't care about my grades, either, but good grades meant I didn't have to fight with my parents to stay in school. The quicker I graduated, the quicker I could move even further away, and leave behind all of the people who thought they knew me, along with all of their opinions on how I should live my life. They all had ideas about what was best for me. Maybe I didn't have enough courage to face it, but I'd certainly gathered enough strength to run away.

Driving back, instead of trying to swallow my fears as I had in the past, I marinated in my anger, letting it ferment into something that felt like strength and courage. The sun glinting through the pine trees on that drive looked a lot like hope to me. The rolling two lane highway felt like my road to freedom.

Back at school, I went to every class, read every chapter, studied every night, and worked whenever I could, even picking up another part-time job at a fast-food restaurant. Hoarding my hourly wages and tips, I saved every penny, preparing for the worst-case scenario. If my grades didn't improve, I needed to be able to support myself.

When not caring began to feel more and more like courage, I told all of my friends that I wanted to date Emmett. I walked around announcing it as if everyone I knew cared and needed to know.

Savanna already knew how I felt and had always been fine with it, as long as it didn't cause her any trouble. She hesitated only slightly when I told her about my decision to come clean about it when we talked on the phone one night.

She said, "Are you sure about this…?"

When I assured her I was very certain, she asked, "So… do your parents know?"

"Not yet. I need a little more money saved in case they try and make me come home when they find out," I told her, twirling the cord of the receiver around my finger.

"Hmm. I'm not sure I could do that," she said.

"Well, no need to worry about that right now," I said firmly. "First things first. We're not even dating again yet. I'll tackle that when it's time." I surprised even myself with how calm I felt inside.

When I told Jeanette my plans, she instantly brightened. As I expected, she adored the drama of it all, and began talking about it incessantly. Laura May and many others didn't say anything at all in response. Not because they were okay with me and Emmett dating, but because they were so self-absorbed, they really didn't care what I did.

My strange and wonderful artist friends seemed to enjoy my news the most. One friend was elated when I told her. We hung out with her from time to time, and she'd recently confessed that she liked girls instead of boys. She laughed and clapped her hands, and said, "Well, finally! Now they'll be talkin' about somethin' other than me!"

Only the conversation with Carol Anne was difficult.

"Whaaaaaat?" was her initial response, so I repeated it.

"You've met Emmett," I said. "Well, I'm in love with him, and I'm hopin' that one day we'll be together."

"I don't understand. I mean, I'll go out with almost anybody. But never a nig. How could you? I mean, why would you do that? Ugh!" she said, flipping her bangs back off her forehead.

"What difference does it make? And what makes you think I give a flying shit what *you* would do?" I asked, setting my jaw. Suddenly she seemed ugly to me.

"Whatever." she said. "People are gonna call you names, ya know. Ugly names. And nobody'll go out with you. But if you don't care, I certainly don't." Then whirling away, she put both of her hands up in the air as she stalked back to her room and slammed her door.

• • •

One night in February, Emmett came over for dinner and I talked him into spending the night. Around two in the morning, it started to snow. I'd only seen snow maybe once or twice in my life, since it didn't usually snow that far south, so I begged him to go outside with me. In the yard behind my apartment building, we played in the snow under the silver moonlight until my fingers and toes hurt. My nose red and running, Emmett showed me how to roll the snow into a miniature snow man.

As I watched him, I thought about how he was like everyone I loved, all rolled into one person. I could be myself with him. We could do anything, talk about anything, and I could be anything with him. Special, smart, patient, and kind, he also didn't put up with any of my bullshit. He knew me inside and out. He knew everything there was to know about me: the good, the bad, the silly, the ugly, the scared, everything. And yet he still loved me.

He didn't think of me as someone who had to be fixed. He thought of me as someone to be enjoyed, celebrated, and discovered. He believed that I, like everyone else would and should change and evolve over time. His only expectation was that I be loyal to him.

Relentless once I'd made up my mind, I began showing up at his apartment all of the time, inviting him to mine, and never said a word if he wanted to go out with someone else. Instead, I tried to keep him so busy that he didn't have time. I stopped by after my fast-food job smelling like hamburgers, bringing one home for him, prepared just as he liked it. After classes, I helped him study, helped him do his laundry, helped him clean his apartment, and cooked for him whenever he'd let me. I worked and went to school, slept at Emmett's when he let me, and invited him to stay over at my house.

I still went out occasionally with girlfriends, but not very often. I didn't feel like partying anymore. I didn't want to meet anyone new or date anyone else, and I didn't want stay over at anyone else's house. If I was alone and had a panic attack, I practiced my deep breathing, and when that didn't work, I resorted to jumping jacks again. I continued to open the windows when I lit the stove, and showered with the bathroom door open, but I acknowledged my fears without letting them take over. Still certain I would die one day, maybe even one day soon, I figured I'd better hurry up and live.

One night, Savanna called and asked me to go out to Larry's where the football players hung out. "Maybe Emmett and Peter will be there," she said brightly when I agreed. We found them there, but Peter was already drunk by the time we arrived. Some people are happy drunks, always smiling, laughing and hugging when they've had too much to drink. But not Peter. He was regularly cussing out people and getting into fights when he went out. Savanna didn't know any better, but I did, and I told her, "Look, we need to steer clear of him tonight."

"Come on. Let's just go say hello," she said, as she pulled me with her to where they sat at the bar.

Peter turned around on his barstool when we walked up beside him, and his eyes and face were blood red. Completely ignoring Savanna, he pointed his finger at me.

"I never did like you much," he growled.

"Oh Peter, you don't mean that," Savanna giggled, hitting his arm playfully.

"Oh, yes I do," he said, turning completely around to face me. He pointed his finger dangerously close to my face as he drunkenly wagged it at me. Then he slurred, "You…need to leave Emmett…alone!"

"I love him, Peter," I told him quietly.

"You're always yankin' his chain, sayin' you love him, and then you run off with other people. Leave him the hell alone!" he said, the redness of his face moving to his ears and scalp.

If I'd been a guy, he probably would've hit me, so I tried to speak in a soothing voice. As I pulled Savanna away from him, I told him, "I promise, I'm not goin' to hurt him, Peter."

I heard him yell, "You better not!" as I dragged Savanna out of the bar and into the parking lot.

"What's goin' on'?" Savanna asked as I pulled her towards her car. As another group went into the bar behind us, I heard Peter's voice from inside yell, "I'll kick your ASS!" but I wasn't sure if he meant that for me or somebody else.

• • •

Around the beginning of May, I moved out of my apartment and into a large house closer to campus with Jeanette, Carol Anne, and three other roommates, lowering my rent significantly. Thankfully, my grades were better that spring semester, and my parents, encouraged by the improvement, agreed that I could stay. But still, I wanted to be prepared in case anything went wrong.

Carol Anne wasn't happy to have me as one of her roommates, but since they needed another roommate, the others agreed that I could move in. She had failed several classes in the spring, and was grouchily continuing in her struggle to both graduate and find a fiancé. Living with her had its challenges, and she enjoyed pointing out that she'd been right. Other guys did quit asking me out, and people did call me names like "nigger lover," "white trash" and "cleat chaser," sometimes even to my face, so who knows what horrible things they said behind my back. But I'd been right, too. I really didn't give a rat's ass anymore about what anyone else thought.

• • •

Brittany's murder trial stretched on for months. Her parents, her sister, a few others of our friends, and her date from the night before she was killed were all asked to testify. Although the papers followed every detail, I wasn't interested in hearing any of it. When I thought of her, I didn't want to think about Tucker or the details of what he'd done to her, and I wanted to keep it that way. None of it mattered to me anyway, since knowing how she died or why wouldn't bring her back.

Tucker was convicted of Brittany's murder. I'd heard that her mom had asked for leniency at his sentencing, asking the judge not to sentence him to die in the electric chair for the sake of their child. My mom called one night and said, "I just wanted to call and let you know that it's all over now. He was sentenced to life in prison." Later she added, "I'm just glad that now everybody can finally move on."

Everyone else certainly seemed to have moved on. Everyone went about their lives, working, going to class, and going out on dates. Even the newspaper reporting had moved on. I heard that Brittany's parents adopted Amy and moved away. But *I* still wasn't ready to move on. I didn't want to act as if nothing had ever happened. I wanted to remember everything about my best friend. I wanted to cherish who and what she was, and what she'd wanted from life. I treasured all of the things that had made her wonderful, and I'd hidden them deep down inside, where the emptiness had once been, and where my anger still burned.

There, deep inside of me, I kept her safe.

Chapter Twelve

In August, before classes had begun, we were lying in bed at nine in the morning, reluctant to get up. Emmett asked, "What's that?" rubbing the corner of my hip.

"I dunno," I said, looking down at the lump on the left side of my abdomen. "That's weird," I said, turning to lie on my back. Just to the right of my left pelvic bone, a peach-sized lump protruded from the otherwise flat surface.

"Yeah, that's weird," he said. "You should get that checked out. Does it hurt?" He asked, leaning on his elbow.

"No. It doesn't hurt," I said, pressing on it, testing it for pain as I tried to push it down or move it to the side without success. "Do tumors hurt?" I asked, scrunching my eyebrows, concerned.

I'd been sure for quite some time that I would die before long. Ever since Brittany's murder, it'd just been just a matter of how it would happen, and how soon, not if. Certain now, almost a year later, that I would die from a tumor, I called and made a doctor's appointment.

"Why the gynecologist? Do you think you're pregnant?" Emmett asked when I told him about the appointment.

"Don't see how I could be. I've taken the pill forever, and I haven't missed a period or anything. I called the primary doctor and they said I should go to the gynecologist first," I told him.

But I'd heard about a girl in Tricia's sorority who'd had a similar lump, which turned out to be an ovarian tumor. Savanna's grandmother had died from ovarian cancer, and she didn't have any symptoms at all until they discovered a grapefruit-sized tumor. Mine looked smaller than that, so maybe we'd caught it in time.

"So what brings you in today?" The doctor asked later that week.

"I think I have an ovarian tumor," I told him. "I have this lump in my abdomen, just to the right of my left pelvic bone. It doesn't hurt or anything. But it's pretty large, about the size of a peach," I said, rubbing the area through the paper gown.

"Well, why don't you lie back on the table and let's see what we've got here," he said, helping me get into position to be examined.

"Are you sexually active?" he asked, as he pushed gently on the different areas of my abdomen.

"Yes, but I'm on the pill. Have been for years. I haven't missed any of my periods," I told him calmly as I watched his hands press on my bare stomach.

"Experiencing any vomiting? Light headedness?" he asked.

"No," I said.

"You haven't felt sick at all?" he asked, looking at my face while he continued to examine me, pushing higher on my rib cage.

"I had an ear infection back in March," I said, not sure if that's what he meant.

"Did you take anything for it?" he asked, helping me sit up on the table.

"Yes, I took an antibiotic. I went to the medical center at school and they gave me a prescription," I explained.

"Well, young lady, I don't think you have a tumor. It's more likely that you're pregnant," he said, patting my knee.

"What? No!" I said, looking at him as if he had two heads. "That can't be. I haven't missed any of my periods and I told you I'm on the pill!"

"Antibiotics can counteract the active agents in birth control pills, rendering them ineffective," he explained.

"How can you be sure? It's gotta be a tumor!" I said. Incredulous, my mind raced, trying to understand. I'd been prepared to be told that I had a tumor, even played out the discussions we'd have regarding surgery and treatment. But this?

"That's likely the baby you feel," he said calmly. "We'll do a blood test and an ultrasound to confirm, take some measurements, and see how far along you are, and then we can talk some more." He said patting my knee once more before he turned and left the room.

Once the tests were complete and I was dressed, I sat on the exam table as I wiped my eyes and mumbled, "I can't do this! Twins?! I'm still in school. My parents are gonna kill me!"

"You do have options. You aren't a minor anymore. At twenty-one, you're considered an adult. You do, however, need to think carefully and consider your options quickly. At sixteen weeks, you don't have a lot of time," he said. Taking a deep breath, he continued, "Now, Birmingham has a clinic that performs late-stage abortions—"

"I don't think I can do that. Not at sixteen weeks," I said quietly, looking up at him. Brittany and the image of her fetus key chain flashed in my brain.

"I understand." He sighed.

"If you choose to have the twins, you can, of course, continue to see me. It'll be considered a high-risk pregnancy, so I'll need to see you every three weeks," he continued.

"I can't take care of twins!" I said, choking on the words and quietly starting to cry again.

"I understand this is overwhelming. Perhaps, if the father is still in picture?" He asked.

"He's in school, too," I told him.

"There are other options," he said and sighed again. "There's a place, a home for girls in your…situation. It's run by a group I've worked with in the past. They provide care for the mother during pregnancy, including taking them to doctor appointments and they arrange for adoption once the birth takes place."

"I don't know if I can do that, either," I said, crying and shaking my head hopelessly.

"Well, you have a lot to think about. I'll ask the nurse to give you all of the information for the options we've discussed today,"

After a pause, he continued. "If you have any questions, you can certainly give me a call or make an appointment to come back and see me."

Then, when I didn't reply, he wished me luck and left the room.

Keeping my head down, avoiding the prying eyes of the ladies in the waiting room, I stumbled out of the doctor's office into the bright, unforgiving summer sun, with the black and white sonogram image showing two heads hidden deep inside my purse.

• • •

"I'm afraid it's our only option," Emmett said as he sat on the worn-out coach in his apartment, his elbows resting on his knees.

"I dunno. Maybe we could do it. I could move in and we could live here," I sniffled. "I could work until you get out of school."

"It's not okay to raise two babies in an apartment with a bunch of guys partying all the time, with girls in and out. That's not okay," he said and shook his head, clasping and re-clasping his hands.

"Maybe we could get our own place? I could work when you're not in school. Maybe you could work, too?" I suggested, grasping for ideas.

"You can't earn enough, and I'll lose my scholarship if I get a job. Ever since I got hurt, they've been looking for a reason to cut off my scholarship. If I'm ever going to get a real job, I've gotta graduate." He shook his head hopelessly. "What'll their life be like, with both of us working minimum wage? We've gotta think of what's best for them, now."

"I know you're right," I sighed.

In the week following my doctor's appointment, other than going to work, sleeping, and crying, all I did was think about what I should do. Ruling out a late-stage abortion was easy; deciding what to do next proved to be much more difficult. I desperately wished I still had Brittany. She would've helped me figure out what I should do. I'd called the number on the brochure for the home for unwed mothers that the nurse had given me, made an appointment, and drove to Birmingham to check out the place.

The faith-based group's mission was to provide "girls in my situation" with alternatives to abortion, so they ran a home for "unwed mothers," which I was now considered to be. The home was out in the middle of nowhere. Managed by a couple who lived onsite, the home provided housing, meals, medical care, and transportation to doctors, all free of charge. After giving birth, the mother and father, if the father could be located, had thirty days to sign the final adoption papers, and then it would be over. If the parents were twenty-one, no further consent would be needed, although the woman at the home strongly recommended that we notify our parents to ensure that they wouldn't contest any future adoption.

"That place for unwed mothers did seem nice," I told Emmett. "They said I can go there any time. All I have to do is call them and set a date," I said, taking a deep breath.

"If you go, can we change our mind?" he asked, rubbing his hands together.

"Yeah. We have until thirty days after they're born," I told him.

"I just don't see any other way," he admitted.

"I don't even have to tell my parents," I said. "I could just go. Sell all my stuff and go there. Disappear. Send them a letter later, lettin' them know I'm okay," I said.

"No. I won't let you do that. They don't deserve that!" Emmett snapped. "You have to tell them."

• • •

"Pack your stuff up. I'll be there first thing in the morning," Mom said in a low, guttural voice. Hearing her, I could picture the angry look on her face.

"There's no need for all that. I'm gonna sell my stuff and go there from here," I said, trying hard not to cry.

"Do what I said. We'll talk about this tomorrow," she growled through gritted teeth before she abruptly hung up.

The following morning, Mom and I crammed everything we cared about saving into our cars, leaving most of my things behind in the rented room. Jeanette, Carol Anne, and my other roommates didn't know what was going on, but they knew enough to stay hidden until my angry mother was gone.

On the drive home, intermittently crying, I watched the passing trees and fields along the familiar two-lane highway, and wished I was going anywhere in the world but home. Consoling myself with thoughts of Brittany's mom, memories of how angry she'd been at first, but then eventually finding a way to be happy about the baby, I prayed that my parents would also find the same path to happiness and forgiveness.

When we arrived home, Grace wasn't there. I was sure she'd been sent somewhere to avoid witnessing what was about to happen, but my dad sat in his chair in the den, waiting.

I forget now, how those difficult, long discussions began, and thankfully I don't remember much of what was said. I promised myself that I'd forget the mean and hateful things we said to each other as we screamed and yelled, each of us trying to regain control of the conversation with the volume and poison of our words. The range of emotions flashed across their faces. Even while shock, disappointment, concern, and anger changed the tone, volume, and content of their words, their eyes betrayed their one true emotion, pain. All they'd ever wanted, all they'd ever worked for, was that I would have the best of everything in life. Clearly my situation was not what anyone would consider to be what was "best."

Steeling myself, and distanced from them as I sat across the room alone on the couch, I forced myself to detach. After announcing my age and corresponding status of adulthood, I highlighted the fact that this was my and Emmett's decision, not theirs. Since my proclamation was met with dead silence, I explained why we had decided against abortion. They stared at me silently as I launched into all of the reasons why Emmett needed to stay in school. After stressing how difficult this decision was for us, I told them that adoption seemed to be the best option, not for us, but for the babies. Afraid that they would see this as an opportunity to jump in, and in an attempt to prove my maturity and the thoroughness of my research, I told them how things would work with the organization, the home, and subsequent adoption process. Out of breath and out of options, I finally stopped talking.

"Well, I respect your decision not to have an abortion," my dad replied calmly.

"You need to think about what's best for the baby now," my mom added.

"Babies," I corrected, and watched the multitude of emotions that crossed her face, inspired by just that one little word.

Then my dad said, "Don't go off thinkin' that all this's because he's black either."

"Well, now we'll never know, will we?" Mom spat out in disgust, shaking her head. "We might've liked him, but you never trusted us. You never even gave us a chance to get to know him." In a dizzying shift from disgust to sadness, and then to anger, she added, "Ya know, nothing's gonna change for him. He'll get off scott-free. He doesn't have to quit school, go off to some home, or anything. He gets to go on just like nothing ever happened."

Eventually, after several days of angry and painful discussions, punctuated at times with shouting and tears, my dad provided their final opinion. We sat in the den once again, my mom clasping her hands and lips tightly, as if doing so helped her remain silent. Then Dad cleared his throat, announcing his intention to speak.

"We'll take you up to Birmingham next week to that place you found. Once the babies come, if you decide to follow through with adoption, you can come home and live here with us, but you'll need to work and finish up with school," he started. "Otherwise," he continued grimly, "you'll need to be out on your own."

After a pause, he continued. "If you change your mind about all this," he said slowly and sadly, "I want you to know that you'll be choosin' the hardest possible road I could ever think was possible." His eyebrows scrunched together with concern as he continued. "I can't even imagine all of the problems and hardships you'll face if you decide to do something different."

I nodded my understanding, and simply replied, "Yes, sir." After all, what else was there to say?

That night at dinner, Mom suggested that I go stay down at the beach condo they'd recently bought. "It might be good for you to stay down there instead of being here trapped in the house while you wait for us to take you up," she said. "Nobody's down there this time of year, and it'll give you some time to yourself so you can think about everything."

Lynne came by the house that night after dinner to drop off her old maternity clothes. She found me in my room reading, and stood in the doorway for a minute, quietly looking at me before saying, "I hope you know this is killing Mom and Dad." I just stared at her in response.

Then, in one quick motion, she took a few steps into my room, set a brown paper grocery bag of clothes on the floor beside my bed, and backed up to the door again, as if she was afraid to come in the room.

"Mom thought you could use these. You don't have to give 'em back when you're done. I don't want 'em back," she said, then turned and left, quietly closing the door behind her.

Although the thought of being all by myself at the beach house stirred up familiar feelings of fear, I agreed that it was a good idea for me to wait down there. Anxious to escape the pain and disappointment reflected in my parents' and sisters' faces, and the overwhelming, constant weight of shame, facing my fear of being alone wasn't all that scary.

Out from under watchful eyes, at the beach I finally had the opportunity to call Emmett. Needing to unload, we talked for hours that first night as I walked him through the details of my discussions with my parents. As we talked, we reexamined every alternative, only to settle once more on adoption as the only viable solution.

Plagued once again by panic attacks, I couldn't sleep. Although imminent death no longer scared me, and instead promised escape and relief, my body still shook and my heart raced with fear. Alone, I paced the floors of the condo. One morning after a long and sleepless night, an hour or so before dawn, I walked down the stairs and out to the beach. After walking up and down the beach for an hour, searching for peace like it was a shell hidden somewhere in the sand, I sank to sit in the sand and stare out at the gulf.

Only the birds and the crabs were witness to my quiet prayers. "Please God, please!" I cried softly, rocking as I held my knees. "I'm so alone. I don't know what to do. I'm scared. Where are you?" I pleaded as the waves broke a few feet away at my feet.

I thought of Brittany, and finally I understood. Like her, I didn't want to be sad and alone. Although I hadn't intended on getting pregnant, now that I was, I wanted to be happy about it.

I wanted to be happy to be having my babies. That's all Brittany had wanted. She didn't want to be sad and ashamed.

Why couldn't she be with me? We could've been happy together with our kids. We would've helped each other! I thought miserably. Again I prayed, "Please God. Please. Where are you?" I said it over and over, until I heard a response.

The voice was powerful and startling. Maybe I heard it, maybe it came from somewhere inside me, or maybe I just felt it or thought it. But its power startled me.

In a booming voice, I heard, "I AM HERE!" and immediately I sat up straight. The voice commanded the full attention of my mind and body.

And that's when I knew that I wasn't alone. We were all there, together. Me, God, Brittany, and the babies inside, all of us. We were there together on that beach.

I wasn't alone. I had never been alone, and I would never again be alone.

As the rays from the sun grew in strength, the warmth and certainty of the voice permeated my soul. Feelings of strength, comfort, connection, and the certainty that it would all be okay soaked every corner of my mind and body as the sun rose over the water. I looked around and the birds and the crabs, the waves and the sun, and the wispy clouds that floated in the pale blue sky above all reassured me. No matter what happened, He, no they, would always be with me.

Smiling through my tears, I *knew* and I *believed.* Like a crazy person sitting on the beach alone, I laughed out loud, giddy with the knowledge that I had the courage to do whatever I needed to do.

Chapter Thirteen

Since everything had already been said, the five-hour drive to Birmingham with my mom was very quiet. There also wasn't much to see. It had been eight years since Hurricane Fredrick had come through, the tornados cutting wandering paths through the forests along I-65, and they'd long since been overgrown. It was oddly reassuring to know that time could heal even the deepest of wounds.

We drove to the same place I'd visited only a month before, and the same woman greeted us, and politely shook our hands before leading us to a private office. She provided my mom with an overview of the organization and the program, and she'd obviously had a lot of practice. As she talked and my mom nodded, I wondered if this was how these conversations usually went. The lady was polite but reserved, almost careful, and appeared to be steeling herself for emotional outbursts and hysterics. Once she finished her speech, she presented us with a glossy folder holding a packet of admission paperwork. Mom reached out to take the packet, but the woman smiled sweetly at her but handed the paperwork to me, saying softly, "Oh, thank you, but we don't need your signature."

After I signed my consent, releasing my medical records, affirming my intent to abide by the rules, and releasing the organization from any unforeseen complications, the woman gave us the address and directions to the home, which was an hour away.

After traveling a long, lonely county road lined with barb wired fences and clusters of cows, we turned into a long driveway leading to a huge two-story house. The driveway, lined with split rail fencing, led to a large front porch with half a dozen rocking chairs. The house looked comfortable and homey.

As my mom lifted my light suitcase from the trunk, the irony of the moment sunk deep. Tears welled in my eyes at the contrast between this moment and the more hopeful one when they'd dropped me off for my first semester at college. But before a tear could fall, the front door flew open and a young woman dressed in faded jeans, a worn pink sweater, and brown work boots called, "Well, hellooo there!"

With long purposeful strides, she reached the back of Mom's car, plucked the suitcase from her, and held out her hand to shake my mom's.

"I'm Tracy. Nice to meet ya," she said as she smiled at my mom. Then she quickly turned to me, and with a big grin said, "And you must be Erin!"

Her boots were dusty, with dried mud on their heels, and she was wearing Levis. I followed her up the steps and into the house. The inside was just what you would expect. In a huge great room with vaulted ceilings and worn hardwood floors, sat a huge brick fireplace and several heavy sofas covered in sturdy fabric, with a large braided rug in the center. It looked and smelled clean and well-worn.

Despite the size of the place, no one else was around. There was a dining room with four large tables that resembled picnic tables, with benches finished in a dark stain and varnished to a shine. Next came an equally large kitchen, but from where we stood we could only see two commercial refrigerators, the kind used in cafeterias. The back of the house had floor to ceiling windows, and outside them lay an expansive deck, from which we could see an aging red barn, a corral with several horses, and a large vegetable garden and pasture.

"This's quiet time for the girls, so they're all in their rooms," Tracy said as she sat on one of the sofas and gestured for us to join her. "We have sixteen girls here right now, and you make seventeen. There's room for twenty. Candy's in labor, so by tomorrow, we should be back down to sixteen." She smiled and brushed her bangs off her forehead.

She looks like she belongs here, I thought, sizing her up. Not just because of her clothes or her boots, but because of everything else about her. She didn't wear any make up or jewelry aside from her gold wedding band. Her hair style said wash and wear, her manner said she had things to do, and her hands looked hard-working.

Then, as a tall, dark-haired man in jeans, boots, and a flannel shirt stomped in from the kitchen, she introduced us to her family, saying, "This is my husband Luis, and my sons Elias, Lane, and Adam." Three little boys followed Luis, a blonde of about seven, a brown-haired boy of about six, and another smaller blonde, who looked about three or four, and who had his thumb in his mouth.

"Hello," Luis said, shaking my mom's hand, then added, "Boys, say hello."

Again following birth order, the three little ones each said hello before following their dad from the room.

"Go get cleaned up," Tracy called after them as they left. Turning to me, she said, "We follow a strict schedule in the house. We get up at six, eat breakfast at seven. Bible study is at eight, then chores, lunch, quiet time, dinner, devotion, and one hour of TV. After TV, there's one more hour of quiet, then lights out at ten. Luis does all of the outside work, and I take care of the girls who live here."

Pointedly looking at my mom, she continued, "Telephone's not allowed, unless it's an emergency. I'll give you the number in case you need it," she told Mom. As Mom nodded, Tracy continued, saying, "You can call anytime if you just want to ask me how she's doing. And, of course, you can write. It's a PO Box to protect the girls' privacy. We only leave the ranch to go to the doctor, and afterwards we let the girls go to Walmart. On Sundays we go to church here in town. Parents can come visit on Saturday, but I wouldn't recommend coming every week. No other visitors are allowed, no friends, other family, or even the father of the child. We've found that other visitors just upset all the other girls."

I wanted to dislike her, wanted to hate her as the warden of this place of detention, but I couldn't. Genuine, strong, purposeful, and delightfully matter of fact, all I could manage to feel was comfort and admiration. Her smile was real, and her hazel eyes danced back at me when I smiled at her.

My mom and I cried in the driveway when she left to begin her long drive back. Although I wasn't sad and didn't feel lonely or scared, I deeply regretted having caused her so much pain, worry, and sadness. My tears were for her, rather than for myself.

"Now then, let's get you settled," Tracy said as she put her strong arm around my shoulders and led me back into the house. "I'm putting you with our other older girl. I figure you two need the most privacy. She's quiet. Just turned seventeen," she explained as she picked up my small suitcase and led the way through the hallway.

"Each floor has a bathroom that you girls share," she said, gesturing to the bathroom on the first floor as we passed it. "Both floors keep a schedule. You get twenty minutes to shower, either at night or in the morning, whatever the schedule says."

"How old are the other girls?" I asked, looking into the bathroom.

"You're the oldest, then there's your roommate Samantha, who like I said is seventeen. Rachelle's our youngest at fourteen. Everybody else is either fifteen or sixteen," she said as she reached the end of the hallway and began climbing the carpeted stairs.

Oh my God! I thought as I followed Tracy up the stairs. *They're all younger than Grace!*

The next day, I began to meet the other girls, except for Candy, who Tracy had taken to the hospital in the middle of the night.

"That's what happens," my roommate Samantha told me as we lay in our beds that night after lights out. "Girls go into labor and you never see them again. You never hear what happens, and they never come back," she said darkly.

Samantha cried a lot, but she didn't talk much, so as roommates go, she seemed like she'd be a pretty good one. Neat, clean, and quiet, even when she cried herself to sleep, she was very considerate. Luckily, and unlike everyone else, Samantha wasn't anxious to tell me her story or talk about her baby. All she said was that she was from up around Muscle Shoals, and that she was almost eight months pregnant.

My experience at my old Christian school and at home proved invaluable as I adjusted to the strict house rules, participating in Bible study, and doing household chores I was assigned. Given Candy's sudden departure, I picked up her assignment, which was listed as post meal kitchen clean-up. A sixteen-year-old girl named Heidi, from a tiny town outside Huntsville, was my chore partner. Her long hair fell to her waist, except for the poufy bangs that she obviously teased and sprayed so they reached high over her forehead. She told me she was a Seventh Day Adventist, so she couldn't cut her hair, wear make-up, jewelry, or pants.

"Are there any other rules?" I asked.

"Not really anythin' different from what they have here. Except'n we can't date until we turn eighteen," she said, swinging her long hair.

I really wanted to ask her how she ended up pregnant if she wasn't even supposed to date until she was eighteen, but I didn't.

"How long've you been here," I asked.

"Seven months," she said, and with a rub of her belly, she added, "I'm almost nine months, and boy, am I ready to get back home!"

"So, how is it here?" I asked.

"Oh it's alright. Only thing is you should only 'spect to get over to Walmart once a month, after your doctor's appointment. So ya gotta be frugal with your good lotion and such," she said with her arms deep in the metal sink, suds up to her elbows.

"Are you always on kitchen duty?" I asked, picking up a dishtowel and beginning to dry a clean dinner plate from the drain.

"Nah. Chores are assigned every week and rotate, but Tracy lets us swap up, as long as we don't fight about it," she said as she rinsed a sudsy plate and set it in the drain.

"Do we have to do anything really hard? Like anything outside?" I asked as I put the dry plate into an open slot above the counter.

"Nah. And you can't *ever* go into the barn or the corral. We aren't allowed 'round the horses. They're gentle and all, but it's a hard and fast rule. Just in case something were to happen. If you wanna get outside, ya can sit out on the porch or walk 'round in the pastures, as long as the horses aren't out there. But you can't walk out on the road, unless we're goin' to church, and ya can't ever walk out in the woods."

"We walk to church?" I asked.

"Yeah. Sunday mornings. My preacher says for a coupla months, it's okay if I go on Sundays, too. He says it's better than not goin' at all. But we only walk if it's nice. If it's raining we take the van. It's a little Baptist church just down the road. Not far at all," she said as she pulled the plug to let the water drain.

As each girl shared their individual stories with me, I withdrew further. As they proudly shared horrid tidbits, describing in detail the drama they'd caused, I decided not to share mine. Like Samantha, I told them as little as possible.

After Luis led devotion that night, we gathered in the TV room and Tracy let one of the girls pick a movie for us to watch from a small collection. The room was lined with bookshelves on all sides, spilling over with more books than they could hold. As everyone settled in, shifting on the sofas, chairs, and pillows on the floor, trying to find comfortable positions, I walked closer to the shelves to read the titles. Turning, I found Tracy watching me, and I asked, "Are we allowed to read them?"

Over the heads of the other chattering girls, she grinned and said, "Of course. You can read anything you want, whenever you want."

Turning back to smile at the shelves, I realized that I had found my escape. Even if I read a book a day, I still wouldn't be able to read all of them before the babies came.

The next day during quiet time, I took the book I'd chosen the night before and went out to the pasture. With the horses safely in the corral, I sat in the tall grass, enjoying the cool breeze and the warm fall sun on my skin. Tracy, Luis, and the boys were working in the barn, and I could hear their voices but not their words. They sounded happy. The rest of the girls had disappeared into different rooms, either to nap or they'd paired off and were talking while they crocheted or knitted.

"What're ya reading?" Tracy asked, surprising me as she plopped on the ground by my side.

"Jane Eyre," I told her, showing her the book.

"Ah. A dark romance. Chock fulla difficult times and forbidden love. Ends well, though," she said, looking up at the sky. "So, how are you doing so far?"

"Okay, I guess." I hesitated, not sure how I was expected to answer. After all, I'd chosen this place, so what was I supposed to say? She remained quiet while I thought about it. She seemed to want to hear my answer. *How exactly do I feel?* I thought, while she waited patiently. *Relieved mostly, to be away from the tension at home.* Instead of explaining, I simply added "It's peaceful here. I like that."

"That it is," she said wistfully to the sky.

After a few minutes of sitting in silence, she said, "You can talk to me if you need to, ya know. I know it's hard for you, being so much older than the other girls." Then she said brightly, "You know, I'm only seven years older than you are."

"I didn't know that," I answered a little glumly, carefully turning the closed book over in my hands and examining the cover, keeping my finger between the pages to save my place.

That meant she'd married Luis and had Elias when she was around my age. Hers seemed such a different, easier path than the one I'd chosen.

As if she could read my mind, she continued, "I know right now it looks like my life's always been easy, but it hasn't. My parents hate Luis, and they didn't want me to marry him. I haven't talked to my mom since Lane was born, and she's never even seen Adam." She said this as she picked at the grass in front of her.

"No way. Why?" I asked, incredulous. I searched the side of her tanned face to see whether she was making it up to make me feel better. *Who wouldn't want their daughter to marry him? He seems like a good man, hardworking, good looking and… he's white,* I thought.

"Well, for one thing, they think he's too religious. But it's complicated. Seems it's always pretty complicated when it comes to parents, daughters, and the men they want to marry," she said, looking at me and smiling. "But I guess you'd know all about that, too, now wouldn't ya? See," she said, pushing at my arm, "we have lots in common, don't we?"

How would she know that? I thought as my body recoiled away from her involuntarily. *I haven't said anything to anyone….*

"By the way," she quickly continued, interrupting my thoughts, "The doctor wants me to bring you in on Monday. Since you're havin' twins and all, he doesn't wanna wait 'til the regular monthly appointment when he sees the rest of the girls. We'll leave the house around ten," she said, getting up and dusting off the butt of her jeans. "Well. Better get back to work. Enjoy your book." And before I could answer, she was striding across the pasture and back to her family in the barn.

• • •

"It'll be a couple of weeks before you get out again, so do ya wanna go by McDonalds before we head home?" Tracy asked as she drove the white twelve-passenger van on the hour-long trip to the doctor's office.

"Yeah. Sure," I answered disinterestedly. The only thing I seemed to crave these days was milk, so I didn't care what we ate.

"Ooh. Can I get a shake?" I asked, suddenly realizing there was something I wanted and asked with the enthusiasm of one of her children.

Laughing, she said, "Of course you can. Gotta enjoy it while you can."

She went on to explain how some girls have to go on special diets. No salt if you swell, low-calorie if you gain too much, high-iron if it gets too low. Not used to openly chatting about pregnancy, the conversation made me uncomfortable. So I blocked her out again, and turned to watch as the fields and pastures turn into neighborhoods, schools, and stores.

Everyone in the doctor's office knew Tracy. She strode in, speaking to everyone, her heavy boots clopping even though the reception room was carpeted. She knew the nurse behind the desk by name, and after checking in, she followed me back to the examination area without ever sitting in the waiting room. Knowledgeable about all things related to pregnancy, she praised the results of my weight and blood pressure, and ushered me into the examination room, telling me to change into the paper gown as she closed the door. The doctor who entered later had dark hair and a dark shadow of stubble. After what he called a pelvic exam, he helped me sit up and told me to get dressed, saying he'd be back so we could talk.

Once I was dressed, Tracy and the doctor joined me in the exam room, where I learned that pregnancy is measured in weeks, percentages, centimeters, pounds, and inches. My goal, he said, was to make it at least to thirty-six weeks of the forty-week full term, to grow my uterus to at least thirty-six centimeters so the babies had plenty of room, and in the meantime, not to gain more than another twenty pounds.

"You're already seventy five percent effaced and two centimeters dilated, which unfortunately means you're to go on full bed rest immediately." He turned to Tracy and said, "Only let her get up to go to the bathroom, and of course for her appointments with me. Otherwise, she stays in bed." Turning back to me, he added, "You need to lie on your right side as much as possible."

"You understand how serious this is, young lady?" the doctor said, putting his hand on my knee. Based on my blank face and blinking eyes as I refocused on his face, he assumed I didn't, and continued in a harsher tone of voice. "If you do not stay on complete bed rest, you will go into labor and your babies will not survive. And if you have them any time before thirty-two weeks, even if they do survive, they will have severe complications and developmental issues." Taking a deep breath, he continued: "It is critical that we get you to thirty-two weeks, and it'd be best if we can get you to thirty six-weeks."

The look on my shocked face, my widening eyes, and the tears that started to pool in them convinced him that I understood the seriousness of the situation, so with a quick pat, he turned once again to Tracy.

Meanwhile, my mind drifted to the consequences of being bed-ridden. Although I didn't like the idea that I had to stay inside, I didn't necessarily mind getting out of chores. The best part, I realized with the tiniest of smiles, would be no more going to church.

I'd always liked going to church, but going with the girls from the house had been humiliating. All sixteen of us, all pregnant, and all besides me in their mid-teens, walked the mile to church right in the middle of the two-lane road at eleven o'clock in the morning. Tracy's little boys skipped and played around us, and Tracy and Luis waved at every neighbor whose house we passed. We filed into the tiny church, taking over two long wooden pews up front and right in the middle. Everyone looked at us, most openly gawking as we walked in. Occasionally people turned their heads towards us during the service, craning their necks with looks of curiosity, followed by a shake of their heads in disgust or pity. At the end of the service, the minister stretched out his hands over the congregation and prayed for us. Calling us specifically out to God, as if He needed reminding, the minister said, "And Lord, we also pray for the sixteen young souls here among us, who carry the heavy burden of the tiny souls within them."

"See you in two weeks" the doctor said, his pat on my knee snapping me back to attention.

A list of vitamin supplements and reminders later, Tracy and I were safely back in the van and turning out of the parking lot. She drove a lot like she walked, purposefully, determined, and clearly in a hurry.

"I know this's scary," she said, looking from me, to the road, the rearview mirror, and the cars around us. "I've had plenty of girls on bed rest and their babies turned out just fine."

Still on the verge of tears, I turned to blink and stare out of the window, not wanting to see her face when I asked, "Will anyone adopt them if they have severe complications and developmental issues?"

"Of course they will, darlin'," she answered, patting my leg before she turned the van into a parking space at McDonald's.

"There's a long list of couples that want these babies. So yes, absolutely, yes," she said and killed the ignition. "Don't you worry about alla that," she added while she waited patiently in her seat.

"If something was wrong with them, if something bad does happen, I'd have to give 'em up, then. I mean, I don't know how I'd take care of two healthy babies as it is. But two sick ones? With problems? I mean, I guess I wouldn't even have a choice, would I?" I said as I searched her hazel eyes for answers. "I need to tell Emmett. He needs to know," I pleaded.

"One thing at a time now," she said. "Let's do what the doctor said. That's what you and I can do." After smoothing my hair, she added softly, "The rest we'll just have to leave in God's hands, sweetie."

Then she said with a big grin, "You can call Emmett and tell him when we get back to the house. Now, let's go get you that milkshake!" and she hopped out of the van.

• • •

Back at the house, Tracy said, "Make your call from in here," opening the door to her family's apartment. "I'll close the door so you have some privacy, but don't stay on too long."

We weren't supposed to make phone calls or have contact with the fathers of our babies, but on the way home, Tracy said, "I think this counts as an emergency. And since you're twenty-one and keep your mouth shut, I think it'll be okay."

"Erin? Where are you?" Emmett said with panic in his voice. "Are you okay? I've been so worried!"

We hadn't spoken in over a week, not since I left home, so I rushed to reassure him. "I'm fine. I'm here at the home. It's okay. I'm okay. I went to the doctor today. Tracy said I could call you. I'm not supposed to, but she said it would be okay."

So much had happened, I could've spent hours explaining it all, but it was important for me to keep it short. Tracy was taking a chance on me, and I couldn't let her down.

"What'd the doctor say? Are you alright?" he asked, obviously still worried.

"I'm okay, but I have to go on bed rest. He thinks I might go into labor early, and if I go too early, the babies might have a lot of problems. I thought you should know," I said, slowing down, realizing I couldn't tell him that they might not make it at all.

"Are they okay?" he asked, his voice sounding even more concerned.

"They're fine right now, right where they are. I just have to go on bed rest so we keep them there as long as possible," I explained, trying to sound confident.

"Okay," he said. "But what if that doesn't work? What does the doctor mean? What kind of problems will they have if you go into labor early?"

I didn't want to scare Emmett, but didn't he deserve to know? They were his babies, too. So as calmly as I could, I said, "I don't know. He didn't really say. But Tracy told me she's had plenty of girls on bed rest and the babies all turned out fine. The doctor wants to see me every two weeks, and he's gonna keep a real close eye on me. I'm sure we'll be fine. I just wanted to make sure I called you and told you I was here, and that everything's fine so you wouldn't worry."

"Who's Tracy?" he asked, confused.

"She's the lady in charge here. She's a really good person. You'd like her." I explained what I could, trying to sound upbeat. So much had happened in such a short time. I felt overwhelmed by the sudden feeling of isolation.

"Okay. So you're okay?" Emmett sounded less concerned, hearing the brightness in my voice.

"Yes, I am. Really, I'm fine. Everything's fine, but I can't stay on the phone," I told him, looking at the closed door. "I'll write you a letter, okay?"

"Yes. Please write! And take care of yourself okay? I love you," he said, sounding a little better, but still with that weird choking hint of concern in his voice.

"I will, and I love you, too," I said, quickly hanging up before I choked.

Crying quiet tears, I sat on the sofa in the small den of Tracy's apartment, trying to gather myself. I needed to stay strong and do this on my own. Burdening him with what ifs just to make myself feel better would be futile and wrong. Staring past my growing belly and down at my white sneakers, I felt both huge and small at the same time. But then the song of a bird outside the window caught my attention.

Perched on a barren branch of a leafless tree just outside the window, a tiny, tattered brown bird opened his beak wider than seemed possible. All alone, he sang his song almost as if he were desperately trying to attract my attention. Slowly I smiled with the realization that he'd been sent to remind me. This tiny bird, like the waves, the sun and the sand, were reminders that God and His universe of souls swirled around me once again. I drew in a deep, shaky breath. "You're not alone!" they all sang, and the relief was instant and palatable.

Suddenly Tracy burst into the room, searching for me, and when I turned to greet her, I was smiling. Grinning back at me in response, her eyes danced when she said, "Well. That must've gone well!"

• • •

All of my things were moved to a bedroom on the first floor hall reserved for girls on bedrest. Following the doctor's orders, I only left the bed in order to use the bathroom, shower and change clothes. Every meal was served from a tray brought to my bed, and the entire house crowded into my room for Bible study and nightly devotion. The room sometimes felt like a well decorated prison cell. Since I'd only been at the house a short time, not many of the girls bothered to visit me, but Heidi swung by every morning after breakfast with a new book for me to read. Tracy, although incredibly busy taking care of the house, the girls, the garden, and her family, always managed to visit me several times a day.

"Whacha readin' now, bookworm?" was her typical greeting as she breezed through the open doorway. As I lay on my right side, she leaned her chair back on two legs and we talked, laughed, and became friends. Like Brittany, when we were together, everything was fun and we could talk about the silly things and the important ones with equal ease. Tracy didn't just accept who I was; she liked me. And I admired everything about her. She asked questions, listened to the answers and rarely shared her opinion. She believed that sometimes we all make mistakes, but that didn't make us bad people. And eventually I opened up entirely to her as we shared our stories, our worries, and our dreams for the future.

In our daily conversations I found out that Luis had graduated from State and sought work in the forestry service, but then he felt a calling to come and work for the home. Tracy said she'd always wanted to live out in the country to raise her family, so she'd agreed. "I know we were brought here for a reason," she said, "and I know we've helped quite a few girls who've come through here this past year."

Growing up in a very small town, she also understood what it felt like to live where everyone thinks they already know everything about you. She'd always wanted to leave her town, too.

As the days stretched into weeks, Heidi and another girl left to give birth as I slept, ate, and read. Unable to go outside, I left the curtains open wide so I could watch the leaves as they changed colors and blew away in the wind. After several weeks alone, my cell had become a sanctuary. But then Rachelle, the fourteen-year-old, was put on bed rest, too.

Unlike Samantha, Rachelle didn't cry herself to sleep at night and unfortunately talked incessantly. Within hours of joining me, I knew that her relationship with her parents had been bad for years, and that she resented them for many reasons, the final blow was them sending her away to the home.

"I wanna keep my baby, but I'm a minor so I got no choice. Why are you even here?" she asked, rolling her eyes and tossing in the bed next to me. "If I was twenty-one, I sure as hell wouldn't be here. What's wrong with you, anyways?" she spat.

Not bothering to respond, I turned away from her and faced the wall so I could think. She had asked me a very interesting question. Lying in the dark, at first I was astounded that I'd ended up in the room with her at all. *How in the hell did I end up here?* I thought. But as I lay there, I realized that everything had been leading me to this time and place.

It had always felt like I was trying to pull away and go my own way, but I'd hedged my bets, played the middle, kept my options open, and tried to go in several directions at once. My lack of courage had led me to gradually lose myself. But now, this time, I'd have to commit.

This decision, this crossroad in my life, was more than just about the babies. This was that important point when you choose between childhood and adulthood. If I had been a minor, I could have chosen to do what my parents said, then go home, pick up where I'd left off, and spend the rest of my life resenting them for making me do what they thought was best.

But adults make their own decisions, anticipate the consequences, and accept them without blame. They're honest and don't feel the need to defend their decisions. With a flood of admiration and respect, I recognized that's what Brittany had done. She'd chosen the path that she thought was best, as an adult, without excuse or apology.

Deciding what to do would be a critical decision but how and why I made the decision was almost more important. I needed to make a choice as an adult, based on what was best for the babies, not best for me, and I needed the courage to do it without blame, excuses, or apologies, just as Brittany had done. If I could decide it this way, I could be proud of my decision for the rest of my life.

• • •

Since the doctor wanted to see me every two weeks, Tracy and I made the long trip into Birmingham in the van alone. Relishing the trip for more than just the time away from Rachelle, I looked forward to having time with Tracy and the opportunity to call Emmett afterwards.

"So have you two decided what you're gonna do yet?" Tracy asked one day as we made our way back from my doctor's appointment.

Encouraged by the doctor's response to my progress and the prognosis for the twins, I could finally talk about it without gulping back tears. "Not for sure yet, but we're leaning towards going through with the adoption," I told her. "We keep talkin' about it, but every time we talk, it really seems to be the best choice. We really want to do the right thing here. It's too important."

"And that's what y'all think'll be best?" she asked, keeping her eyes on the road.

"To do anything else seems selfish. The only reason not to go through with it would be because we don't want to give 'em up. They'd be better off with parents who are married, have good jobs, plenty of money, and can give them everything they need and want. They'll love 'em and can take care of 'em. I wanna be proud of our decision, and I think I can be proud of giving them to a good home. I think it takes a lot of courage to do what's best for them, even when it hurts this bad."

"You're right. It does," she said and nodded. "So have you thought about what you might do afterwards?" she said, glancing at me as she drove.

"I'll go back. Find a job. Finish school," I said grimly.

"Gonna go back home?" she asked, keeping her eyes glued to the road.

"No," I answered quickly.

"Have ya told your parents yet? That you're not plannin' on goin' home?" she asked, glancing back and forth between me and the road.

"Not yet," I sighed.

"Why not?" she asked, but when I didn't answer, she didn't press. Just like Brittany, she knew when to leave me alone with my thoughts.

• • •

My parents came to visit one Saturday before Thanksgiving, both wearing their worry and pain on their faces. Tracy shoed

Rachelle out to the couch in the TV room so we could have privacy. They sat awkwardly in the straight-backed kitchen chairs at the foot of my bed while we attempted to make conversation about things that didn't revolve around my pregnancy and the decisions looming ahead. The unasked question hung between us like a low dark cloud until finally my mom was brave enough to ask.

"Have you decided what you're gonna do yet?" she asked, clasping and unclasping her hands.

"We still think adoption would be best. We don't want to give 'em up, but we think it'd probably be the best thing for the twins," I said carefully. "Afterwards, I'm not gonna come back home. I'm gonna go back and work, and try to finish school on my own."

My dad nodded in response, saying, "Might take you awhile, doin' it on your own."

"Yeah, but I think it's time," I said, and as we locked eyes, I knew we agreed.

It was a long drive, so they didn't stay long. As we hugged and kissed, saying "I love you," we all seemed relieved that they had to leave.

Not long after they left, Tracy burst in the room, asking, "Do you want milk with dinner tonight?" clearly making up an excuse to check on me.

When she saw that I was reading, not crying, she smiled when I said, "Sure!"

• • •

Thanksgiving was a depressing event a couple of weeks later. Rachelle and I joined the others at the long picnic tables for the special occasion, and many of the dozen or so girls cried through the holiday dinner. Tracy and Luis attempted to make it special for us, cooking turkey and dressing and pies. They even put on "It's a Wonderful Life" in the afternoon, but only a few girls chose to join them in the TV room. Instead, most of them retreated to their rooms and hid for the remainder of the day.

Two weeks later, when I awoke and got out of bed to go to the bathroom, a rush of water poured down the inside of my legs. Rachelle screamed, "Tracy! Erin's water broke!" and jumped from her bed to run down the hall while I stood staring at the soaked carpet between my feet.

Chapter Fourteen

Tracy, ever the bundle of confidence and efficiency, packed everything from my closet into my small suitcase while I sat on a towel on the edge of my bed. Like many before me, I was going to the hospital and wouldn't be coming back. After a quick call to the doctor and Emmett to let them know we were headed to the hospital, Tracy helped me climb into the van. I'd made it to thirty-four weeks, and with her at my side, I was neither scared nor worried.

By the time we arrived, the contractions had started, but they remained pretty far apart, so she said we had plenty of time. Once she checked me in and settled me into the labor and delivery room, I called my mom.

"Hey, Mom. My water broke. I'm at the hospital." I said calmly.

"Who's with you?" she asked.

"Tracy's here now, and I called Emmett, so he's coming later. He's got a final this morning and he's coming right after," I told her.

"If he's gonna be there, I don't think I should come. Is that okay? I don't think I can do it. And you don't need all of us there, do you?" she asked, sounding sad.

"Well I'd like you to be here. But they are his babies and he has the right to be here. I need him to be here," I answered, also sad. Tracy, trying not to overhear our conversation, stood in the corner of the room, looking out of the window.

"It'll be worse with both of us there. I don't think I should come," Mom said. "You've got people with you. That's what I care about. Call me when it's over," she said, her voice cracking on the word *over*.

"I will. Love you," I said, quietly hanging up the phone.

"You okay?" Tracy asked, returning to my side and touching my leg to console me.

"Yeah, I'm fine. I'm just really tired of being sad." I cradled my belly as another contraction began to tighten.

Hours later, after I'd spent a long day enduring contractions and sucking on ice chips, Emmett's roommate drove him an hour through a winter rainstorm so he could be with me for the births. And hours later, our two beautiful, perfectly healthy baby girls were born. For months we had talked about them, expected them, and thought about their futures, but the shock on our faces was unmistakable when we looked first at them and then at each other.

After finding me a burger, my first food since dinner the night before, Emmett and his roommate drove back to school for another day of final exams. He promised to come back after his final the next day, and Tracy said she'd come back after she fed the horses, and so for the first time, I found myself alone with my two beautiful babies. Amazed and in awe, I watched as the two slept, each a mirror-image of the other. Wrapped in the white hospital blankets with blue and pink stripes, wearing tiny little pink stocking caps, they snuggled close together in one bassinet, just as they had snuggled together in my womb. Less than five pounds each, the babies were no longer a concept or an idea; they were perfect, tiny little people.

As I drifted off to sleep, I imagined the kind of life they'd have, living in a large brick home somewhere in a ritzy part of Birmingham, each with her own bedroom decorated in pink.

Dancing lessons, music lessons, and horseback riding lessons would keep them busy as they grew into smart and beautiful young women. They'd have the best of everything growing up, and after going to the college of their choice, they'd be doctors or lawyers, and maybe one day have families of their own. As I dozed, opening my eyes to verify that they were real, I often reached out to touch them when my mind continued to question what I saw.

When I finally slept, in a fitful dream, I saw Stanley and Shannon, the twins from high school. Once again on the bus, I watched as they walked home from the bus stop, the two of them walking alone. As they reached the corner of their street, the other kids continued walking in a cluster, talking among themselves many yards away. But this time, in my dream, the twins turned to look back at me, sitting alone by the window on the bus. They paused on the corner and looked directly at me, as if they knew I'd be watching. The look of sadness on their faces made me gasp audibly and startled me awake.

My heart racing, I jolted upright in the hospital bed and looked over to my two baby girls sleeping peacefully. My mind clouded by the dream, and unable to go back to sleep, with a deep breath I reached for the phone beside the bed and dialed my mom.

She answered on the first ring and I started talking immediately, saying, "Hey. It's me. I wanted to call you and let you know that we're fine. The babies and I are fine!"

"How're you doing?" she asked quietly.

"Good. It hurts still, but I'm good. Just tired. The babies are perfect," I answered carefully.

"Did the doctor say when you'll get out?" she asked, keeping her voice low.

"He thinks it'll be sometime tomorrow," I told her, dreading what would surely be her next question.

"Want me to come and get you?" she asked. Although her voice was soft and calm, in my mind I could picture her pained faced with the receiver held tightly to her ear as she braced for my answer.

"No. Emmett's coming to take me back with him," I said with a wince. I'd caused them so much pain already, I hated to cause more, but there was no going back. I couldn't live under a cloud of shame, and as hard as it might be, for once I was going to act like an adult. It was time.

"I hope you know what you're doing," she said.

"Yes, ma'am. I do. Don't worry. I'll call you later and let you know what's going on. Love you," I said, and without waiting to hear how she'd answer, I ended the call.

Insisting that the babies stay in my room, it was a long and restless night filled with bottles and diapers, emotions and thoughts. Early the next morning, the nurse bustled in with sheets of paperwork for me to complete. Although the labor nurses had been understanding and kind, the regular care nurses were far less compassionate. Whether it was my age, the mention of the charity organization in my medical file, the color of Emmett's skin, the obviously mixed race of my babies, or quite possibly all of these factors, they obviously disapproved of me and my children. Their faces full of distaste, they made huffing and tsking noises as they bustled in and out of my room.

As I completed the paperwork for the birth certificates, carefully printing my full name, checking my race, printing the father's name, checking his race, and printing the babies' names that we'd spent so much time discussing in letters over the past months, I stopped to chew on the pencil as I considered the answer to the next question.

Seeing my hesitation, the nurse asked brusquely, "What's your question?" as she continued moved about the room.

"Baby's race. It says I can only choose one," I said as I studied the form.

"Let me see," she said and snatched the form from my hand. "You check black," she said, handing it back to me, clearly infuriated by the simplicity of my question.

"Why?" I asked, without first considering what I should've expected in response.

Hands on her hips, she exhaled deeply before she answered. "Because they're black. If either of the parents are black, then the baby's black. That's how it works."

"I'm not doing that. They're black and white. They should let you check more than one box," I said as I completed the first form and picked up the next one for the second baby.

"You can't pick both," she said, huffing and picking up the completed form from the tray.

"I didn't," I said, snatching my baby's form out of her hand.

"Well, what'd ya pick, then?" she said, returning both hands to her hips.

"Other," I said and smiled down at the paper. "If they can't be both, then they won't be either."

"You're not doin' it right," she said, throwing her hands in the air and turning to leave the room.

"So?" I said, smiling after her in satisfaction as she left the room.

Once all of the required paperwork was completed and signed, including those that released my babies into the temporary custody of the organization, and Emmett and Tracy returned, the judgmental nurses gave us time to say goodbye to our tiny sweet babies.

Tracy ushered the nurses away sternly and guarded the door so the four of us could have time alone. Not knowing if we'd ever see them again, fear clawed at our throats and our hearts. Then, gently knocking on the door, Tracy stuck her head into the room and said softly, "I'm sorry, but it's time."

As the nurse wheeled the babies back to the nursery, I was seated in a wheelchair and taken down the hall to the elevator. Tracy mumbled reassuring words over and over to us as tears ran down my face. My small suitcase in his hand, Emmett somberly helped me leave the hospital and get settled in the car.

"Nothing's final until you sign in thirty days," Tracy said, leaning in close to me through the car window as I slumped in the seat. Every part of my body and soul smoldered in pain.

As she hugged Emmett tight and then held his broad shoulders at arm's-length, she said, "Let her get some rest now, and then y'all talk it through. Call me if you have any questions or if you need anything."

As he silently nodded and turned to make his way around his roommate's car and into the driver's seat, she added, "You take care of her now."

Leaning down again through the window, she smiled at me and said, "It's gonna be alright. Now don't you worry."

She tapped the roof of the car twice, signaling to Emmett that he could leave, and he slowly he pulled away from the curb. Out the passenger window, I looked up at the windows on the fourth floor, imagining my babies snuggled in their bassinet together, among the others in the nursery. Twisting in my seat, I kept the tall hospital building in my sights until it finally disappeared behind the tops of the trees that lined the highway.

We spent the remainder of the week in Emmett's apartment, sleeping, eating, and talking, examining and reexamining every angle. Everything would be possible if we followed through with the adoption process, and nothing was predictable if we changed our minds.

Meanwhile, the twin-dream continued to haunt me every time I slept. Even the pain medication the doctor had prescribed couldn't mask the sadness in the faces of Stanley and Shannon as they looked back at me sitting on the bus. At a few days old, it was already apparent that the girls would never look either black or white. I knew that like Stanley and Shannon, our twins would appear mixed.

Desperately I attempted to explain to Emmett what I thought my dream meant. "Now, I know just about everybody at one time or another feels out of place, feels like they don't belong anywhere, and that nobody understands them. I know all that."

Emmett nodded and I continued. "But because of who they are, who *we* are, they're gonna have it even harder than the rest of us. And they're gonna have to face it a lot earlier. I don't want them growing up feeling like they don't belong anywhere."

His confusion apparent by the quizzical look he gave me, I tried again. "Look, their parents are gonna be either white or black, right? Interracial marriage isn't even legal in Alabama, I don't think. So ya know, they're not gonna be like us. So they're *always* gonna feel different, even at *home*." Seeing that I had his full attention, I took another deep breath and went on.

"Maybe it would be different if they looked white or they looked black. Maybe then they could go to white parents or black parents, and have some time to grow up before they realized they were different. Their parents could tell them about us later, when they were older. "

"What're you sayin'?" Emmett asked.

"I don't want them spending their life not fitting in, even at home. I don't want them wondering why they're different from their parents, even when they're little kids. But they're gonna know that they're different right away."

Choking a little, I gulped and continued. "And because of that, they're gonna wonder why they're different. They're gonna wonder whether we gave them up just because they're half white and half black. They might even grow up thinking it was my fault or your fault, maybe think something terrible happened, and maybe even hate one side or the other because of it. I don't want them growing up wondering, and hating different parts of themselves. *We* could make sure that never happened. We could show them *every day* that being different doesn't matter. That none of that matters. —" Exhaling, I paused as his mouth twisted in thought.

"I don't want that either. I really wanna raise them ourselves. I do. But how would we take care of them until I get out of school?" he asked, obviously upset.

"I don't know," I said and sighed. "But that's what we've got a couple of weeks to figure out."

Over the next couple of days, we continued talking, our ideas coming out of the blue. Since it was always on our minds, we didn't have to explain or provide context. We said things like, "I didn't grow up with everything I ever wanted, and neither did you." and "Our parents always worked hard to give us everything they could and that meant just as much, didn't it?"

Several days later, I called my mom and told her about our plan to head back to Emmett's parents' house to spend the Christmas holidays with them. We kept the conversation brief and she didn't object. Before we hung up, she said "Thanks for letting me know. I love you."

Over the holiday, we explained to Emmett's parents why we believed it was important for us to raise our babies ourselves. Admitting that we couldn't provide what they needed, much less what they deserved, we expressed our willingness to work hard to deserve a chance.

Emmett told them emphatically, "We can't raise them here. That wouldn't be good for us or for them. I've got to finish school and get my degree so I can get a good job and we can move somewhere else. I just need a little more time until I graduate."

Listening quietly, nodding their heads, his parents never questioned us or commented until the day after Christmas, when his parents asked us to join them at the kitchen table for a discussion. Sitting at the head of the table, Mr. King cleared his throat as he began, "We appreciate you two spending time explaining how you're thinking about the whole situation. You two are adults, and this is your decision, but the two of us've talked about it and here's what we're willing to do."

He went on to explain that if we decided to keep the babies, they would help us under "certain conditions." The babies and I could live with them as long as Emmett stayed in school and finished his degree. If he messed around and lost his scholarship or dropped out, we'd have to move out. While he was in school, they would provide the basics and make certain the babies had what they needed, formula, diapers, a crib, and clothes, and would ensure that they went to the doctor. I could live with them, take care of the babies, and eat with them as a member of their family, but they wouldn't give either of us any money. Once Emmett graduated, and it needed to be as soon as possible, he'd have to get a job and take over right away, and we'd need to move out. All we needed was a year and a half until Emmett graduated, and they were willing to give us that chance.

On the surface, it might've seemed like a difficult decision to move in with someone else' parents, but Mr. and Mrs. King were so kind and gracious, so accepting and welcoming, I was ready to move in without hesitation. Emmett and I talked all night, trying to determine whether this really was the right thing to do, and ultimately we agreed to accept the many gifts we'd been given. We agreed it would be extremely difficult, but I wasn't worried. I'd come from a long line of hard-working people and knew we could do it, too.

The next morning I called Tracy and excitedly told her of our decision. I could hear her smiling into the phone as she promised to contact the agency and call us back with the date, time, and place to meet. Before she hung up, she said, "I can't wait to see you again so I can give you both a great big 'ole hug."

And then I called my mom and asked if I could swing by so we could talk, and so I could pick up some of my clothes. Once again Grace wasn't home, so the three of us sat in the den together. After announcing our decision, providing the reasons and explaining the agreement we'd made with the King's, I paused for what I assumed would be an overwhelmingly negative response.

My dad just shook his head as he stared at the floor and said, "You've chosen an almost impossible path. I really hope you know what you're getting' yourself into, because this isn't just about you anymore."

"Even though it's gonna be really hard, I know it's the right thing to do. No matter what, I've gotta do the right thing." I felt empowered by the words he'd spoken to me throughout my years, even if he may not have realized that they'd inspired me.

"It's gonna be more than just hard," he said, continuing to shake his head.

"If you're gonna try and do this, why in the world would you stay here? It's gonna be even harder here," Mom said, obviously alarmed. "Are you just doing this to throw it all back in our faces? Are you doing this just to get back at us for something?" she added, raising her voice.

"No, this has nothing to do with you! I wish we could live somewhere else, but we can't just yet. We've got to get Emmett out of school first, and then we'll move away somewhere, where it'll be easier," I said, trying to stay calm and reminding myself that I didn't need to defend our decision.

"Are y'all gonna get married? I don't even think it's legal, is it?" Mom, asked, looking at my dad.

"No, we can't get married yet because he'll lose his scholarship. Plus, if I stay single, then if something bad happens with the babies, I can get help from the state. We'll get married once he gets out of school," I explained, trying not to become defensive.

"So let me get this straight; you're gonna live here, live with his parents, with two kids but not married, and he's just going off to school like nothing ever happened? And you're going to go on welfare?" Mom asked incredulously, obviously getting angry.

"No. I'm not going on welfare," I snapped. But after taking another deep breath, I continued in a softer voice. "I know it sounds bad, but it's the right thing to do. It'll be okay. We're gonna make sure it's okay."

"I really hope you know what you're gettin' into," she said finally, shaking her head and lowering her voice. "I just don't know how this could be the best thing for you or the children."

Dad ended the conversation by stating, "Well, I guess you're gonna do what you're gonna do."

After I packed my clothes and loaded them into Emmett's mom's car, Mom walked me to the back door and said grimly, "I need you to give me your house key back."

Although initially taken aback by the request, I recovered quickly and nodded. I removed my keys from my purse and handed her the whole ring, which held my house and car keys.

"You'll need your car, won't you? You'll have to pick up the payments and pay the insurance, of course, but it's your car," She said as she worked to remove the car key from the metal ring.

"Yeah, but no. I can't afford it. I won't be able to work for a while, but thank you," I said, before giving her a hug, telling that I loved her, and that I'd call her in a couple of days. Driving back to the King's house that day, although the distance was less than two miles, the two houses felt a thousand miles apart.

The following day, as Mr. King went to the Air Force base to buy cases of formula and huge packs of diapers, Emmett and I gassed up his mom's car and drove the five hours to pick up our twin girls and bring them home. We'd been apart for twelve days, and that was twelve days too many.

Tracy and the polite woman from the organization met us in the parking lot and handed us our precious babies, who were sleeping in their car seats. They also gave us a small bag of clothes, bottles, and other little things they'd acquired along the way. As we cheerfully hugged Tracy goodbye, accepting her wishes of good luck and promises to be included in her prayers, we were blessed once again when the woman from the agency told us that the organization, the doctor, and the hospital had forgiven all of our medical bills.

• • •

The first three months passed in a blur of bottles, diapers, and sleep snatched in two- or three- hour increments. Although Emmett went back mere weeks after we brought the twins home, to me, caring for the twins never felt overwhelming.

Although incredibly small, the girls were incredibly healthy and grew quickly. As they began to sleep for longer periods of time, the three of us developed a routine, and days became more like days and nights more like nights. After spending months in a home for unwed mothers on full bed-rest, the relative isolation felt normal and I loved my new role as a mom. Determined to be the best mother I could be for my girls, going out or seeing friends no longer interested me. My head and heart were focused on doing what was best for my twins, and as a result I lost contact with most of my friends and rarely spoke to my family.

But Tracy called every couple of weeks to check in on me, and one day she told me she was on her way to Mississippi and that she wanted to bring her three boys by for a quick visit.

"I brought you Adam's old crib," she said, gesturing to her van parked in the driveway as we sat in the King's den. "I figured the girls must be getting too big to sleep in one crib by now."

"Thank you! Yes, they are!" I said and grinned.

"Yeah, I figured," she said, nervously wiping her hands on her jeans. "Well. Wanted to let ya know that we're movin'…"

"No, really? Where?" I asked, surprised.

"Mississippi. Luis got a job with the forestry service. We bought a small ranch out there, 14 acres and a barn for some horses. We already quit the home. Moved out last week. That's where we're headed now, to our new place."

"Wow, that's great! Any idea what they're gonna do at the home?" I asked, trying to imagine the place without Tracy.

"I dunno. But I don't think they were too sad to see us go," She laughed. "After you left, we had two more girls keep their babies. When we gave notice, they didn't even blink. Just asked us when we were moving out!" We both laughed at that.

"I'm so happy for you guys! It's what you've always wanted. That's so cool. Aren't you excited?" I asked.

"We are! It's so weird, though. I mean, we were only there at the home less than a year before you came. And they told us it would be several years before they got another opening in the forestry service. But then, right after you left, they called. We decided you were the reason God called Luis to that home." She beamed at me, hitting my shoulder. After smiling broadly at each other, we turned to watch our children play together on the floor at our feet.

As we hugged goodbye that day, we promised to call and write letters so we wouldn't lose track of each other. Before she got into the van, Tracy held my shoulders and searched my face. I watched as her gaze grew soft and unfocused, and stood quietly, somehow understanding that I should wait for her to finish. Then her eyes focused and her face lit up in a huge grin. She said, "Ya know, it's all gonna be alright. Y'all are gonna be alright!" And then, with one last quick hug, she hopped into her van with her boys and left.

• • •

Just as at the home, my only real outings were the "well baby" monthly checkups for the girls. By default, my childhood pediatrician became theirs. A wizened gray-haired doctor for more than thirty years, he laughed we he saw me at our first visit, and said, "Well, hello there. I see you've been busy since I last saw you. These two little ones will be my very first set of biracial twins. Let's see what we've got here."

When we left the doctor's office that day, as I wheeled the girls out in the twin stroller Mr. King had bought for them, a blonde haired woman held the door open for me.

"Oh, my gooooodneeeessss!" she squealed when she saw the girls. "Wouldya look at them? Aren't they the sweetest things? And so taaaaan! Do you set 'em out in the sun so they look like that?" she asked as I pushed the stroller through the open door.

I chuckled and said, "No, ma'am," as I continued walking across the parking lot towards Mrs. King's car. As I picked up each baby and strapped her carefully into her car seat, I glanced back at the woman who was still standing at the open door, watching me with a confused look on her face. I laughed to myself and shook my head.

• • •

The Kings' enjoyed spending time with the girls each night when they came home from work, and they constantly reassured me. Without hovering or offering unwanted suggestions or advice, they answered my questions about how to care for my children and praised me for all the time and attention I gave them. They often told me I was a good mother. Ever gracious and kind, they treated me as a family member, and it was easy to be grateful for the chance we'd been given.

As the girls grew, I made myself more and more useful around the house, looking for things I could do to make the King's lives easier. My parents had taught me that as a member of a household you have an obligation to chip in whenever you can, and gradually I began picking up what needed to be done. Respectfully, I offered my help, and added routine household chores, laundry, and cooking dinner to my daily routine.

Emmett took the maximum number of credits permitted, working hard to graduate as quickly as he could. He came home weekends and on breaks whenever he could, and we talked on the phone as often as possible, keeping it short to stay within the phone budget his parents had given us. Since his dad had been in the military and often stationed apart from the family throughout the years, Mrs. King often reassured me she understood what it was like trying to raise the girls without Emmett. She cheerfully reminded me that it was only for a short period of time and helped me stay focused on the future.

As the months passed and the girls grew, we became a tight-knit little family, and as we got closer, I learned more about my future in-laws. I would sit rocking the girls to sleep as Mr. King told me stories. He came from a large family, with thirteen brothers and sisters, and from a small town just east of where my parents grew up. Like everybody else there, they'd been very poor when he was starting out. He left to fight in World War II, joining the Army before he even graduated high school, serving our country back when they segregated black soldiers even in times of war. After the war, he returned to finish high school in town, where they sent the older black students back from the war. That's where he met his future wife, who was six years younger. After graduating, he rejoined the service but chose to enlist in the Air Force, and fought in Korea and in Viet Nam. He return to visit his family whenever he had time off, and sent money home each week to help his parents and large family. He proudly showed me the bullhorn his great grandfather had used to call in the other slaves from the fields. He told me his dad had given it to him just before he died. He told me that in 1965, just a year before I was born, that he remembered when the Voting Rights Act was signed.

He said that his dad proudly walked for over an hour in his Sunday suit to the polls in order to vote for the first time.

Mrs. King grew up in a small town just outside of the city, and came from a much smaller family. When she graduated from high school, her mother, aunts, and, older sister worked extra jobs to scrape together the money to send her to college. Back in the early 1950s, she said it was highly unusual for black women to go to college. At the time, there were only certain schools that would admit her, but by working part-time whenever she could, and with the help of her family, she graduated from A&M. Afterwards, she worked as a teacher in the town where Mr. King grew up. She even taught a few of Mr. King's much younger brothers. Eventually, the two of them married and moved to wherever Mr. King was stationed. She raised four kids while he fought in Korea and Vietnam, and during that time, she finished her Master's degree. They'd spent over twenty years living far away on military bases in Germany, Turkey, Nevada, and Oklahoma, among others.

Emmett was their youngest child, and once he graduated, all four of their children would hold college degrees. They had overcome more obstacles than I ever could have imagined. Not only was I deeply proud to join their family, their stories also made me feel stronger and more confident in our decision to keep our new young family together.

And although they believed in the strength of family, the Kings never pried or spoke ill of my parents. I called my mom occasionally, and sometimes I spotted her driving slowly by the Kings' house, but we didn't spend time together. Since I'd been deemed a bad influence by most, neither of my sisters could risk a visit. I had made my decision, so I focused on my new family. I knew I had hurt them all deeply. The rift felt too deep to overcome.

The topic was rarely broached, but once, Mrs. King told me, "You gotta understand how it was when we all came along. This is a hard thing for anybody."

Mr. King quietly chuckled and said, "Well, we'll have to just wait and see. Blood's always thicker than beet juice."

• • •

By the summer, the girls had grown even more beautiful. They were fat and happy, always smiling and laughing, and I loved being the mom to such special little girls. They were so much a part of my life, the focus of every thought and decision, that I couldn't imagine life without them. Emmett stayed at school over the summer, taking the maximum numbers of credits in order to graduate the following May. But he came home for a week in between semesters.

I was anxious to earn a little extra money, since taking care of the girls and the house hold chores had grown easy for me to manage. Emmett mentioned that Peter's mom had started a cleaning service and was looking for someone to help out at night over the summer, so I jumped at the chance. Eagerly, I asked Mrs. King, "Would you mind watching the girls a few nights a week so I could work? Peter's mom might have a job for me. It'd be after they went to bed."

Mrs. King agreed, saying, "We can try it for a little while and see how it works out."

When Peter came by during the break to see Emmett and the girls, I asked him to let his mother know I was interested in working for her.

He said, "You'd be willing to do that?" he asked. "Cleaning offices is hard, dirty work."

I said, "Of course I would," I told him. Will you ask her for me?"

As we walked him out to his car, he mumbled, "Ya know, I mighta been wrong about you."

I just smiled and said good night.

A few days later, Peter's mom called me, and soon I had a job cleaning office buildings and medical offices a few nights a week. By the fall, Mrs. King was comfortable watching the girls at night since they went to sleep easily, and I'd proven that I wouldn't take advantage of the situation by running off at all hours of the night. And so she agreed that I could continue working. Weeks later, she said I could work more nights, so in addition to cleaning buildings, I took another job working the night-shift at a call center.

When the girls turned one, I baked pitiful-looking birthday cakes, one for each of them, decorated with pink and yellow icing. Emmett finished his finals the day before their birthday, and then drove the three hours home, arriving just in time to celebrate with us.

A year later, everyone we knew in town had found out about us, and from what little we'd heard, we had apparently caused quite a stir. Although we consciously chose to minimize any drama by limiting where we went and who we saw, it was inevitable that we heard what people were saying about us. Other than the few close friends that we held dear, we shielded our fragile little family from as much gossip as possible. Our friends fiercely protected us as much as they could from the ugly gossip. If they experienced blow back in their own lives, they never mentioned it to us. Imagining how difficult the rumors and opinions about our situation had made it on my family, we tried to keep a low profile until we could move out of town.

Anxious to begin our lives together, and at times frustrated that we were still so dependent on Emmett's parents, we kept our focus firmly on the future. Finally, the following spring, Emmett graduated and came home while he looked for a job. By then the girls, at eighteen months, were walking and talking, and as smart as whips, always happy, giggling, and jabbering as they played. Imagining our future together brought us so much joy, and we were married within a month of his graduation at the small church his grandparents had attended. I handwrote our invitations and Emmett's uncle performed the ceremony, which was very small and traditional. A college friend of ours played the guitar, and I wore a rented dress. Afterwards, we held a small reception of punch and cake in the fellowship hall that still smelled of the fish-fry from the night before.

Peter was Emmett's best man, Lorna was my maid of honor, and Mr. King walked me down the aisle. Less than fifty people attended our little wedding, including a few of my cousins and several of our close friends. Most of our guests were Emmett's family members who lived in the area.

Determined to leave Alabama, Emmett searched for positions in newspapers from large cities across the country. All during the week, as summer turned into fall, we mailed letters and resumes in response to jobs listed in the want ads. Since Emmett could now watch the girls during the day, I quit my night jobs and took a full-time day job as a receptionist in a real estate office so I could earn more money. We continued to save every penny to finance our move, which we hoped would happen soon.

When the girls turned two, I baked two more pitiful looking-birthday cakes and we celebrated another year. Days later, one of Emmett's sisters, the one who lived in L. A., called and told him about a job opening at the company where she worked. She explained that even if that job didn't work out, there were many more opportunities in the L. A. area than in

Alabama. She offered him a place to stay with her while he job-hunted. So as soon as the holidays passed, Emmett flew to L. A. Within weeks he was hired and started work, and with his first few paychecks, he bought a car and put a deposit on a two-bedroom apartment. Elated, I packed what little we owned into cardboard boxes, shipped them to our new address, and used whatever remained from my savings to buy three one-way plane tickets to California.

Before we left town, I called my family and told them the great news. Grace, who by then had graduated from high school and was already working, came over to the Kings' to say goodbye. Lynne wished me luck over the phone. Unwilling to go against her husband's wishes and see me in person, she said sadly, "Maybe y'all can finally fit in out there."

A few days before we left town, I borrowed Mr. King's car and took the girls to my parents' house for a final good bye. Dressed in their cutest matching dresses, we sat on the sofa in their den. Still concerned that at twenty-three, we were still too young to be moving to a huge city thousands of miles away, they reluctantly agreed it was for the best.

"It's just too hard here," my mom said. "I'm sure it's different way out there."

"That's what we're countin' on," I told her.

"Sounds like he's got a really good job," my dad said.

"Yes, he does," I said and nodded proudly.

"Maybe in a couple of years, y'all can come back and visit?" my mom asked.

"Yeah, or maybe y'all can come out and visit us one day?" I said.

As we hugged goodbye, I knew in my heart that time and distance would heal what had broken between us. We all cried a little and said "I love you" a lot as we repeatedly hugged each other goodbye. They'd always loved me, believed in me and wanted the best for me, and I knew they still did. Sometimes it's hard for parents to know what the best will be for their children. Now that I'd become a parent, I understood that, too.

Then, Mr. and Mrs. King solemnly drove me and the girls the three hours to the airport in New Orleans. I'd chosen a direct flight to L.A., rather than have to change planes with two toddlers. My in-laws had grown so attached to the girls while we'd lived with them that it nearly broke their hearts to see us move so far away.

"I know this is the right thing," Mr. King said as he hugged me goodbye. "But I'm gonna miss you and those girls somthin' terrible."

We all cried and hugged as we said goodbye at the gate. We promised to call often and visit soon. Our mix of races and ages confused the passersby, and our quiet hugging and crying nevertheless created something of a spectacle. Uncomfortable that everyone who passed by us openly gawked, I knew that leaving the south was the right thing to do. Once on the plane, with me on the aisle and the girls seated between me and the window, I busied myself making them comfortable for the five-hour flight as people stopped to stare as they walked down the aisle, some commenting about the twins.

As we settled in before take-off, a small brown bird flew by the window and landed on the wing. Once settled on his perch, he opened his beak wide in song. Although I couldn't hear his tune, I knew he'd been sent to remind me that I wasn't alone. Tears ran down my cheeks as I smiled at the bird and pointed him out to the girls. As they clamored to see, I thought of the frightened girl I'd been not even eight short years ago on the first day of P. E. class and as the older but still frightened girl I'd been three years ago, sitting there, crying on the beach.

There was a time when I'd been fearless, and it seemed that with the help of some special people along my way, I'd found my courage once again.

As the plane's engines rumbled to life and the bird flew away, I thought of Emmett waiting for us to join him at the other end of our journey. He'd worked so hard to graduate and find a good job in a place where we could start our lives together. The love of a lifetime, he'd loved me for who I'd always been, and had patiently waited for me to discover who I could be.

And then my mind flashed to a picture of Brittany, and again I felt the warmth of her smile so freely given. I remembered our conversation by the creek that very first time I'd spent the night at her house. She'd said she wanted to be important. And she *had* been incredibly important to me. I'd said that I wanted to be interesting, and thinking about it, I snorted out loud, realizing that I certainly *had* become interesting.

As I looked down at the beautiful, "coffee with milk" colored faces of my sweet little girls and listened to their sweet voices calling me "Mama," I realized that these two precious girls were already interesting and important, and so very much more. As the plane taxied down the runway, I thought of the wonderful adventure ahead that we would share as a family. And my chest, which had once felt so empty, and later had burned in anger, swelled with pride.